CODY BAY INN: AUGUST DREAMS IN NANTUCKET

A Nantucket Romance Novel

AMY RAFFERTY

© **Copyright 2021 Amy Rafferty — All rights reserved.**

This is a work of fiction. Names, characters, places, and incidents either are products of the author's imagination or are used fictitiously. Any similarity to actual events or locales or persons, living or dead, is entirely coincidental.

All rights reserved. No part of this publication may be reproduced, stored in, or introduced into a retrieval system, or transmitted, in any form, or by any means (electronic, mechanical, photocopying, recording, or otherwise) without the prior written permission of the copyright owner.

The author acknowledges the trademarked status and trademark owners of various products referenced in this work of fiction, which have been used without permission.

The publication / use of the trademarks is not authorized, associated with, or sponsored by the trademark owners.

Formatted by Author Services by Sarah

Cover Design by Primal Studios

Amy Rafferty

AUTHOR

STAY UPDATED WITH ME

Thank you so much for purchasing or downloading my book! I am grateful to all my amazing readers.

To stay updated on all my latest books, newsletters, freebies and beautiful photos from the fabulous locations I write about, why not join my VIP group?

I will send you regular pictures of La Jolla Cove, San Diego and the Florida Gulf Beaches where I try to spend as much time as I can. I live in San Diego, my own 'Garden Of Eden' and I am in love with the sea and the beaches in the area. They inspire me to write lots of beachy mystery romance fiction to share with my awesome readers like you. Click here to join ME!

You will be asked for your email. You also get a FREE BOOK whenever you sign-up!

CLICK ON MY LOGO/PICTURE ABOVE FOR
NEWSLETTER & FREE BOOK

FREE BOOK

To get your FREE copy of Cody Bay Inn Prequel - Nantucket Calling, go to https://www.amazon.co.uk/dp/B0992NFTY1

CHARACTER LIST

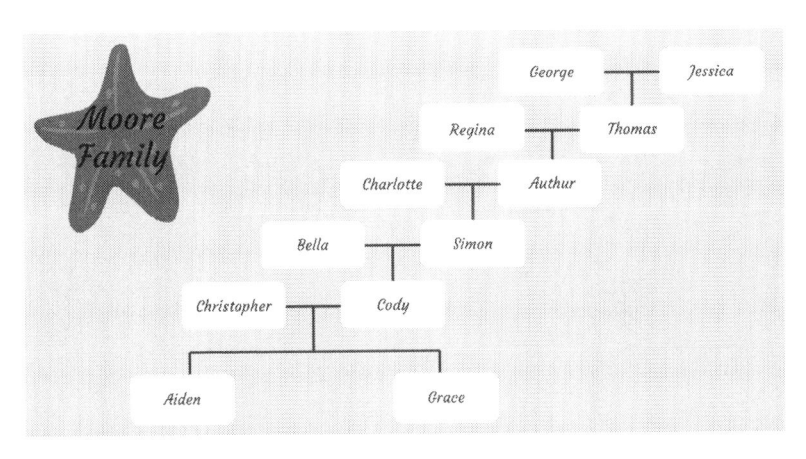

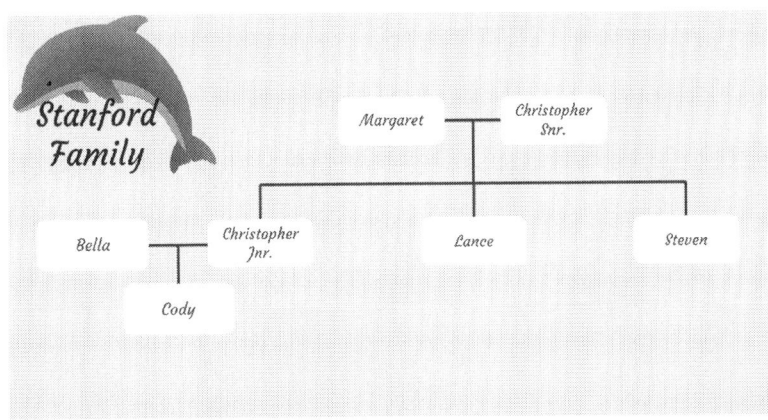

Moore Family

- George — Jessica
- Regina — Thomas
- Charlotte — Authur
- Bella — Simon
- Christopher — Cody
- Aiden
- Grace

Stanford Family

- Margaret — Christopher Snr.
- Bella — Christopher Jnr.
- Lance
- Steven
- Cody

Connie Taylor - Widowed
Nancy Honey - Connie's adopted daughter
Fern Taylor - Connie's younger sister

Dr. Grant Baxter - Widower
Michaela Baxter - Deceased wife of Dr Grant Baxter
Carla (Charlene) Newton - Daughter of Dr. Grant and Michaela Baxter
Luis Vern - Michaela Baxter's older brother
Annie (Vern) Decker - Michaela Baxter's older sister
Dr. Rose Decker - Annie's daughter

Chapter One
AN UNEXPECTED VISITOR

"I'm here to see my son," Margaret Stanford eyed the young woman in front of her with disdain. "I will not leave here until you show me the way to Christopher Stanford's room." She looked around the Inn with distaste. "Why he has to stay here to recover is beyond me."

"I'm sorry..." Nancy's eyes narrowed. "Who are you?"

"Miss Honey," Margaret Stanford glared at Nancy, "You know perfectly well who I am. Now stop stalling and get my son!"

"I would," Nancy looked at Margaret smugly. "But I'm watching the front desk, so I can't run off to do your bidding."

"Where is Cody?" Margaret said angrily. "Let's hear what she has to say about you being rude to a customer's mother."

"Ah," Nancy nodded. "I see your mistake now. You think that Christopher is a customer here. Well, he's not; he's a guest of *Miss Moore*," she informed a shocked Margaret. "As your son is a guest of *Miss Moore*, I am not at liberty to disturb him. You'll have to speak to *Miss Moore* about that."

"Then call Cody," Margaret raised her voice. "I'm getting tired of your sass."

"Sass?" Nancy raised her eyebrows. "I'm shocked that people still use that word." She shook her head. "While I'd love to rush to

1

do your bidding and not subject you to my *sass*, Cody is not here. But you can go to the Marine Life Center. You'll find her there."

"I hope Christopher is not with her," Margaret glared at Nancy.

"I believe he is," Nancy looked at Margaret, "and before you get all prickly about that, his doctor and brother are with him."

"What in the blazes is that?" Margaret took a step back as Sheba, the Moore's large Baby Doll cat, hopped onto the front desk. She sat wagging her tail, eyeing Margaret.

"It's a cat!" Nancy told Margaret with a straight face. "You know, a small domesticated carnivorous feline?"

"I know what a cat is, Miss Honey," Margaret's cheeks were stained with angry red. "Now, call the Marine Life Center and get Cody to bring my son back here. I will not set foot in that smelly place."

"I don't think the sea life at the Marine Life Center would..." Nancy was stopped mid-sentence by her mother, Connie Bright, who came from the kitchen.

"Nancy, don't you have to go get ready for a shift?" Connie gave Nancy a warning look. "Hello, Margaret." She looked at Margaret coldly. "Did you arrange to see Christopher today?" She opened a diary on the desk marked *C. Stanford's visitors*. "I don't see your name in the visitor's logbook."

"Why would I need to make an appointment to visit my son?" Margaret hissed.

"His doctor has a strict guest protocol for Christopher at the moment," Connie explained to Margaret. "We are under strict instructions to only let approved visitors see him."

"That's absurd," Margaret scoffed. "I'm his mother; I don't need an appointment."

"Actually, mother," Steven Stanford walked through the front door of the Inn, "you do."

"Steven," Margaret greeted her eldest son a little frostily. "Where is your brother? And what is this nonsense about having to make an appointment to see him?"

"Christopher had brain surgery not too long ago," Steven

reminded her. "We have to keep him as stress-free as possible, and you, Mother, tend to raise people's blood pressure."

"That's nonsense," Margaret fobbed it off. "Why would I stress Christopher out?"

"Oh, oh," Nancy put her hand up. "Please, can I answer that?"

"No!" Steven and Connie said together and glared at Nancy.

"I was going to be medical about it," Nancy said with a pout.

"I warned you, Mother," Steven reminded Margaret, "on many occasions not to talk about work and everyday life pressures to Christopher until he was well enough to cope with them again."

"Christopher has responsibilities to the company," Margaret's eyes narrowed. "As it is, I am left to deal with the board of directors on my own, and you know I don't trust any of them."

"You've never let anyone get the better of you, Mother," Steven raised his eyebrow. "I'm sure you're handling the board and the company just fine on your own." *You probably prefer it that way too,* he thought. "Christopher needs peace and calm right now."

"Then why the hell is he a *guest* of Cody Moore?" Margaret sneered. "This place couldn't be peaceful for him."

"Actually, Mother," Christopher's voice had all heads turning towards him as he walked into the Inn. He was wearing board shorts, a cotton shirt, and a cap to cover his head. "It is very peaceful for me here."

"There you are my beautiful baby boy." Margaret rushed over to Christopher. "As soon as I got back to Nantucket, I came to see you and take you home to the Stanford Estate."

"Mother," Christopher swallowed, pinched the bridge of his nose, and closed his eyes, "I've had this conversation with you, and I'm not having it again."

"I must insist that you come home with me, Christopher," Margaret said stubbornly and linked her arm through his. "You know how I feel about these people." She didn't care who heard her.

"Well, Mother," Christopher unlinked his arm from hers. "I'm not going to the Nantucket estate. I'm staying here with my doctor." He turned as Dr. Carla Newton walked in.

3

"Do I know you?" Margaret's eyes narrowed as she looked at Carla.

Carla had stopped the instant Christopher turned around, and she'd seen Margaret Stanford standing beside him. Her face was pale, and her features looked like they'd turned to stone.

"And my nurse practitioner," Christopher turned Margaret's attention away from Carla to Nancy. "Nancy."

"You're a nurse practitioner?" Margaret looked at Nancy in disbelief.

"Amazing, isn't it?" Nancy folded her arms over her chest and leaned back. "What did you once say to me?" Nancy tapped her lips. "Oh, that right—I'd never amount to anything, and you'd be surprised if I managed to stay out of jail."

"Nancy," Connie warned her. "Christopher's not looking well," she whispered, pointing out his pale face and glassy eyes.

"Shit, I knew that shrew was going to do this," Nancy's jaw clenched. She looked at her watch. "It's time for his therapy, anyway."

"Mother," Christopher said through clenched teeth, "I promise as soon as I'm able, I will come and visit. Right now, I'm late for my therapy."

"I'll see you out," Steven stepped up to his mother. "I promise I will bring Christopher around to the estate in a few days."

"Fine," Margaret reached up and kissed Christopher on the cheek. "Call me."

"I will, Mother." Christopher gave his mother a small smile.

"Are you sure we haven't met before?" Margaret stopped in front of Carla. "You look familiar."

"I..." Carla swallowed. She was saved from answering when Margaret's attention was caught by the Moore family returning home.

"Mom," Aiden immediately stepped between Margaret, Grace, and Riley when he saw her. "What is she doing here?"

"It's okay, honey," Cody smiled at Aiden, "take Grace and Riley to the dining room. I'll join you in a bit."

Riley had immediately hidden behind Aiden when he'd seen

Margaret, and Grace had frozen on the spot. Aiden picked Riley up and took Grace's hand, pulling them past Margaret and giving her a cold look.

"No manners," Margaret clucked and gave Cody a condescending look. "I see they are as wild as you were."

"It's good to see you too, Margaret," Cody held her head up high. "If you'll excuse me, I have hungry children to feed."

"Stay, sit, stop...." Harper West, a teenage friend of the Moore siblings, ran into the Inn. "TINY!" Harper shouted as the huge English Mastiff broke loose from her grip and flew towards Margaret Stanford.

"What on earth is that..." Margaret's eyes grew huge.

"Sit!" Cody commanded, and Tiny automatically sat and skidded a few paces forward, stopping just shy of knocking into Margaret.

"I don't think this is the place for you to stay with all these animals," Margaret said haughtily, turning back to Christopher.

Margaret jumped and spun around when Rage, the Moore's brindle Staffordshire terrier barked a few times. "Good grief, another one?" Margaret breathed, eyeing the smaller dog.

"The animals are fine, Mother," Steven assured her, stepping around Tiny and guiding Margaret out of the Inn. "Let's get you back to your town car."

"*L*et's get you to the therapy room," Nancy stepped up to Christopher. "You look like you're going to fall over."

"Thanks," Christopher smiled down at Nancy. His head was starting to ache, but he tried to push the pain away. "I think I could lie down." He looked around at Cody and Carla. "I'm sorry about my mother." He gave them a tight smile. "I'll make sure she doesn't come back here."

"Don't worry about that now," Cody smiled reassuringly at Christopher. "Let me help you to the therapy room."

"Thanks," Christopher hated being dependent on anyone. But

it did bring him closer to Cody, and right now, that was one of his top priorities, working things out with her.

"Come on," Cody linked her arm through Christopher's, "I'll ask the kids to bring you something to eat because you skipped lunch."

"Oh, I thought you wouldn't notice that," Christopher grinned as they walked through the Inn's kitchen and into the Moore's house that joined the Inn. "I still feel bad about turning your sun lounge into a therapy room."

"Are you kidding?" Cody said to him. "Aiden has already made plans to turn it into a gym once you no longer need therapy. I think he's asked for gym equipment and a sauna for Christmas."

"Nothing big then?" Christopher laughed.

"Oh, Grace wants a jacuzzi, and I believe Riley wants a real dragon," Cody shook her head.

"Riley's wanted a dragon since he could say the word," Christopher told Cody as she helped him onto the bed.

"Is that comfortable?" Cody made sure the bed kept his head elevated.

"Perfect," Christopher's eyes locked with Cody's. His heart thudded in his chest as he saw the emotions flitter through her eyes.

"Good," Cody said, breaking eye contact. "I'll go get Nancy."

"Thank you," Christopher stifled a yawn. "Carla said I can join in pizza night one Friday," he told Cody when she put some fresh water next to him.

"The kids will be thrilled," Cody smiled at him. "Just don't expect to choose the movie, though."

"I enjoy the movies they choose," Christopher told her softly. "I missed so much." His features changed, his sadness and regret were reflected in his eyes.

"You're here now," Cody gave his hand a little squeeze. Christopher closed his hand over hers and held it.

"Cody..." Christopher's voice became hoarse, "I..."

"I'll go get Nancy," Cody pulled her hand from Christopher's and stepped back. "I'll also get you something to eat."

"Thank you," Christopher sighed.

Christopher had started to mend bridges with his children, but with Cody, there was still a lot of debris from their shattered relationship in the way. That was going to take time to sort through. He put his head back and closed his eyes. Christopher wished he felt like himself again. Although he'd lived with that thing in his head for so long, he wasn't sure who that really was. The doctor told him that his erratic behavior, blackouts, and disorientation was caused by the tumor. But how did they know that? How could they say what part of the erratic behavior was caused by it?

Christopher found himself worrying that the mood swings were actually part of his natural personality. Both his mother and his father were prone to them. Christopher had read that some people with anger issues exhibit some of the same symptoms as the tumor had caused him. Christopher was afraid of being alone with his kids in case he really did have anger issues. He'd rather die than ever lash out or hurt his kids. Christopher's head started to pound. He concentrated on his breathing like Nancy had taught him. Breathe in clean air to fill his body with a cleansing breath. Hold for a few seconds as it washes through him, picking up negative energy and calming him. Then expel all the negativity and pain.

As Christopher started to relax, images of the past few weeks spent with his kids and Cody filled his mind. Christopher was sure that his remarkable recovery was due to the love and support of her amazing children and their big-hearted mother. Christopher still didn't know how he'd ever had the strength to let his family go all those years ago. He gave a small laugh, and Christopher's heart filled with love as he thought about a conversation he'd had with Grace four weeks ago.

FOUR WEEKS AGO

"Let me help you with that, Mr..." Grace bent down to pick up Christopher's hat he'd dropped on the floor, stopped, and took a breath on her way up. She closed her eyes and shook her head. "I'm sorry, Dad." She looked at Christopher with a tight smile.

"Gracie, sweetheart," Christopher grabbed her hand and smiled at her. "It's okay. I understand, and I'm comfortable with whatever you're comfortable calling me."

"I'm glad you're staying with us at the Bay," Grace smiled at Christopher.

"I'm so glad I'm staying here too." Christopher looked into Grace's big blue eyes that were so much like his own. Other than the eyes, Grace looked so much like her mother, Cody.

"I used to make Aiden look for monsters in my cupboard and beneath my bed before I went to sleep at night." Grace twirled Christopher's hat in her hands.

"All kids are afraid of monsters, honey," Christopher smiled at his daughter.

"Oh no, I wasn't afraid of them," Grace surprised Christopher by saying. "When I was little, I can remember Aiden telling Mom that you were the monster in his closet."

Christopher's heart ached when he heard that. Images of his bad moods rocking the house tormented and torched his already shredded soul.

"I'm so sorry, honey," Christopher's voice was hoarse.

Grace smiled at Christopher. "Every night after I'd brushed my teeth, I would sit on the floor between my bed and the closet and sing our song."

"Oh?" Christopher looked surprised. "You sang our song on your floor every night?"

Grace nodded, "I did." Grace looked down at Christopher's hat in her hands. "When I was finished singing, I'd quickly jump into bed and call mom or Aiden to come to check for monsters." She looked up at Christopher. "I'd hold my breath in anticipation each time Aiden would peep under the bed or in the closet."

"Why?"

"Because each night, I was hoping that we'd find you in the closet," Grace gave a small laugh. "I thought if you heard our song, you'd know how much I missed you, and then you'd come back to us."

Christopher looked at his daughter in awe. After everything he'd done, his beautiful child had tried to fearlessly call him home each night even when she'd thought he was a monster.

"But every night, I was disappointed not to find you there," Grace sniffed. Her eyes sparkled with unshed tears. "I even made Mom take me to singing lessons in case I wasn't singing our song right."

"Oh, honey, I...." Christopher swallowed down the emotion burning in his throat. "I'm sure your singing was as beautiful as it was when you sang to me in the hospital."

"Thanks, Dad," Grace kissed him on the cheek before gently placing his cap on his head. "We can't let your head get sunburned."

"Thanks, sweetheart," Christopher smiled lovingly.

"I want you to know," Grace said, "I never stopped loving you, Dad. Mom always said that you were where you needed to be when you left us. I now know that you were." She smiled at him. "Riley's mother needed you as much as you needed her, and now we have the sweetest little brother. He talks a little too much...." She rolled her eyes, "But we wouldn't have it any other way."

"When did you get to be so wise?" Christopher held her soft hand. "I can't believe I have the world's most special kids."

"Trust me," Grace warned him, "a few months in and you'll see we're just normal teenage siblings."

"I doubt that," Christopher said with pride swelling his heart. "My kids are amazing individuals."

"Wakey, wakey," Nancy pulled Christopher out of his light slumber. "I know you're tired, but we need to give your brain a workout and then stretch you out."

"I know," Christopher stifled a yawn and took the pills Nancy handed him.

"Let's get started," Nancy perched herself on the high stool next to his bed and took out her flashcards. "We are going to get a little more complex today. Let me know if at any time you are struggling."

"I will," Christopher sighed, hating that he felt like an invalid.

"Can you believe the nerve of that woman?" Connie shook her head in disgust. "I grew up with Margaret, and I never thought she'd turn into what she is today."

"Oh?" Cody looked up from the shopping list in front of her on her desk. "So she wasn't always the town bully then?" She laughed.

"No," Margaret shook her head. "Before we got to high school, she was sweet, kind, and caring even though she always was the most popular girl in school." She sighed. "In high school, something changed inside, and as beautiful as she was, and still is, mind you, there was no longer anything beautiful about her."

"She most definitely is still a very beautiful woman," Cody agreed with Connie. "I'm sure she has her reasons for turning out the way she has."

"Could've been her controlling father," Connie raised her eyebrows. "That man was so strict, and her parents were determined that she was going to marry within her station."

"Wow," Cody shook her head. "What is wrong with people with money?"

"There are some really great people with money," Connie assured Cody, "just some rich people live in their own wealthy bubble and think they are above everyone else."

"They forget that they are human like the rest of us," Cody sighed, remembering what her gran used to say, "it's only their wealth that is different. It doesn't make them any better or any worse than everyone else."

"Your grandmother used to love saying that," Connie smiled. "I miss her. I miss both your grandmother and grandfather so much. They were such a help when Nancy came to live with me."

"Will you ever tell me the whole story about Nancy's parents and how you got to adopt her?" Cody asked Connie.

"Cody, you know I haven't even told Nancy that," Conned smiled. "One day, when Nancy is ready to hear her story, it will be up to her to tell those she wants to share it with."

"Now you sound like my grandmother," Cody shook her head.

"I have a feeling that some mysteries are about to unravel," Connie said cryptically. "I've felt it in the gentle breeze that has tickled me and whispered in my ear of late."

"You've even taken over my grandmother's role as the Cody Bay soothsayer," Cody laughed. "I guess I better go find the kids and see if they'll come help with this long shopping list."

"Well, honey," Connie stood up from the chair in front of Cody's desk. "It's not my fault both the Inn and your new restaurant are the huge success they are. It's the magic of the Bay and its new owners."

"I'll go with you to the store," Carla said from the door, grabbing Connie's and Cody's attention. "I need a few things, and it will be good to look around the town."

"If you're sure," Cody smiled at Carla. "I hate shopping on my own and find I get things done a lot quicker if Connie's long shopping lists are divided up."

"Cody hates shopping," Connie gave Carla a tight smile.

Cody had noticed Connie instantly stiffen when she'd heard Carla's voice. She'd also noticed the shock on Connie's face when she'd seen Carla walk into the Inn for the first time. For some reason, Connie was always tense and on guard around Carla. Cody was sure Connie knew Carla from somewhere. Margaret Stanford had also seemed to recognize Carla. A prickle ran up Cody's spine.

There was something more to Carla Newton, Cody suspected. From the moment Cody knew that Carla had accepted the post at Nantucket General, Cody had thought there was a deeper reason for Carla accepting the job.

As with everything or everyone that passed through Cody Bay, the mysteries would unravel as they should and reveal their truths when the time was right. For now, Cody and Carla were going grocery shopping, and Cody was happy to have the help—she really did hate grocery shopping.

Chapter Two

THE TRUTH CAN EITHER SET YOU FREE OR IMPRISON YOU

Carla Newton stood staring out over the Atlantic Ocean from her balcony with a cup of coffee in her hand. She loved this time of the morning. The world was just waking up, and the air was still fresh and pure. Everything was quiet except for the flowing sound of the sea. Carla's mind went back to the previous day when she'd come face to face with a woman who'd been the source of her nightmares for the past twenty-eight years.

Carla shuddered. She couldn't believe that she'd frozen the way she had when she'd seen that woman. *Good grief!* Carla was nearly forty-seven years old. She'd headed up hospital departments and gone head to head with some of the toughest people in the world, but she'd frozen the moment she'd looked into the eyes of that woman.

Carla closed her eyes, pushing back the memories that still haunted her and the guilt that ate her up from the inside. But that was one of the reasons she was back in Nantucket. To try and finally put the past behind. Carla knew there were some things she'd never be able to make amends for, but at least she would finally stand up to and own the truth. She turned and walked back inside her room, glancing at the letter on the desk. Carla wasn't the only one who needed closure, and although it scared the hell out of her, she knew it was time.

"You're doing remarkably well, Christopher." Carla jotted down information on her tablet. "I'm glad to see that you're keeping your head covered in the sun."

"My kids make sure I've got a hat on before I leave the house." Christopher put his hat back on.

"Good for them." Carla smiled and looked at her watch. "Nancy should be here by now." She frowned. "She's usually so punctual."

"She really does run on a prompt schedule," Christopher shook his head. "You and she have that in common." He stood and did some balance tests. "In fact, the two of you could be sisters. You have a lot of similar features."

Carla stopped and looked at Christopher as tiny shock waves zinged through her body. *No!* She frowned. *Could it be?* Her frown deepened. *No, it wasn't possible.* Carla shook the thought off. But if she was correct in her estimations, it all added up.

"What is her story?" Carla asked as conversationally as she could.

"I'm not too sure," Christopher admitted. "Nancy doesn't talk about herself much. But, she loves to tell me stories about my kids growing up."

"Your kids do treat her like a big sister," Carla pulled a sad face. "I would've given anything to have had an older sibling."

"Oh, don't you have any brothers or sisters?" Christopher lay on the bed, and Carla started his physical therapy while they waited for Nancy.

"I had an older brother," Carla told him. "He died of Leukemia when he was eleven. I was seven at the time."

"I'm sorry to hear that." Christopher breathed through the exercises. "My second eldest brother was killed in a car accident when I was fourteen."

Christopher had his eyes closed so he didn't notice the stricken look on Carla's face at the mention of the accident that had changed his and Cody's family's lives forever.

14

"Steven told me about the accident," Carla said softly. "I'm sorry about your brother." Christopher couldn't understand just how sorry Carla really was about his late brother Lance.

"It was a surreal night." Christopher closed his eyes for a minute to regain his composure.

Carla could see how much that fateful night still ripped Christopher apart inside. The gut-wrenching guilt started to throb through her like an open wound. Carla tried to shake it off and calm herself by thinking of the patients she had to see that day. Her head shot around when the room door burst open.

"I'm so sorry I'm late," Nancy rushed into the room and started to sanitize her hands. "Things were crazy at Dr. Baxter's surgery."

Carla stopped what she was doing and stepped aside for Nancy to take over.

"How is Dr. Baxter?" Christopher asked Nancy. "Has he recovered from his stroke?"

"Stroke?" Carla's eyes widened. "When did he have a stroke?" She hoped the panic she'd felt at the mention of the doctor having a stroke wasn't reflected in her voice.

"About five months ago," Nancy told Carla. "Luckily, one of the other nurses at his practice was able to get Dr. Baxter to Nantucket General in time."

"Thank goodness for that." Carla breathed a sigh of relief. "Why didn't you become a doctor?" She asked Nancy. "I was looking at your resume, and you could've quite easily become one."

"I love what I do." Nancy shrugged. "Being a nurse practitioner, I get to help people in ways doctors can't."

"That's true," Carla agreed with Nancy. "Your mother must be so proud of you."

"She is," Nancy gave Carla a smile.

"How long have you been at Cody Bay?" Carla asked Nancy.

"Since I ran away from my foster parents," Nancy glanced at Carla, whose face had gone ashen. "Are you okay?"

"Yes, why?" Carla asked Nancy as she quickly regained her composure.

"You're usually all cold and business-like," Nancy said truthfully. "In all the weeks you've been here you haven't once joined in with any of the summer festivities, teas, and so on."

"I..." Carla was a little taken aback. "I've been busy settling into the Nantucket way of life and catching up on how things work at Nantucket General." That wasn't a lie; Carla had simply left off some truths.

"I get that," Nancy gave Carla a smile. "I used to be a loner too. Well before Connie took me and became my legal guardian."

"May I ask what happened to your parents?" Carla looked at Christopher when she heard him snoring.

Nancy smiled when she saw Carla looking at Christopher. "He always falls asleep when I loosen his back muscles."

"Christopher told me you have magic massage fingers," Carla laughed.

"I never knew my real parents," Nancy told Carla in answer to her previous question. "I was adopted as soon as I was born by a lovely couple. Trevor and Dotty Honey."

"Why did you run away from them?" Something niggled at the back of Carla's mind as she looked at Nancy.

"The Honeys couldn't have kids of their own," Nancy explained to Carla. "They adopted me when they were in their late forties."

"Oh," Carla raised her eyebrows in surprise.

"My father turned fifty the year of my first birthday." Nancy smiled, remembering him. "He was the kindest, most patient man. When my mother started to get early-onset dementia when I was five-years-old, he had to retire early. So he sold his construction company to take care of my mother and me."

"He sounds like he was one of a kind." Carla watched Nancy carefully. Now that it was pointed out to her by Christopher, Carla could see the likeness between herself and Nancy.

"He was." Nancy looked away to hide the tears sparkling in her eyes. "My mother had other complications and died of pneumonia when I was eight. My father was heartbroken, but he carried on as long as he could because he had me to care for."

Carla's heart broke for the young woman standing in front of her.

"I was eleven when my father died," Nancy swallowed. "I have no other relatives, so I was put in foster care. My foster parents were the Andersons." She shook her head.

"Deke Anderson?" Carla looked at Nancy in amazement.

"Do you know him?" Nancy frowned at Carla.

"Uh..." *Uh oh, Carla, that wasn't very clever.* "He came into the hospital in need of hydration after a weekend alcohol binge." *That wasn't a lie, at least*, Carla thought.

"Sounds right," Nancy's eyes flashed. "I put up with their drunken verbal abuse, wearing hand-me-down clothes from his wife Terry that were too big for me, and going hungry for two years."

"Nancy, that's awful." Carla's heart hurt for her. "How did Social Services not see what was happening?"

"Every time they came around to check up on me, the Andersons would get everything cleaned up and be on their best behavior." Nancy's eyes flashed with anger. "A teacher complained about my bruises to Social Services. Deke liked to use his fists instead of a belt to dole out punishment."

"Oh my God, Nancy." Carla could feel a lump rising in her throat at the woman's tragic story.

"Deke was clever and knew how to turn it around to make it look like I was deliberately hurting myself so they wouldn't lose their foster parent grant," Nancy shook her head. "They also used up the monthly cheques that came to me from the trust fund my parents set up for me."

"How can people do things like that?" Carla was shocked and angry for what the Andersons had put Nancy through.

"I ran away after one night in particular." Nancy cleared her throat but didn't elaborate on the story. "I found my way to Cody Bay. Old Mrs. Moore was a good friend of my Mother's. She took me in. Connie had just lost her husband, who'd had a heart attack, and we kind of found each other."

"I have no words, Nancy," Carla was horrified at what Nancy had gone through at such a young age—how cruel fate had been to her.

"Connie and her husband couldn't have kids." Nancy smiled. "She says that Cody Bay drew me to it at a time when we both needed to fill a hole in each other's lives."

"I'm so happy your story had a happy ending," Carla told her. "Maybe Cody Bay is as magical as everyone has always said it was."

"Okay, big guy," Nancy shook Christopher awake. "Time to wake up from your nap. You're all done for the day."

"Just a few more minutes, Mom." Christopher rolled over and stretched. "I sleep so well during your massages."

"Are you not sleeping well?" Carla frowned at Christopher in concern.

"I do." Christopher shrugged putting his shirt back on. "Most nights."

"Why didn't you tell me this sooner?" Carla asked him.

"I did," Christopher reminded Carla.

"That was about your headaches." Carla pulled out her tablet and scrolled through it.

"I don't get many of those now," Christopher assured Carla. "I have a lot on my mind and have been plagued with dreams."

"What kind of dreams?" Carla and Nancy said at once before looking at each and smiling.

As soon as Nancy's face lit with a smile, her left cheek dimpled, and her big blue eyes sparkled with amusement, Carla saw it. She moved her head from Nancy to Christopher, who grinned back at them. Carla's breath caught in her chest; her heart thudded hard in her chest. She dropped her tablet as the shock hit her like she'd been zapped with a cattle prod.

"Carla," Nancy ran forward and reached out to grab Carla's forearms. "Are you okay?"

"I...," Carla fought to get herself under control.

"Here." Nancy bent down and scooped up Carla's tablet from the floor. "Luckily, there is carpet on the floor, as you have no screen protection on your device."

"Thank you." Carla took her tablet from Nancy. "Sorry, I realized I have to be somewhere."

"Sure," Nancy frowned at her. "Are you sure you're okay? You look like you've seen a ghost."

"I'm fine," Carla lied. She felt like she was suffocating and someone had just punched through the chest. "I'd better be going."

Carla turned and fled from the room. Her mind was reeling, and long-buried memories burst from the deep dark depth she'd buried them in. Carla's urgent need to get to her room blinded her, and she knocked into Steven.

"Whoa," Steven reached out and steadied Carla. "Where's the fire?"

"What?" Carla looked up at Steven.

"Are you okay?" Steven's smile changed to a frown as he looked at her worriedly.

"I..." Carla breathed. "I'm sorry, I'm late for a conference call consultation."

Steven stepped aside and let her pass. "Call me later for an update on Christopher," he called after Carla.

"I will," Carla promised as she fled to her room.

*Carla let herself into her room and put the *do not disturb* sign on the door. She stripped off her clothes and did what she always did when a panic attack hit her—she jumped into a hot shower. Carla scrubbed her body, hair, and nails until she felt like she'd scrubbed her panic away.

She'd started getting panic attacks at the age of nineteen, the year her life had changed forever. Carla remembered her mother having panic attacks, and every time her mother had one, she'd take a shower. When Carla asked her why she did that, her mother had told it helped her wash away the panic.

After her shower, Carla pulled on a flowing sundress and picked up the letter on the desk. She stared at the name on the letter—*Miss Charlene Baxter*. Her hands trembled as she shoved the letter into one of the desk drawers and slammed it shut. Carla was not going to let the ghost of Charlene Baxter haunt her anymore.

It was time to find out the truth and to finally come clean about her past. Carla had dragged the secrets trapped in her heart around with her for far too long now.

Carla was no longer a powerless and scared nineteen-year-old girl, she reminded herself again. She was a strong, independent woman that had fought her way to the top of her profession. Carla had to stay focused on her mission and not get side-tracked or allow her emotions to interfere with what she had to do. And her first step to redemption was letting the people who thought they could control her know that Charlene Baxter had died a long, long time ago—Carla had made sure of that!

Carla picked up the phone and dialed a number. It was answered on the third ring.

"Dr. Newton," a deep voice drawled from the other side. "It's been a while."

"Hello, Brandon," Carla greeted her ex-husband. They'd had an amicable divorce sixteen years ago, and they were closer now than they'd been when they were married. "I know and that's my fault."

"It is," Brandon agreed with her. "You've missed our past two dates."

"The first one wasn't my fault," Carla reminded him. "You were the one that stood me up."

"I know," Brandon laughed. "So I hear you finally went back to Nantucket."

"You really do have ears everywhere, don't you?" Carla was amazed the news had reached Brandon so fast.

"I just hope you know what you're doing, Carla." He said softly. "Why would you ever take on the Stanford case?"

"Sucker for punishment?" Carla gave a little laugh. "Steven needed me." Her voice dropped. "I owed him that much."

"Honey, we've been over this a million times," Brandon's voice held an edge of anger. "You don't owe that horrible family anything. And I hope you're staying away from that ass of a father of yours."

"I am," Carla's heart warmed. Brandon had always been very protective of her. "It was why she'd been drawn to him in the first place. He made her feel safe. "I have not gone around there."

"Good," Brandon said. "Where are you staying?"

"In the most magical place on the island," Carla looked out her bedroom window over the sparkling Atlantic Ocean. "It's beautiful here. You need to come here for a vacation or at least look over the proposal I sent you. They need good surgeons here, Brand, and you're the best I know."

"I'm considering it," Brandon promised her.

"Sophie would love it here." Carla knew she was using emotional blackmail now. "You know how much she loves the beach. I know that one of Cody's bungalows will be opening up soon, and it would be a great new start for the both of you."

"Are you using my daughter to blackmail me, Dr. Newton?" Carla could hear the smile in Brandon's voice.

"Is it working?" Carla asked him.

"I promise you, I'm thinking about it," Brandon sighed. "She misses you, you know," he said softly.

"I miss her too," Carla said honestly. "She's growing up so fast, and this is a difficult age for her. Teenage girls need female support."

"Is that your way of prying into my love life?" Brandon laughed. "I'm not ready to go for round three, and I could never do that to Sophie. She's had a rough few years since Tricia pulled a disappearing act on us."

"You mean since Tricia drained your bank accounts, left you with a mountain load of debt, and a five-year-old daughter?" Carla's voice was laced with anger. "I told you I never liked her."

"I know." Brandon sighed. "Speaking of love lives, who are you dating these days?"

"No one." It was not an outright lie. Carla had gone on four dates with Steven Stanford, which couldn't really even be classed as a date because they discussed business. "I've been too busy saving lives and moving to a new town."

"You use that excuse a lot," Brandon pointed out to her. "I hope you're not there to rekindle old flames, Carla."

"I think it's time to put the past behind me, Brand." Carla looked at the drawer she'd shoved the letter into. "Some ghosts won't go away until their business is finished."

"Please be careful, and check in with me at least twice a week," Brandon made her promise. "You know it's going to make some evil people very nervous just to see you back there. God knows what they'll do if you start snooping around."

There had never been any secrets between Carla and Brandon. That had been their one major rule between them since they'd met. Brandon was the one person on earth that knew her entire life story. They may not have worked as husband and wife, but they worked as best friends.

"I already ran into one of them." Carla's voice dropped. "She didn't recognize me, though."

"You went to great lengths to change your appearance," Brandon pointed out. "At least you know it was all worth it."

"I'm not too sure," Carla told him honestly. "I also think I've found the child."

"You have?" Brandon asked.

"That's why I was calling," Carla admitted. "Do you think you could get that PI you know to help me get some records and do some digging?"

"Do you think that's wise?" Brandon asked her. "I don't like him to think he's doing us any favors."

"Us?" Carla asked in surprise.

"Yes," Brandon said sternly. "Us. You don't think I'd let you do this on your own, do you?"

"No," Carla smiled suddenly, realizing she'd reached out to him because she knew Brandon would be her rock and not let her navigate what she had to do on her own. "Thank you, Brand."

"Anytime, Tinker Bell," Brandon used the nickname he'd given her since the day they'd met at a costume party where she was dressed as Tinker Bell. "Send over what you need dug up, and I'll get you the information you need. But now that I'm pretty sure I know what you're up to, you have to promise to check in with me every day."

"Deal," Carla breathed a sigh of relief. She no longer felt so alone.

"Love you, and I'll send you the info as soon as I have it," Brandon promised.

"Love you too, Brand." Carla hung up feeling a lot better.

Chapter Three
THE DIRT BIKE INCIDENT

Steven Stanford looked at the young woman sitting in front of him and shook his head.

"You're not fourteen anymore," Steven raised his eyebrows as he stitched up her eye. "Look at you." He sat back and pulled off the latex gloves. "You look like you were in a bar brawl."

"I wish it was that exciting," Nancy mumbled and winced when she touched her split lip.

"Why were you on the dirt bike track in the first place?" Steven asked her.

"I went with Aiden," Nancy told Steven. "But you can't say anything to Cody."

"That shouldn't be a problem," Steven told her. "Cody is not exactly speaking to me at the moment."

"Oh, yeah, that's right." Nancy looked at Steven slyly. "Which means you can't rat us out."

"What exactly were you and Aiden doing at the dirt bike track?" Steven raised an eyebrow at her.

"That's privileged information." Nancy went to fold her arm across her chest. "Ow!" She grabbed her left arm.

"Ah, yes the arm," Steven turned his tablet around to show her the X-rays he'd just received. "What does that look like to you?"

"Uh oh." Nancy pulled a face. "That doesn't look good."

"It's not," Steven agreed with her. "This is the third time you've broken this arm, Nancy."

"I haven't broken it for years, though." Nancy gave Steven a puppy dog eyes look.

"Nancy, you have an important job now," Steven reminded her. "How are you going to work with a broken arm and your face looking like you came out second best in a catfight?"

"I would say I was the one that won the fight." Nancy held up the index finger of her good arm. "I'll put a sign around my neck to tell everyone I was in a motorbike accident."

"What are you going to tell Cody?" Steven looked up as the nurse brought Aiden back into the room. "You're lucky only Aiden's ankle is sprained, and he has a few cuts and bruises."

"It was so worth it," Aiden grinned. "You should've seen her, Uncle Steven," he said proudly. "Nancy rules on the dirt track."

"I'm sure your mother is going to love hearing that," Steven said and grinned.

"You were at the dirt bike track?" Cody's shocked voice had Aiden and Nancy both turning around in fright.

"Mom," Aiden breathed. "I... uh..." He looked at Nancy for help.

"It was my fault," Nancy took the fall. "I took Aiden to the track to go and practice."

"Of course you did," Cody's face said she didn't believe Nancy. "So you wrote and signed this note from Aiden yourself?" She handed the evidence to Nancy.

"Yes, I did." Nancy stuck to her story. "I wrote that note and signed it from Aiden."

"Mom, I'm sorry," Aiden manned-up. "I've always wanted to try dirt bikes. I knew Nancy used to race dirt bikes, so I asked her to take me and not tell you."

"No," Nancy butted in. "I took Aiden with me. This is my fault, not his. We were going for a ride around the course so Aiden could get a feel for it when this kid skidded out into us."

"Well, Aiden," Cody's eyes narrowed, "you're grounded for a

month." She turned to Nancy, "And you'll be on housekeeping duty with Aiden's help."

"Mom, I've got a sprained ankle." Aiden showed her. "And Nancy has a broken arm."

"You'll both figure out how to do your chores," Cody looked at Steven. "Are they still able to do their chores?"

Steven was so shocked that Cody had addressed him instead of talking around him, he sat in stunned silence for a while.

"Yes," Steven said, "they can do light chores. I'd give them a day, though."

"Are they ready to go home?" Cody asked Steven.

"Nancy needs to have her arm set," Steven told Cody. "But they should be good to go in about thirty minutes. We're still waiting for some of Aiden's tests to come back."

"I'm going to go to the store," Cody looked from Aiden to Nancy. "I'll be back to fetch the two of you in thirty minutes." She turned and left the room.

"That went well," Nancy said.

"For you, maybe." Aiden looked towards the door his mother had just marched out of. "I had plans this weekend."

"That's life, kid," Nancy pointed out to Aiden. "It doesn't work out the way you want it to."

"That just sucks." Aiden looked at Nancy. "But it was worth it."

"Totally worth it," Nancy agreed with Aiden. "But next time, I think we should ask your mom."

"You're kidding, right?" Aiden winced as Steven pressed his ribs. "Hey, that hurts," he grumbled. "Do you really think after this my mother will let me near the track again?" He looked at Nancy. "We have to do it without her knowing."

"You've bruised your ribs," Steven told him. "It could've been worse; you could have broken them."

"But I didn't," Aiden said. He looked at Nancy, "We can't tell her, and now that I'm grounded, we're going to have to sneak out next Saturday."

"You got lucky this time." Steven raised his eyebrows. "You both did." He stood up. "Trust me, Cody won't let there be a next time." He wrote something on his tablet. "I wouldn't go sneaking back to the track anytime soon."

"I'm sure my mom will have calmed down by then." Aiden looked at Steven.

"Don't look at me," Steven told Aiden. "Your mom hasn't spoken to me since you went to Boston."

"I'll help you if you get back in Mom's good books if you help us," Aiden grinned at Steven.

"No," Steven shook his head. "It's up to me to get your mother to forgive me." He looked at his watch. "Now, let's get your arm set as I have an appointment."

"A date, you mean?" Nancy's eyes narrowed. "Ooh, is it Dr. Newton?"

"I'm not going on a date," Steven assured them. "If you must know, renovations are starting on my house. Because the house is being completely gutted, I have to find a place to stay for two to three months."

"Why don't you just come stay at Cody Bay?" Aiden asked Steven.

"Because I'm not in your mother's good books," Steven reminded Aiden. "We've just had a conversation about Cody not talking to me."

"Aiden's right. Cody wouldn't mind," Nancy backed Aiden up. "I know the smaller room next to Dr. Newton is available."

"What about the cottage?" Steven knew it was pointless to ask because Carla wouldn't want him there anyway.

"It's been booked by another Dr. Newton," Nancy told him and grinned.

"Another Dr. Newton?" Steven's brows creased together. "Oh, right." He remembered. "I think he's a relative of Carla's. She's offered him the chief of surgery position here at the hospital."

"Or..." Nancy held up her index finger again, "the male Dr. Newton could be her husband." She gave him a smug smile.

"Ex," Carla had all heads turning towards where she was standing by the door. "Dr. Newton is my ex-husband," she corrected Nancy.

"Carla!" Steven stood up, nearly knocking the equipment cart over.

"I take it you were telling them about our potential new head of surgery?" Carla walked into the room.

"Uh..." Nancy looked at Steven and Aiden, who were not sure how to answer Carla. "Yes, that's what Steven was saying."

"Brandon is a top surgeon; we'll be lucky to get him," Carla informed them. "What happened to you two?"

"Dirt bike racing," Nancy said.

"You're not going to be able to work with your hand like that." Carla eyed Nancy's arm that Steven was setting in plaster.

"I still have one hand." Nancy held up her good hand.

"You're going to have to be careful." Carla stood next to Nancy, who was sitting on a bed and picked up her X-ray. "Have you broken this arm before?"

"This is her third time," Steven was sitting down again and finishing off setting Nancy's arm in a plaster cast. "The first time she broke it, she was fifteen."

"Another dirt bike accident?" She looked at Nancy questioningly.

"Nope." Nancy shook her head and bit her lip.

"She broke it punching a seventeen-year-old hockey player," Steven explained to Carla.

"You hit him that hard?" Carla's eyes widened, and a smile split her face revealing a dimple in her left cheek.

"She did." Steven's heart lurched when he saw that dimple crease Carla's cheek. "Young Nancy was always getting into brawls until she found dirt bike racing and mixed martial arts."

Nancy gave a sheepish grin that showed off her dimple. Steven's breath caught in his throat, looking from Carla to Nancy. *Why haven't I noticed how similar they looked before?* Steven thought. Their eyes, hair, and some of their mannerisms were identical.

"So you were the rebel?" Carla looked at Nancy.

"Nancy doesn't like bullies," Aiden told Carla. "I remember her first broken arm because I decorated it with superheroes." He looked at Nancy. "Nancy always tried to stop bullies from picking on other kids."

"Aiden is quite the artist," Nancy changed the subject. "Some of those paintings on the wall of the Cody Bay Inn entrance hall are done by him."

"Really?" Carla looked at Aiden impressed. "You're going to have to show me which ones."

"They're all his." Steven finished off Nancy's arm and pulled off the latex gloves. "I'll go get you a sling for the arm."

"Wow, Aiden. Are you going to study art?" Carla asked Aiden. "Because I have to say those paintings are brilliant."

"No." Aiden shook his head. "It's just a hobby."

"I've always told him he should study art." Steven stood up and was about to call a nurse to take the suture cart away, when Carla stopped him.

"I actually need that cart if you're finished with it?" Carla asked Steven.

"Sure, I'll get it cleaned up." Steven started to push it again, but Carla stopped him.

"No, that's fine." Carla took the cart before Steven could argue. "I'll do it on the way."

"If you don't mind," Steven thanked Carla before looking from Nancy to Aiden. "I'll be back in a minute."

Steven walked out of the room thinking about the likeness between Nancy and Carla. They had the same unusual violet-colored eyes, dark hair that gleamed a rich red in the sun. Then there was the dimple in the left cheek. Nancy's dimple was identical to Carla's. Dimples were an inherited trait.

Something niggled at the back of Steven's mind as he went to get a nurse to take a sling to Nancy.

"Can you please take a sling to room twelve?" Steven asked the duty nurse. "I have another appointment I'm running late for." He signed off Aiden's and Nancy's charts. "Please tell Nancy and Aiden they can go when Cody Moore gets here to fetch them."

"I will do," the nurse printed out the two release forms.

"Thank you." Steven walked towards his office.

29

His pulse quickened as he thought about the first day he'd Met Carla thirteen years ago at a medical conference at the Atwood hotel in Boston.

THIRTEEN YEARS AGO - ATWOOD 5-STAR HOTEL, BOSTON

Steven had been looking forward to this medical conference for months. It was a talk on brain tumors and the new treatment that would soon be available. He'd been consulting every neurologist, neurosurgeon, oncologist, and even herbalists to find help for his younger brother.

Steven knew there must be some way to help Christopher. The medications were no longer helping Christopher, and his mood swings, blackouts, and pain were getting worse. Steven was worried about Christopher's family as well. He'd all but begged Christopher to tell his wife what was going on with him.

Steven lived in constant fear of Christopher completely losing control around his family. Christopher had two small children who he doted on and an amazing wife. But Steven feared that Christopher was going to lose them if he kept his condition a secret for much longer—especially as he may need surgery.

Steven found the conference room and walked in. The room was full of medical professionals. He found a seat and sat down, glancing at his watch. The conference would be starting soon and was being given by one of the top neurologists, Dr. Carla Newton. She also specialized in oncology, and Steven was hoping to be able to have a word with her after the conference.

A noise at the door had him turn his head. A tall, well-dressed woman glided into the room. Her head turned in Steven's direction and their eyes locked for a second, making Steven's breath catch in his throat. *Oh, my God, it's her!* He finally let out his breath.

The woman had her phone to her ear and looked away. Steven got the impression that although their eyes had met, she hadn't really seen him. She was concentrating on her phone call. His pulse raced the closer she got to his seat on the aisle. *Had he finally found her after nearly sixteen years of looking for her?* he wondered excitedly.

But as the woman walked closer, he saw the name tag on her blazer—Dr. Carla Newton. His heart sank, and he realized that other than the same color eyes and similar features, that it wasn't the woman he'd been looking for. Steven felt so disappointed, and his heart had sunk to his feet.

When the conference got underway, Steven watched Dr. Carla Newton intently. Some of her mannerisms and her smile brought out the dimple in her left cheek that reminded him of the person he'd lost sixteen years ago. By the end of the evening, after talking to Dr. Newton, Steven still wondered about Carla. *Was it possible she'd had surgery to hide the scar on her face?*

A few times during the evening after the conference, Steven found himself staring at Carla. He was looking for clues that she may be hiding who she really was behind a surgical disguise. Anyone could change their name, although he didn't know why she would've done that. The woman he was looking for had nothing to hide from, or at least nothing he knew of. That same horrible thought struck his heart once again. Unless, of course, she was hiding from him and his family—not that Steven could blame her for that.

When he'd introduced himself to Carla, there was not a flicker of recognition in her eyes. She treated him like she had everyone else who'd gone up to talk to her. Steven had offered to buy her a nightcap to talk to her about Christopher. For the rest of that evening, he'd tried to find out more about her. He'd asked her if she'd ever been to Nantucket, and she'd said, *Of course, hasn't nearly everyone who lives in Boston?*

After the conference, Steven had met up with Carla a few times, and they'd become good friends. Then Carla went off to France for a year, and they'd lost touch as her one year in France stretched into four. After France, Carla was never in one place for long as she traveled around the States until landing the position as head of neurology at Boston General.

PRESENT DAY

Steven pulled an old photo from his wallet and stared at it.

"Where are you?" Steven asked softly and ran his fingers over the photo. "Why do you and Carla look so much alike?"

He knew everyone thought he was in love with Cody, and that was why he'd never married or settled into a relationship for very long. Steven did love Cody, but his love for her was more like the love a brother has for his sister. He looked at the picture again. He'd known the minute he'd laid eyes on Charlene Baxter that she was his one true love.

Only, some love stories don't have happy endings but tragic ones. Unfortunately, Steven and Charlene's love story had been one of the tragic ones, and they'd met a little too late. She'd been going out with someone for years when she and Steven had met. But the connection between them had been an instant one. The minute Steven had looked into Charlene's eyes, he knew she'd felt it too.

Steven and Charlene tried their best to ignore their feelings for each other, but they were too strong. They'd had a secret summer romance that had ended abruptly on the night of Steven's late brother Lance's death. It was a night he'd never forget, and the guilt still made his stomach churn. After Lance's death, Steven had sat at his grave nearly every day asking for forgiveness.

Since the night of the accident, when Stephen wasn't working or sleeping, he was looking for Charlene. Steven lost more than just his brother on the night of the accident. He'd lost everything except his career and his youngest brother. Steven had also lost whatever shred of respect he'd had for his parents when he'd gotten home the next morning after the accident and overheard a conversation his mother was having. He'd carried that conversation with him for almost twenty-nine years. It was the reason he'd walked away from everything the Stanfords stood for. It was also the reason he couldn't bear to be in the same vicinity of a few key residents on Nantucket.

If it hadn't been for Cody and Christopher and the need to protect them, Steven would've left Nantucket many years ago and never looked back. Steven pulled himself out of memories and switched on his laptop to do a search on Dr. Carla Newton. It was something he should've done a long time ago. They'd dated a few times over the past few weeks, but Carla never let him get too close to her.

He started to type on the laptop. *Let's see if you really are who you say you are, Dr. Carla Newton.* But his search didn't bring up much about her personal life, only about her career.

Chapter Four
SEARCHING FOR ANSWERS

Carla wheeled the suture cart into her office and looked at the blood-stained cotton swab. Her heart pounded. She had the material she needed to find out who Nancy Honey really was. Carla picked up the cotton swab and put it into a small clear bag. She opened the top of her desk drawer and pulled out another small clear bag with a DNA sample in it.

Carla shoved the two bags into her coat pocket before cleaning up the suture tray as she promised to before handing it to a nurse who needed it. She rushed towards the lab, not looking where she was going, and nearly plowed Steven over, who was coming out of his office.

"Whoa, are you okay?" Steven automatically reached out to steady her.

Carla's pulse quickened at the feel of Steven's strong hands wrapped around her upper arms. She quickly stepped back out of his hold and mentally gathered her thoughts.

"Sorry," Carla looked up at Steven. "I wasn't looking where I was going."

"I'm glad we ran into each other." Steven grinned. "I was coming to see you to ask if you'd like to have dinner with me tonight at Cody Bay."

"Sure." Carla smiled. "I'd like that."

"I will meet you at the reception desk at seven?" Steven asked.

"I'll be there." Carla glanced at her watch. "I have to go."

"Of course." Steven stepped aside to let Carla pass.

Carla hit the up button on the elevator, and the doors swung open. She waved to Steven as she climbed in, and her hand shook when she pushed the button to take her two floors up. Her heart was still beating a little wildly from getting so close to Steven. Images of a time gone by flashed through her mind, but she shook them off. Carla didn't have time to indulge in a walk down memory lane. She had a busy afternoon ahead of her.

Carla let herself into the lab and walked over to the lab technician who was going to run the tests discreetly for her.

"Hi," Carla pulled the two cotton swabs from her coat pocket. "Here are samples for the test I called about." She handed them to one of the lab technicians.

"I'll get right on these for you, Dr. Newton," the lab tech promised. "I should have the results for you by tomorrow."

"Thank you." Carla signed the form she was handed. "The results must only come to me. This is a rather sensitive case."

"I understand," the lab tech assured her.

Carla left the lab and headed to a consulting room. She had a patient to see before she went back to Cody Bay for Christopher's checkup. But, her mind kept drifting back to the DNA tests being run. Carla couldn't believe she'd not seen how uncanny Nancy's resemblance to her real parents was. But then again, Carla hadn't been looking for a female, she'd been looking for a male. So she wasn't looking that hard for female resemblances.

Her phone beeped. It was a message from Brandon.

I've managed to get the help we need to dig into the information you want. Will have it for you in a few days.
Brand

Carla's heart leaped. She was finally getting somewhere, and as soon as she had all the proof she needed, it was time for a showdown. A showdown that had been a long time coming so she could finally put the past to rest. Although Carla was pretty sure she was about to poke a hibernating bear, it would be worth it in the end, and she would no longer have to carry all this secrecy and guilt around with her.

Carla was on her way to the consulting room when she was paged. She looked at her watch and sighed. Carla was running late, and now she had to make a detour. She hurried to the station where she was being paged and froze when she saw who was standing there waiting for her.

"Ah, there you are, Dr. Newton." Margaret Stanford walked towards her. "I'm glad I was able to catch you."

"What can I do for you?" It took everything Carla had to keep her cool, calm demeanor. Inside she was still a scared, bewildered, and torn-up nineteen-year-old around Margaret Stanford.

"You've taken such good care of my youngest son," Margaret complimented Carla. "If it wasn't for you, we'd be going through all those other treatments Christopher had to have before."

"I'm glad I was able to help him." Carla looked at her watch. "If that's all, I have an appointment."

"Of course," Margaret said. "I understand you must be very busy. I've been told that you've also brought a lot of patients to Nantucket to receive your care."

"You need to thank Steven for that," Carla admitted to Margaret. "I merely do the consulting."

"Don't be so modest." Margaret frowned. "Do you have relatives in Nantucket?"

Carla's pager went off. "Excuse me." She pulled her pager out of her pocket. "I'm sorry, Mrs. Stanford, but I have to go."

"Before you do," Margaret's hand grabbed Carla's arm, making Carla go cold. "I have a dear friend who could use your help."

"Would you like to walk with me, Mrs. Stanford? You can tell me how I can help along the way." Carla suppressed a shudder. She felt like she was walking with the devil.

"About five months ago, my dear friend had a stroke," Margaret began. "Would you be able to give him a consultation as I'm worried that he is not making the progress he should be."

A tingling crept up Carla's spine as another conversation about a stroke victim flashed through her mind. *Surely Margaret wasn't asking her to help Dr. Baxter?* "May I ask who this friend is so I can check their records?" Carla asked Margaret coolly.

"I don't know if you know Baxter's Medical practice on the island?" Margaret waited for Carla's response.

"I've heard about it," Carla told her. *No, no, no!* her mind screamed. "But, I'm sorry, Mrs. Stanford, I'm not comfortable taking on patients without their consent."

"I understand," Margaret said. "Dr. Baxter has given his consent for the consultation." She filed in her purse and brought out the signed document. "Dr. Baxter means a lot to me." Her voice dropped. "Please, we need your help."

"I can refer you to another doctor who has a lot more experience with strokes than I do." Carla looked at the signed paper. "I'm sorry, Mrs. Stanford, but this is not my field."

Carla had stopped outside the consultation room she was supposed to have been in ten minutes ago.

"Please send me the details." Margaret pulled a card from her purse. "Here are my contact details."

Margaret Stanford gave Carla a small smile. "Thank you for your time, Dr. Newton," she said as she turned and walked off.

Carla stood staring after Margaret with a frown on her face. Was it Carla's imagination, or did the formidable Margaret Stanford look a little defeated? Carla had seen the hope fade from Margaret's eyes when Carla had told her she couldn't help her. Carla had waited for the day she saw that defeated look on Margaret Stanford's face.

But Carla didn't feel good about turning Margaret away or having to have lied to her. She felt awful. But there were other reasons Carla couldn't take Dr. Baxter on as a patient—reasons she wasn't ready to share with anyone just yet. Carla walked into the examination room and greeted her patient. She'd ponder on

Margaret's reaction later and the fact that she'd called Dr. Baxter a dear friend!

"*D*ad, please, can you speak to Mom?" Aiden was having a milkshake with Christopher. "She's being unreasonable."

"Son, I'm not going to pick a side here." Christopher took a sip of his tea. He wasn't allowed a milkshake, even though he really wanted one. It was amazing how much Aiden took after him. They both loved vanilla shakes, mustard, fries with ketchup, and M&M's. "You should've been open with your mother and told her where you were going with Nancy."

"I know." Aiden sighed resignedly. "I knew she'd say no, and I was dying to try dirt biking."

"I used to ride dirt bikes at your age." Christopher saw the interest spark in Aiden's eyes.

"Really?" Aiden leaned back in the booth to look at Christopher.

"Yeah," Christopher laughed. "It was a great outlet for me after your Uncle Lance died."

"I'm sorry, Dad," Aiden's voice softened. "That must've been the worst."

"It really was," Christopher admitted. "Losing someone close to you is something you never really get over."

"I know that feeling." Aiden gave Christopher a tight smile. "I remember when Grandad died. I felt like there was this big hole inside of me, and it ached every day. It still does at times. It was the same for Gran."

"Your grandparents were good people." Christopher patted Aiden's hand. "I'll speak to your mother about the dirt bikes, but I can't do anything about you being grounded."

"That's fair." Aiden sighed.

Christopher's heart filled with pride as he stared at Aiden. At his age, Christopher would've made plans to sneak out and go get into more trouble.

"No," Cody expressed herself quite clearly. "Absolutely not!"

"I'll be that at the track with him," Christopher argued. "Steve said that he would ride with Aiden."

"No." Cody shook her head. "Look what happened just yesterday. I'm sorry, but my answer is no, and I won't change my mind."

"Cody, I'll get him all the correct gear, and I'll be right there with him," Christopher pleaded with Cody.

"Sorry, is this a bad time?" Nancy popped her head through Cody's office door.

"No, come on in," Cody invited Nancy in.

"I'm sorry, I want to say I wasn't eavesdropping, but...." Nancy shrugged. "But I was eavesdropping, and I wanted to apologize to you for taking Aiden dirt biking without your permission. But, Cody, Aiden is a natural, and he loves the sport. The accident wasn't his fault; it was mine."

"Am I being ganged up on?" Cody looked from Nancy to Christopher. "How about this? Aiden can't ride or do anything for the next week or so while his ankle heals. During that time his ankle is healing, I promise I'll think about letting him ride dirt bikes."

"Deal," Nancy said excitedly before Christopher could get a word in.

"What she said." Christopher grinned. "I'll go tell him."

"After which, you need to go to the therapy room," Nancy reminded him. "I'll see you there in ten minutes." Nancy left the office.

"How is your therapy going?" Cody asked Christopher.

"I don't think I need it anymore." Christopher sighed. "But I have two doctors and a nurse practitioner that think otherwise."

39

"They are the experts." Cody sat back in her chair. "I know it's been frustrating for you."

"You and the kids have helped me tremendously." Christopher's eyes held Cody's. "I don't know what I would've done without all of you. You helped Riley, and he's so happy again. You gave me a second chance with Aiden and Grace." He swallowed. "The only thing that would make the happiest man in the world is...."

"Mom," Grace burst into the office before Christopher could finish. "Oh, hi, Dad." She glanced at Christopher. "Tiny's gone missing. We've looked everywhere for him."

"Oh, no!" Cody's eyes widened. "Did you go down to the cove?"

"No." Grace shook her head. "That's why we came to you."

"Hi, Aunt Cody." Harper West waved.

"Hello, Harper," Cody greeted the teenager. "Have you got his leash?"

"I have." Harper held up Tiny's leash.

"Let's go." Cody slipped off her sandals and put the sneakers she kept under her desk on instead.

"We'll meet you outside, Mom," Grace called over her shoulder as she and Harper took off.

"I'll come too." Christopher pushed his chair back.

As Christopher stood up, Cody came around her desk, and they collided. Christopher's arms immediately went around her and pulled her to him to stop her from falling over. Their eyes met and held. Cody's hands were pressed up against his chest, and Christopher felt his pulse quicken. They stood lost in each other's eyes when a loud squawking noise came from Professor Squawking's cage.

"Tiny's missing, Tiny's missing," the parrot repeated over and over.

Cody stepped back and broke out of Christopher's embrace.

"I don't think that's a good idea." Cody cleared her throat. "The cove is quite treacherous if you don't know how to navigate it, and you have an appointment with Nancy. We'll be fine."

"I agree with Cody," Carla said from the door, getting their attention. "When I'm done with your checkup, I'll go down to the cove and help look for Tiny. It's not a good idea for you to be there."

"Fine." Christopher clenched his jaw. He hated not being able to do things because of his head. "Please be careful," he said softly to Cody.

"I will," Cody assured him before stepping past him and rushing out the door.

Chapter Five
TINY AND THE BABY SEAL

"I know it's hard." Carla looked at Christopher. "But a few more weeks of taking it easy is worth the lifetime you're going to get to be with your family."

"You're right," Christopher agreed. "It's just so damn hard having to stand on the sideline all the time."

"You know it's not permanent," Carla assured him. "Now come on, Nancy has already called me five times."

"Are you sure the two of you aren't related?" Christopher joked. "You're both so bossy."

Christopher's smile turned to a frown when he saw the look of shock pass over Carla's features before she quickly contained herself.

"I think most people in the medical profession tend to be bossy." Carla led the way to the therapy room.

Christopher's eyes narrowed as he walked slightly behind Carla. Something was going on with her. Christopher was sure of it. And he was pretty sure it had something to do with Nancy and maybe his mother. Christopher had seen the stricken look on Carla's face when his mother had approached her. His mother had also thought she'd recognized Carla.

Ever since the accident all those years ago, Christopher had thought his family was hiding things from him. At first, he'd thought it was because of his skull injury. The doctors had warned him that he might experience memory lapses and exhibit other odd behavior. So Christopher had put his suspicion down to paranoia and his fear that there was something wrong with him that his family wasn't telling him. But over the years, his suspicions hadn't gone away; instead, they'd grown.

"Christopher!" Carla snapped her fingers, bringing him out of his deep thoughts. "Are you okay?" She looked at him worriedly.

"Sorry, I was deep in thought," Christopher told her. "I'm feeling fine. Great, in fact!" He walked into the room and ignored the glare from Nancy.

"You're both late, as usual." Nancy tapped her watch.

"Sorry, there was Tiny trouble." Carla and Christopher grinned at the confused look on Nancy's face.

"Tiny, the dog, has gone missing," Christopher explained.

"Oh, no!" Nancy's eyes widened. "I hope Tiny hasn't gone to that freakin' cove again."

"That's where Cody, Grace, and Harper are headed." Christopher pulled off his shirt and sat on the bed. "Aiden's gone up to the widow's walk with binoculars to keep an eye on them and see if he can spot Tiny."

"Have you been wearing sunscreen?" Carla asked Christopher, eyeing his sunburned back.

"Grace and I went to kick a ball around on the beach yesterday. I got hot and took off my shirt," Christopher kicked off his shoes before lying down. "I didn't know we'd be in the sun for that long."

"You always put sunscreen on when you go out," Nancy scolded him. "You got quite sunburned, which limits your massage today."

"I promise you it's not sore," Christopher assured Nancy and pinched his shoulder. "See."

"There are no blisters on the skin." Carla examined Christopher's back, and when she poked a finger on his sunburn, he flinched. "Not sore, huh?" She raised her eyes at Christopher.

"Okay, it might be a little tender," Christopher admitted. "But I've had worse."

"Just do some stretches and work his neck," Carla instructed

Nancy. "Your scar looks good." She examined his head. "And your hair is growing out nicely. But that doesn't mean you can go without your hat."

"I don't," Christopher told her.

"I'm done." Carla jotted information onto her tablet. "I'm going to go down to the cove and help Cody look for Tiny."

"Hi, sorry I'm late." A tall, handsome man with sandy blond hair and brown eyes walked into the room.

"That's okay." Nancy gave the man a big smile. "Dr. Newton, this is Dr. Andrew Stein. He's Dr. Baxter's substitute. He also does sports massage therapy and agreed to help with Christopher while my arm was out of action."

"Hi," Carla greeted the man. "Nancy will discuss Christopher's treatment with you. If you'll excuse me, I have to go help find Tiny."

Christopher's brows furrowed as he watched the interaction between Dr. Stein and Carla. Carla had stiffened the instant Nancy had mentioned Dr. Baxter. *Mm, interesting!* Christopher thought, before he was introduced to the good-looking Dr. Stein, who had Nancy smiling and blushing like a teenager. Christopher didn't think Nancy ever got embarrassed, let alone blushed.

"Nancy, did you meet Dr. Newton before she came to Nantucket?" Christopher asked her.

"No." Nancy shook her head and handed Dr. Stein Christopher's chart. "She does seem vaguely familiar, though."

"Dr. Newton looks a lot like the picture of Dr. Baxter's daughter he has on his desk," Dr. Stein said as he scrolled through Christopher's therapy chart.

Christopher and Nancy looked at each other. Their eyes both mirrored surprise.

"You're right." Christopher sat up. "Charlene Baxter left Nantucket about twenty-eight years ago."

"Oh, come on!" Nancy looked at Christopher curiously. "You don't think Carla's Dr. Baxter's long-lost daughter, do you?"

"She could've had reconstructive surgery to remove that angry red scar from her face," Dr. Stein added to Christopher's suspicions.

"We need to see that picture." Christopher started to put his shirt on.

"I agree," Nancy backed him up and grabbed her purse. "I'll drive."

"What about your wrist?" Christopher pointed out.

"Nope," Nancy shook her head. "I can drive with one hand; you haven't been cleared to drive."

"Wait!" Dr. Stein looked at Christopher. "What about your therapy?"

"It's canceled for today," Nancy told Dr. Stein.

Dr. Stein picked up his things while Nancy waited impatiently for Christopher to finish getting dressed.

"I'll still pay for the session," Christopher assured Dr. Stein as he jumped off the bed.

"I'm not worried about the money. I'm more worried about what the two of you are up to." Dr. Stein followed them out of the room. "I put the photo in the top left drawer of the desk, by the way. I won't be back in the office for another hour or so."

"Thanks," Nancy called, hurrying to her car with Christopher in tow.

*

"*B*e careful, girls," Cody called over her shoulder. Cody followed the rocky path which took them to the cove on the far side of the Inn. It was a treacherous walk. The rocks were always wet and slippery from the spray of the waves crashing against them.

"We're following you, Mom," Grace assured Cody. "These rocks are really slippery today."

"We're almost at the bottom." Cody looked at the small section of sand. "Luckily, it's still low tide. I just hope Tiny didn't try to go fishing in the cave again."

"There's a cave?" Harper asked excitedly. "Why didn't anyone tell me?"

"Probably because we knew you'd want to check it out!" Grace hopped onto the sand next to Cody.

"I get that." Harper grinned. "Can we check it out now that we're here?"

"Let's see if Tiny is here first." Cody turned to survey the small beach.

"Listen." Grace cocked her head, turning her ear towards the cave. "I think I can hear Tiny barking."

Cody, Grace, and Harper took off at a sprint towards the small cave opening in the opposite cliff walls.

"Oh, wow." Harper looked at the cave that was slightly raised in the sand. "There's a step up to the arched doorway."

"I know, it's so cute. When I was little, I would pretend it was a doll's house," Grace told Harper as they followed Cody up to the entrance.

When they got there, they could hear Tiny barking loudly.

"He's in there." Grace looked at Cody. She took her mobile phone out and switched on the flashlight.

"Don't go near the sand," Cody warned them, switching her phone's flashlight on.

"Why not the sand?" Harper looked confused. She, too, switched on her phone's flashlight.

"The sand tends to give way, and you could get sucked into the bottomless trench." Grace pointed to the large pool in the middle of the cave that looked dark and foreboding.

"Is it really bottomless, though?" Harper followed Grace and Cody along the rock shelf, keeping an eye on the ominous pool.

"No." Cody turned and grinned at Harper. "But it is really deep, and we have no idea what is in that pool. Neither do we want to."

"Good, because I'm pretty sure that some weird sea monster lives in that black pit." Harper shuddered.

"Tiny," Cody called and whistled. "Where are you, boy?" she called when the barking died down.

"I think he's near the seaside of the cave." Grace stopped and listened when Tiny barked again.

"Is that bad?" Harper asked Grace, trying to look around her.

"At least there's no bottomless water trench." Grace grinned. "It's kinda cool, but we have to squeeze through that hole." She shone her light to the entrance to another cavern. "It's a little slimy and disgusting."

"It's just moss." Cody laughed at Grace's look of disgust. "Tiny's stopped barking again. I hope he's not in trouble because, even together, the three of us are not going to be able to lift him."

"There he is." Grace pointed to where the large dog was standing with his back to them and barking at something. "What's he barking at?"

"I'm not sure." Cody shone her light towards Tiny. "Tiny!" she commanded.

Tiny turned around and ran towards them and did a spin and bark before rushing back to the bank of rocks he was barking at.

"There must be something behind that rock shelf." Harper pointed as they walked cautiously to where Tiny was barking.

"Oh, no!" Grace stopped at the rock shelf that plummeted down into a small, jagged rock pool below. "It's a baby seal."

"Hey, boy." Cody scratched Tiny's head as she came up next to him and Grace. "It's still alive, but it's badly injured." She shone her flashlight onto the little seal.

"We have to help it." Harper looked around the cave for a way down. "There!" She pointed to what looked like a rocky path down to where the seal was.

"Harper, it's too dangerous." Cody looked at her watch. "When the tide rises, the water fills the crevice up from the sea entrance to the cave."

Cody shone her light down over the shallow rock pool to the mouth of the cave. "You don't want to get stuck down there when the tide comes in, and we have no way of lifting it."

"You can use my doctor's coat," Carla said from behind them, making Cody jump and Harper and Grace scream in fright. "Sorry!" She held up her hands. "I didn't mean to scare you."

"Carla, what are you doing here?" Cody asked her.

"I promised Nancy, Christopher, and Aiden that I would come and lend a hand," Carla told them.

"I'm so glad you did." Cody shone her light on the path Harper had found. "I think I may be able to get down there."

"I'll come with you," Carla volunteered.

"Grace and Harper, we'll need you each positioned where we can pass the seal up." Cody looked at the baby seal. "It is still very young, but they are heavy, and it is going to try and wiggle free."

"In other words," Carla continued for Cody, "you need to ground yourself as best you can, so it doesn't knock you off balance."

"I'll text my mom to let her know we have a...." Harper moved her phone around in the air. "Shoot, there's no signal."

"Go and call your mother. There should be a signal outside the cave," Carla instructed Harper. "Grace, go with Harper and call Aiden to tell him what's happening before he tries to come to the cove."

"Okay," Grace and Harper said at the same time.

"In the meantime, Carla and I will make our way down to the baby seal." Cody placed her watch and phone on a rock, so they didn't get wet. "We have to hurry because the tide is already starting to come back in." She pointed to the water rising in the cavern below.

Tiny barked a few times at Cody and wagged his tail excitedly.

"Tiny, stay!" Cody commanded the big dog, who automatically sat. "Stay," she warned him as she and Carla made their way to the jagged path.

"Okay, here we go," Carla took a breath. "This is going to be fun."

"Hold on to the rocks and watch your footing," Cody warned Carla. "One wrong step and we end up in a bloody heap on those sharp rocks."

"Delightful," Carla drawled sarcastically.

"I'd like to say I've done this before, and don't worry." Cody grinned. "But we've always stayed away from this part of the cave because it's not that safe."

Cody jumped onto the sand. The baby seal immediately started to make mewling noises like it was calling for its mother.

"It's okay, little one," Cody cooed as she slowly walked closer.

"Here." Carla took her white coat off and handed it to Cody. "The poor little thing looks very young."

"It is," Cody managed to edge closer. "Shh, little one." She kneeled next to the baby seal. "I need you to distract the little guy," she said softly to Carla.

"Okay." Carla moved to the other side of the seal, taking its attention away from Cody.

Cody threw the coat over the baby seal. She reached over and rolled its little body into the coat before lifting it and cradling it in her arms. As she held the seal, she felt the water come up to where they were standing.

"It's okay, little one," Cody soothed. "Its body temperature is very low." She looked up at Carla. "We have to get it out of here quickly."

Carla nodded and headed up the path they'd come down. She climbed the first part on her hands and knees until she was at a place she could stand firmly. Carla crouched down and reached towards Cody, who passed the seal up to her.

"Got him," Carla carefully stood up as Grace and Harper rushed back into the cavern.

"My mom and Carter are on their way," Harper called down to Cody.

"Mom, the tide." Grace pointed to the water that was now almost knee high.

"I see it." Cody looked back and caught sight of Carla's stethoscope rising up with the water. "Carla, your stethoscope. It must've dropped out of your coat pocket." Cody pointed to the object floating not too far away from her.

"Cody, leave it," Carla called to her as she passed the seal to Grace, who was standing just above her.

"I've got..." Cody reached out to grab the stethoscope. She

slipped and skidded as a wave of water pushed into the cavern, knocking her against the rock wall.

Cody felt the rock connect with the back of her head and back. It knocked the breath out of her. She struggled to get her footing and fight off the grey mist starting to fog her brain and clear the whooshing sound in her ears.

"MOM!" Cody could hear Grace, but she sounded so far away. Cody turned to look towards the sound before she knocked back against the rocks again. She heard the crunch of her body hitting the hard surface. The last sound she heard was someone calling her before the cold, wet world around her went black.

Chapter Six
RESCUING CODY

"Cody!" Carla screamed as she watched Cody get bashed against the side of the cavern again. "Go get help!" She turned towards Grace and Harper before wading into the water.

"What about my mom?" Grace's face was pale. "Mommy!" she screamed.

Tiny started barking and running up and down the rock cliff. He stopped and jumped, splashing into the water. He sank like a stone into the fast-filling cavern.

"Tiny," Grace shouted and ran around the rock cliff. She looked towards where Carla was swimming towards Cody. "I think I can dive in." She looked at Carla.

"NO!" Carla reached Cody and managed to pull her onto her back. She treaded water and positioned herself behind Cody to pull her back towards the path. "You go and call Aiden to get an ambulance to the Bay."

Tiny had popped up and was doggy paddling next to Carla. Grace nodded and ran from the cave.

Carla hit the rocks and felt them scrape along her back, but she didn't care. Her heart was pounding. She protected Cody's body as much she could while she pushed herself up the shingly rocky path. Carla's adrenaline was pumping through her; she barely felt the sting of the rocks cutting into her flesh. When she got to a position where she could sit, Carla pulled Cody's body up against her and gave her the Heimlich maneuver until Cody started to cough and splutter.

"My head," Cody mumbled and passed out again.

Tiny started to bark and push Cody's foot with his head.

"It's okay, boy," Carla said to Tiny.

She felt Cody's pulse. It was strong, and she was breathing. Carla looked up at the path above her. It was not too far from the top, but it was rock and shingle. Carla couldn't drag Cody over that—it would rip her back to shreds. She looked at the water rising rapidly around Tiny's ankles and creeping up to them.

"Cody." Carla tried to wake her.

"Need a hand?" Carter Ellis, Harper's soon-to-be step-father, put a hand on Carla's shoulders.

"Oh, thank goodness." Carla breathed a sigh of relief. "We need to hurry. I don't like Cody's head wound. She hit the rocks pretty hard."

"On it." Carter helped Carla up, stepping around her to take hold of Cody. "My young intern up there will help you."

"Here, take my hand." The young man held his hand out to Carla and pulled her up before going to help Carter get Cody onto the ledge.

"How are we going to get her up to the Inn?" Carla picked up Cody's phone and watch.

"We're not," Carter told her. "We have a boat waiting in the cove." He had Cody in his arms as they made their way through the cave to the entrance.

"There's an ambulance on its way," the young man informed Carla. "They'll meet us at the Cody Bay jetty."

"She's cold," Carla noticed. "Can I have your windbreaker?" she asked the young man.

"Sure." The young man pulled his jacket off and wrapped it around Cody.

They cleared the cave and were greeted by Lana West, Harper, and Grace.

"Mom," Grace called.

"It's okay, Gracie," Carter smiled at the young woman. "Let's get her into the boat."

They all climbed into the waiting boat, including Tiny. Carter took the controls and roared the boat off towards the Cody Bay jetty.

Christopher stood on the jetty, pacing.

"Where the hell are they?" Christopher said through gritted teeth, looking out at the sea.

"There." Steven pointed. "And there's the ambulance."

The paramedic parked as close as they could before retrieving a gurney and rushing to the jetty as Carter steered the boat to a stop. Carter hopped out of the boat while his intern passed an unconscious Cody to him. He gently put Cody on the stretcher as Carla jumped out of the boat and started barking orders to the medics. When they were ready, they rushed Cody towards the ambulance."

"Dad." Grace ran into Christopher's arms. "Can we go with them?"

"Dr. Newton's going to take good care of her," Christopher hugged his daughter and kissed the top of her head. "Why don't you go get some dry clothes on, and Uncle Steven will bring you and Aiden to the hospital." He looked at Steven questioningly.

"Of course," Steven nodded.

"I'm going to go with the ambulance, okay?" Christopher gave Grace another encouraging squeeze before walking off towards the ambulance.

"Why don't we go fetch Aiden, and you can get some warm clothes on." Steven stepped up. "I'll take you, and we'll let Christopher go with Dr. Newton in the ambulance."

"Is Mom going to be okay, Uncle Steven?" Christopher heard Grace say as he left. "How is she, really?" He asked Carla as he climbed into the ambulance.

"She has a gash at the back of her head," Carla examined Cody as the ambulance took off. "I don't think she's broken any bones, but I won't know for sure until we get some x-rays."

"What the hell happened?" Christopher asked and sucked in his breath when he noticed the blood staining Carla's back. "Carla, your back is bleeding."

"It's nothing," Carla shrugged. "Just a scrape."

"It doesn't look like a scrape," Christopher eyed the rips in her shirt.

"It's nothing, really," Carla assured him as the ambulance pulled into the emergency bay of Nantucket General.

"You know you're going to have to go through to the waiting area, right?" Carla told him as they hopped out of the ambulance.

"I know where to go," Christopher said and walked next to the gurney as the medics wheeled it in.

"I need Miss Moore taken straight to the x-ray department," Carla informed the duty nurse, who nodded and made the arrangements. Another nurse brought her a clean coat and a new stethoscope. "Thank you." She slipped the coat on.

"Dr. Newton, your back," the nurse said as she helped Carla with her coat.

"It's fine." Carla took the tablet from the duty nurse in charge.

"You need to get that looked at," Christopher's eyes narrowed.

"When I'm sure Cody's okay." Carla looked up at Christopher. "Didn't I tell you to go to the waiting area?"

"You did, but I ignored you," Christopher gave her a cool look. "I need to be with Cody."

"You need to be in the waiting area, and the longer you stand here arguing with me about it, the longer you're keeping me from attending to Cody." She raised an eyebrow at him.

"Fine. But let me know how she is the moment you know something." Christopher stalked off. He felt so helpless and had to swallow down the fear clawing at his throat.

"Dad," Grace rushed towards him with Aiden hobbling behind her. "How is Mom?"

"I'm not sure yet. Dr. Newton is with her now." Christopher ushered them to a chair.

"I'll go find out what I can," Steven said and walked off.

"I was so scared." Tears welled up in Grace's eyes. "Tiny and Dr. Newton dived into the water after Mom." She swallowed. "Mom was just floating there."

"It's okay, honey." Christopher pulled Grace to him and held her. "I'm sure she's going to be okay. She has the best doctors with her, and Dr. Newton managed to get to her in time."

"How is she?" Carter, Harper, and Nancy rushed into the waiting area.

"We don't know yet." Christopher looked up at Carter. "Thank you."

"I didn't do much," Carter smiled. "Dr. Newton, Cody, Grace, and Harper are the heroes."

"How is the baby seal?" Aiden asked Carter.

"It's touch and go, but you know Lana," Carter shook his head. "She won't stop until she tries everything she knows to save it."

"Where's the other hero?" Harper asked.

"Tiny?" Grace asked, and Harper nodded.

"He's back at home being hosed down by my mother and Riley." Nancy laughed. "Not a job I wanted to stick around for."

"No, me either." Grace shook her head. "Tiny loves to swim, but he hates being bathed."

"What's taking so long?" Aiden looked down the empty hallway.

"Steven has gone to find out." Christopher put his hand on Aiden's shoulder. "Your mother is a fighter."

"She nearly drowned." Aiden looked at Christopher. "That cave needs to be closed off. Tiny continuously goes in there."

"We can look into doing something to stop him going in there." Christopher looked at Carter. "Is there any way to close off the cave?"

"I'll take a team down there at the next low tide." Carter nodded. "I'm sure we can find boulders to block up the entrance. It is a hazard, especially if guests from the Inn wander in there."

"Thank you." Christopher breathed a sigh of relief.

"Here comes Uncle Steven and Dr. Newton." Grace stood up.

"I see we have a full house." Carla looked up from the tablet in her hand. "Cody had a few stitches at the back of her head, a few bruised ribs, some nasty cuts on her back, and a concussion." She reached out and took Grace's hand. "Your mother's going to be sore for a while, but she's going to be fine."

"Thank you." Grace hugged Carla. "Can we see her?"

"Of course, but I think only you, Aiden, and your father." She looked apologetically at the rest of the people waiting to hear about Cody. "The rest of you can see her tomorrow because we're keeping her overnight to make sure there are no complications."

Christopher slowly let the breath he'd been holding out. His heart was hammering like a jigsaw while he listened to what Carla had to say about Cody. Christopher knew now more than ever that he never wanted to spend another day apart from Cody and his children. These past weeks had been some of the most physically painful, but they'd also been the happiest days he'd had in many years, and he never wanted to have to walk away from his family again.

Christopher followed Aiden and Grace to Cody's room. He hesitated at the door, not sure if he should intrude on Cody's time with Aiden and Grace.

"Come on, Dad." Grace put her small hand in his large one and pulled him into the room with her.

"Mom," Aiden said gently before kissing Cody on the cheek.

"Hey, honey." Cody slowly opened her eyes. "How's the baby seal and Tiny?"

"Mom!" Aiden shook his head. "You nearly got killed saving a baby seal."

"No," Cody corrected Aiden. "I nearly got killed saving a stethoscope."

"What?" Christopher hissed.

"Dad," Grace warned him softly. "Remember, we can't upset her or you for that matter, and as I'm the only one that has not been injured, I'm now in charge."

"Sorry, honey." Christopher sighed. "It's been a tense day."

"Tiny's fine," Grace caught Cody up on the events that

followed after she'd been knocked out in the water. "We're still waiting for Aunt Lana to let us know how the baby seal is."

"The poor little thing." Cody swallowed. "Is there some water?"

"I've got it." Christopher picked up one of the bottles, opened it, and placed a straw in it for Cody. "Small sips."

"Thank you." Cody took the bottle from Christopher and took a few sips.

"Carla is going to keep you in the hospital overnight," Christopher told Cody. "Do you mind if I take the kids out for dinner?" He gave Cody a smile. "I'm still an awful cook."

"You don't have to do that," Cody smiled. "Connie will make you all a meal."

"I think it would be nice for Aiden, Riley, me, and Dad to go out for supper for a change." Grace looked up at Christopher. "That is if Dr. Newton says you can drive and go out."

"He can go out, but I haven't cleared your dad to drive just yet." Carla stepped into the room. "I'm sure someone at the Inn will drive you."

"We'll find someone if your mother says it's okay." Christopher looked at Cody hopefully.

"Of course." Cody nodded. "But please, get someone to drive you."

Christopher saw the fleeting moment of fear flash through Cody's eyes, and he understood.

"I will," Christopher promised.

"Okay, Moore family." Carla looked at her watch. "I'm taking the night shift, so I'll be here with your mother the whole night. But right now, Cody needs her rest."

Grace and Aiden said goodbye to Cody. Christopher smiled, reached for her hand, and gave it a squeeze. "I promise I'll take excellent care of them."

"I know you will." Cody's eyes met Christopher's, and they held for a moment before Carla's voice intruded.

"I'll call you if there are any changes," Carla promised Christopher as he started to leave the room.

"Thank you," Christopher said softly and placed his hand on

Carla's back. She flinched and winced. "You need to have your back looked at." He said softly before leaving the room.

Before Christopher left the hospital, he found Steven.

"Are you busy tonight?" Christopher asked Steven.

"Well, I was supposed to have a dinner date, but it's been postponed, so no." Steven shook his head. "Why do you ask?" His eyes narrowed as he looked at his younger brother.

"I want to take the kids out for dinner, but I'm not cleared to drive," Christopher explained. "I was hoping you'd join us and drive us." He grinned.

"Sure," Steven replied. "I'll pick you up at seven?"

"Can you make it six-thirty?" Christopher asked.

"Yeah." Steven nodded. "I'll see you all then."

"Oh, and Steven." Christopher lowered his voice. "You need to get Carla to have her back seen too. It is pretty scraped up from saving Cody."

"I will," Steven promised and patted his brother on the shoulder before walking towards Carla's office.

Chapter Seven
DR. BAXTER'S OFFICE

Steven knocked on Carla's office door.

"Come in," Carla called.

"Hi." Steven stepped into the room, wheeling in a cart. "I'm here to take a look at your back." He picked up a gown and handed it to her. "I'll give you ten minutes to put this on, and there are some clean scrubs here too for you to change into when we are done."

"My back's fine." Carla waved him off. "Just a few scrapes."

"You scraped your back against rocks in a dark, dank cave." Steven's eyes narrowed. "Should I remind you of what even a small cut on rocks like that can do?"

"I've had a shower." Carla pointed to the scrubs she had on. "See, I even washed my hair with soap because I left my shampoo at the Inn."

"Did you clean up the wounds with disinfectant and put some cream on them?" Steven asked her. "Or asked someone to check in case you needed stitches?"

"No." Carla shook her head. "I haven't had time. I had to sneak a shower in between consultations and checking up on Cody."

"I'm not leaving until you let me look at your back." Steven held out the gown to her. "As we're not having dinner together tonight, I promised Christopher I'd take him and the kids out."

"Cody will be happy to hear that," Carla said. "She didn't want Christopher driving."

"You can go tell her as soon as I've sorted out your back." Steven looked at his watch. "I promised to pick them up at six-thirty, and they'd feel so let down if I'm late because you wouldn't let me take a look at your back."

"Fine." Carla pushed her chair back and stood up. "Give me five minutes." She snatched the gown from him as she walked around her desk.

"I got you some more clean scrubs." He cocked his head to look at her back. "You may want to use the top as you've already bled onto the one you have on."

Carla nodded as she backed Steven out the door and closed it when he was over the threshold.

Steven stood patiently waiting outside Carla's office door until she opened it wearing the gown and green scrub pants.

Steven smiled. "It suits you." He laughed.

"Funny." Carla pulled a face. "Can we get this over with? I have a lot to do."

Carla positioned herself on the bed in her room with her back to Steven.

Steven sterilized his hands and pulled on a pair of latex gloves. He gently pulled the gown apart and sucked in his breath.

"This is not just a few scrapes." Steven picked up a swap and dabbed it in disinfectant.

"I know," Carla said softly. "I checked in the bathroom a little while ago when I showered."

"I'm going to disinfect them, and it's going to sting." He gently touched the swab to one of the angry gashes that ran down her back, looking like she'd been clawed. Carla flinched and drew in a breath. "Sorry, it's going to sting a lot."

"I don't think they need stitches," Carla said.

"I do think we need to put a dressing over them to stop them from bleeding onto your clothes." Steven cleaned up the wounds before applying an antiseptic cream to them. "You're going to need to change the dressing every time you shower until they start to heal." He put two thick dressings over the worst of the scrapes.

"Thank you," Carla stood up. "Can you close the curtains around the bed?"

"Of course." Steven handed Carla the clean shirt and closed the curtains.

He walked towards her desk, and an envelope caught his eye. It said something about a DNA test on it. He looked towards the closed curtains before leaning over to get a better look. It definitely was a DNA test. Steven frowned before giving himself a mental shake. The mystery surrounding Carla was getting to him. Even Christopher and Nancy thought Carla was hiding something and was not who they thought she was.

"I'm done." Carla opened the curtains pulling Steven out of his deep thoughts.

"I'll check in with you tomorrow." Steven smiled at Carla before leaving her office.

Whose DNA report was that? Steven wondered as he walked towards his office to get his keys. The envelope only had Dr. Newton's name on it. *Is Carla Charlene's sister?* He frowned. If she was, that would mean that Dr. Baxter must've had a love child because Carla and Charlene were roughly the same age. Steven's frown deepened as he climbed into his car. Actually, Steven didn't know Carla's exact age or date of birth. A thought struck him. But it must be in her hospital employee file.

Steven picked up his phone and called his assistant to ask her to send him Dr. Newton's employee file. Steven had already known Carla's reputation and the work she'd done, so he hadn't paid any attention to her file. He pulled out of the parking lot and headed towards Cody Bay. Steven was hoping to have a shower and change before picking up Christopher and the kids. But he was already running a few minutes late.

As Steven headed towards Cody Bay, his mind was full of questions about Carla. Steven and Carla had made an instant connection when they'd met at the medical conference. He knew they'd both felt it. Steven's search on Carla had drawn a blank. So, earlier that day, he'd decided to head to the one person who may have known Carla, Dr. Baxter. Only the doctor wasn't home, and his housekeeper had said he'd gone to the surgery. Steven didn't find Dr. Baxter at the surgery, but he did find Christopher and Nancy snooping around the doctor's office.

Earlier that Day

Steven arrived at Dr. Baxter's office. Another day he'd arrived at the doctor's office flashed through his mind, but he shook the painful memory away. Steven should've demanded the doctor tell him where Charlene was on that day, but Steven had not been in the right frame of mind. Lance had just been killed, Steven's father was badly injured, and Christopher was in a coma. The news Dr. Baxter had to tell him there had been another cruel blow that shattered the last fragment of his heart left intact. Steven had avoided Dr. Baxter as much as he could after that day. That was all in the past now. Steven needed information that only Dr. Baxter could give him.

Steven squared his shoulders and walked into Dr. Baxter's surgery room. He'd been surprised to see no one was manning the front desk. When he'd heard a noise coming from the direction of Dr. Baxter's office, Steven had cautiously made his way down the passage. He was not expecting to find Christopher and Nancy snooping around Dr. Baxter's office.

Nancy was going through Dr. Baxter's drawers to find a photograph of Dr. Baxter's daughter while Christopher stood guard.

"What the hell are you two doing?" Steven pushed the door to Dr. Baxter's office.

"Steven!" Christopher looked guiltily at his older brother. "What are you doing here?"

"I asked first." Steven folded his arms across his chest.

"We were looking for this." Nancy held up a photo of Charlene Baxter.

Shock waves had pounded through his veins when he saw the picture. He clenched his jaw and narrowed his eyes.

"Why are you looking for a picture of Dr. Baxter's daughter?" Steven looked from Nancy to Christopher.

"Because we think Carla Newton looks a lot like Charlene Baxter," Christopher said honestly.

"Let me see that." Steven walked over to the desk and took the picture from Nancy.

Steven's heart was pounding, and it took everything he had to stop his hands from shaking as he looked at the beautiful smiling face of Charlene. The one thing Steven remembered the most about Charlene was that she always seemed to have a smile on her face.

"Dr. Stein was right," Nancy said. "Charlene Baxter and Carla Newton could be sisters."

Steven stared at the photo, picturing Carla in his mind. They were right, of course. But Carla had high cheekbones, a straight nose, and was lean, trim, and fit. Charlene was curvier, with a fuller face and a cute turned-up nose. Charlene also had a bright red scar on the side of her face that ran from her temple down to below her cheekbone. Carla didn't have the scar, but both women had the same shaped violet eyes framed with thick black lashes, naturally shaped pink lips, a dimple in their left cheek, and thick deep red hair.

"I can see the resemblance." Steven handed the picture to Christopher. "But you two shouldn't be in here snooping through Dr. Baxter's things."

"Why are you here?" Nancy leaned back in Dr. Baxter's plush leather office chair and steepled her fingers.

"I came to meet the new doctor," Steven lied. He looked at the picture over Christopher's shoulder and then at Nancy. "You know, you look a lot like Charlene, Nancy."

"So I've been told." Nancy looked pointedly at Christopher.

Steven looked back at the picture. "Nancy, do you think Charlene could be your biological mother?" He looked at Nancy questioningly.

"If I tell you two something, will you promise to keep it to yourselves?" Nancy's eyes narrowed as she looked from Steven to Christopher.

"Sure," Christopher said.

"Absolutely," Steven promised.

"About five months ago, right before Dr. Baxter's stroke, he was making a house call and had left his prescription pad in the office. He called me to ask if I would bring it to him," Nancy started to tell her story. "It wasn't in the right top-hand drawer where it usually was, and he'd left the bottom left-hand drawer unlocked."

"Was it unusual for him to leave it unlocked?" Christopher asked.

"Yes," Nancy nodded. "That drawer was always locked."

"I take it you snooped in the drawer?" Steven raised his eyebrows.

"I was looking for his prescription pad!" Nancy shrugged unrepentantly. "I came across a whole lot of returned to sender letters addressed to Charlene Baxter and this." She opened her purse, pulled out a letter, and put it on the desk. "This one was still on his writing pad."

Steven stepped forward and picked up the letter. Christopher put the photo down on the desk in front of Nancy and stepped up next to Steven to look at the letter.

Dearest Charlene

I know nothing I could do or say could ever make up for the past. Letting you leave Nantucket was one of the hardest things I've ever had to do. When you left, you took what was left of my heart with you. I wish there'd been another way, and if there were, I would've gladly taken it. But I would do anything to keep you safe, and I was not going to let them get to you as well. You were better off as far away from both Nantucket and Boston as you could go. When my old friend agreed to take you under her wing in England, I knew you'd be safe and in good hands. You have no idea how proud I am of you and everything you've accomplished in your life.

You've returned every letter, birthday, and Christmas card I've sent over the past twenty-nine years. I hope one day I'll get to see your beautiful smile and hear your voice again. Maybe by then I'll be able to tell you everything. What I can tell you is that one of my biggest regrets to come from my business was what we did to you. I never meant for you to get tangled up in the middle of my affairs.

I know I shouldn't be doing this, but it has eaten me alive all these years and what I'm about to tell you will probably only make you hate me more. But you at least need to know this truth. Your baby wasn't stillborn. Nor was your child a boy. We told you what we did to protect you and the child. I can't tell you too much, only that she is very much alive, healthy, and as beautiful, strong, and intelligent as her mother. I've secretly looked out for her over the years and made sure she was safe. She was placed with a wonderful family until they both passed on, and then she was taken in by a kind woman who reminds me a lot of your mother.

If you ever read one of my letters, I hope it's this one. If anything happens to me, I need you to contact Pete Williams. He'll know what to do, and he has all the information you need to know. Please promise me, whatever you do, you'll stay away from the Stanfords. They're not to be trusted.

Love always,
Your father

Steven looked up at Nancy, "This doesn't prove you're Charlene's daughter."

"Really?" Nancy's eyes narrowed. "So that story about the child being placed with a nice family until they died didn't sound at all familiar to you?"

"Nancy has a point." Christopher frowned at Steven. "How do we find out how many newborn babies would've been adopted on Nantucket the year Nancy was born?"

"Dr. Baxter has also always shown an interest in me," Nancy cocked her head. "Kind of like you." She raised an eyebrow at Steven. "Which begs the question, if I am Charlene's daughter, would that make your late brother, Lance, my father? I know she was dating him before the accident."

"What?" Christopher's eyes widened with shock.

"You're right," Steven admitted. "Lance and Charlene were a couple back then."

"Charlene was at Lance's birthday party that night of the accident as well," Christopher told Nancy.

"That's correct," Steven confirmed. "Charlene was there."

"She was at the accident scene with you." Christopher pinched the bridge of his nose. "I remember now. You were trying to get me to wake up, and I looked into a pair of violet eyes. I thought I'd dreamed it."

"Yes, she was," Steven admitted. "So, where do you think Charlene's been all these years?" He turned to Nancy, changing the subject.

"I got this address from some of the more recent letters Dr. Baxter sent to Charlene." Nancy turned the letter over, and Steven froze. He knew that address.

"He never sent the one about the baby though?" Steven asked Nancy.

"No." Nancy shook her head. "But it was the last letter he'd written before his stroke."

"So you two think that Carla might be related to Charlene?" Steven's eyes narrowed as he looked from Nancy to Christopher.

"We think Carla is Charlene," Nancy confirmed Steven's own suspicions.

"They look similar but not identical." Steven's mind refused to believe it.

"Are you looking for excuses because you're dating her?" Christopher looked at his brother curiously.

"We're not dating," Steven denied. "We're friends."

"Uh-huh." Nancy raised her eyebrows. "I've seen the way the two of you look at each other." She rolled her eyes. "Anyone can see the two of you have something."

"So you two think that Carla is not only here for the position at the hospital or to look after Christopher?" Steven asked. "You think she's here to... find you?"

"I do," Nancy confirmed. "You see, after I found the letter about the baby, I decided to write to Charlene. I didn't say who I was, only that I was sure she was my biological mother."

"You believe that drew Carla here to Nantucket?" Steven looked at Nancy. He was not convinced, or rather he didn't want to believe what she was saying.

"I know it did," Nancy said. "Cody put me on housekeeping duty as my punishment for taking Aiden to the dirt bike track. My mother made me start by going to take some fresh towels to

Carla's room right before Christopher's therapy session. I found the letter I'd written to Charlene in Carla's room."

"God, Nancy, you've got to stop snooping!" Steven hissed and ran his hand through his hair. *Maybe Carla was related to Charlene and....* He closed his eyes for a second and drew in a breath. Who was he kidding? Steven had thought many times that Carla and Charlene were one and the same.

Steven felt like his chest was being compressed, and he needed air. But he couldn't exactly rush out of the office; it would look suspicious. Instead, he gave himself a mental shake to get his emotions and thoughts together.

"Christopher and I are trying to find out what happened to Charlene to make her become Carla." Nancy put the documents back into her purse.

"I think you two are crazy." Steven shook his head. "I also think you should both stop snooping into some else's life."

"I'm trying to help Nancy find her biological mother," Christopher defended his actions.

"I know you're bored, little brother." Steven gestured at Christopher with his hand. "But I think it's best leaving the past where it is." He turned to Nancy. "I know you're curious about your biological parents." He ran a hand through his hair. "But maybe you should go speak to social services and find out from them if they knew who they were."

"I'm pretty sure I know who my mother is." Nancy glared at Stephen. "I'm also pretty sure that your late brother might be my father. Why else would Charlene's father tell her not to go anywhere near the Stanfords?"

"I can think of at least ten reasons," Steven muttered and once again ran his hand through his hair. "Dammit, Nancy, you are going to stir up a hornet's nest if you and Christopher continue digging into this."

"If Lance is my father, that would make you both my uncles." She gave them a cheeky grin, ignoring Steven's warning. "So, uncles, are you going to help me find out who Carla Newton really is or not?"

"I'm in." Christopher raised his hand and looked at his brother with raised eyebrows.

"Fine," Steven said through gritted teeth. "But, we have to be careful and keep each other informed of what we find at all times. I cannot stress this enough. Someone went to a lot of trouble to cover up Nancy's birth and who her parents were."

"Proceed with caution." Nancy saluted him. "Got it!"

"I hope so." Steven shook his head and sighed.

Chapter Eight
A PAINFUL PAST

Carla walked into her office after checking on Cody and stared at the envelope on her desk. She'd been avoiding it the whole day. Carla sat down and picked it up. It was time to open it. The lab had put a rush on it for her. She took her letter opener, slit the top, and pulled out the folded document.

Carla slowly opened it up and read it. Tears welled up in her violet eyes as she stared at the results. Her hands shook as she shoved the test back into its envelope and stuffed it into her purse. It was time to pay Dr. Baxter a visit. She looked at her watch and yawned. But first, Carla had two hours to catch up on some sleep. Her head and back ached.

Carla set her alarm, pulled a blanket out of the closet, switched off her office light, and laid down on the bed. When she closed her eyes, her mind was filled with memories of the day her mother died. It was one of the worst days of her life.

May 1991
Charlene had walked home from school as her mother hadn't picked her up like she usually did. When she got to

the house, Charlene saw that her mother's car was parked in the driveway. Charlene frowned and walked into the house.

"Mom?" Charlene went through to the kitchen, but her mother wasn't there.

Her mother wasn't in the living room, laundry, or back garden.

"MOM!" Charlene shouted up the stairs.

She stood looking up the stairs when she heard a crash. Charlene's heart thudded in her throat as she sprinted up the stairs. "Mommy," she called and ran into her mother's room. Charlene's breath caught in her throat as she stood in the doorway, frozen. Her mother was lying on the floor with the phone in her hand.

"Hello?" Charlene heard a voice coming from the other end. "Ma'am, are you there?"

Feeling like she was moving through a bad dream, Charlene forced herself to rush to her mother's side.

"Ma'am, if you can hear me, we have an ambulance on the way," the woman on the phone said.

That's when Charlene saw that her mother had dialed 9-1-1.

"Hello," Charlene took the phone from her mother. "It's my mom. She's collapsed on the floor." Her voice shook with fear.

"Who is this?" the woman asked.

"I'm Charlene, her daughter," Charlene explained to the woman.

"Hello, Charlene," the woman's voice was calm. "Your mother called 9-1-1 because she wasn't feeling well. Hold tight, honey; the ambulance is almost there."

"I can feel she's still breathing," Charlene's father was a doctor, and she was going to study medicine in the fall.

"That's good," the woman said and kept Charlene talking until the ambulance got there. She raced down to meet them as they swooped into the house.

While the paramedics were working on her mother, Charlene tried numerous times to get ahold of her father, but no one seemed to know where he was. She rode along with the ambulance to the hospital, and when she was there, she tried her father again and again. Charlene sat alone in the waiting room to hear about her mother. She was so scared and had to fight down the tears that were threatening to overflow.

As the minutes ticked by, Charlene couldn't sit still. She sat, then she stood and paced, chewing down her nails. After not being able to reach her father, she'd called her boyfriend. He was there within twenty minutes and sat with her while they waited to hear about her mother.

"Where is my father?" Charlene looked at her watch. "Why is it taking the doctors so long?"

"I'm sure they'll be here as soon as they can," Charlene's boyfriend put his arm around her shoulders and pulled her to him.

"Thank you for being here with me," Charlene smiled into his blue eyes.

"I would never leave you alone during a time like this." The hint of anger in his voice surprised her.

"The doctor's coming." Charlene stood up and felt her heart sinking at the look on the doctor's face. She'd seen that look a few times when she'd volunteered at the hospital. "No!" The tears she'd been fighting back dripped over her eyelids and splashed onto her cheeks. "No!" She shook her head.

"Where's your father," the doctor asked softly.

"I..." Charlene swallowed. "I can't get ahold of him." Her eyes bored into the doctor's. "I want to see my mother."

"Charlene..." The doctor steered her towards the chairs. "Why don't you sit down?"

"NO!" Charlene's voice rasped, and she shook her head, refusing to budge. "I want to see my mother."

"I'm sorry, your mother had an embolism." The doctor looked at her. "I'm so sorry, Charlene, but she didn't make it. If she'd got here even twenty minutes earlier...." He shook his head and pinched the bridge of his nose. "I'm so sorry. Your mother was part of this hospital, and we all feel your grief."

"NO!" Charlene's mind refused to believe what he was saying to her. "Where's my mother?"

"Charlene," her boyfriend put his arm around her, but she pulled away.

"I WANT TO SEE MY MOTHER!" Charlene's throat burned as she screamed.

"Charlene?" her father rushed into the waiting room. He looked from the doctor to Charlene's boyfriend. "What is going on here?" His cold eyes fell on Charlene's boyfriend. "What are you doing here?"

"Supporting your daughter," her boyfriend's eyes narrowed angrily on Charlene's father. "Unlike you, who couldn't be reached."

"Calm down," the doctor barked. "This isn't the time for accusations."

"Where's my wife?" Charlene's father ignored her boyfriend and asked the doctor.

"I'm sorry," the doctor told Charlene's father what he'd told her.

The following week went by in a blur up until the day of the funeral. Charlene sat on the stairs while their house was filled with people. She didn't remember who was there or who wasn't, and she didn't care. Charlene wanted them all to leave so she could curl up into a little ball and cry. She'd done a lot of that this past week.

"Hey, kiddo," her mother's older brother, Luis Vern, plopped down on the stairs next to her. "How're you holding up?"

"Truthfully, I wish everyone would go home." Charlene gave her uncle a teary smile. "I can't believe Mom's gone." She swallowed and sniffed, wiping at her cheeks. "How did this happen, Uncle Luis?"

"I don't know, love." Luis put his arm around Charlene's shoulders and let her cry. "We're going to be okay." He kissed the top of her head. "I'm taking that job as the Stanfords' head of security."

"I'm glad you're going to be staying in Nantucket," Charlene whispered.

"I'll be right down the road if you need me," Luis promised her. "Would you like a soda?"

"Sure." Charlene nodded.

"I'll be right back." Luis stood up and walked towards the kitchen.

While Charlene was waiting for Luis to come back, she heard voices coming from the study. They sounded like they were arguing. Charlene got up and quietly walked to the door, which was slightly ajar.

"What are you doing here?" Charlene heard her father ask someone. She crept closer, wanting to take a peek through the door.

"I came to pay my respects to your wife," a familiar female voice replied.

"You shouldn't be here," her father's voice was low.

"I wouldn't leave you alone at a time like this, darling," the woman said.

Charlene felt her heart jolt at the woman's words. She peeked through the door and froze as she saw the woman standing far too close to her father. Charlene's mind reeled as she recognized the woman with her father. At first, her brain rejected the idea of what she was seeing.

"I should've been here," Charlene's father stepped away from the woman.

"We couldn't have known," the woman said softly and once again closed the gap between them. "This is not our fault, darling. You shouldn't feel guilty."

"If I'd answered the phone, I could've got to the house in time." Charlene's father stepped away from the woman and ran his hand through his hair. "I think we need to take a break from us for a while."

"WHAT!" the woman hissed. "No." She shook her head. "You've got to stop blaming yourself for what happened to your wife."

"I can blame myself," Charlene's father hissed and turned back to face the woman. "I should've been here for my family; instead, I was unreachable because I was with you."

The fog cleared from Charlene's mind. She couldn't believe what she'd just heard. Her father had been having an affair with that dreadful woman! As the reality of what she'd just witnessed and heard sank in, Charlene felt the last pieces of her once secure world shatter. She turned and ran up the stairs, not stopping when her uncle called her. Charlene fled into her bedroom, locked her bedroom door, and then collapsed on her bed sobbing.

Present Day

"Dr. Newton," the nurse's voice penetrated Carla's restless sleep. "We have multiple incoming from a bus accident."

Carla sat up and nodded at the nurse. "I'm on my way."

"I've got a clean coat for you and a new stethoscope." The nurse put the items on her desk.

"Thank you," Carla pulled her hair into a messy bun and hopped off the bed.

She pulled on the coat and hooked the stethoscope around her neck before following the nurse to the emergency section.

"Your family will be here in a few minutes to take you home," Carla told Cody. "Remember, you need to take it easy for a few days. You'll need to come back in seven days so I can take out your stitches."

"Thank you." Cody smiled at Carla. "How am I ever going to repay you?"

"You would've done the same for me." Carla signed off Cody's chart. "I've already asked Nancy to keep an eye on you."

"Great!" Cody laughed.

"Mom!" Grace rushed into the room, followed by Aiden and Christopher, who was carrying a big bouquet of flowers in one hand and Riley in the other.

"Hi!" Cody hugged her kids and stood up for a hug from Riley. "Thank you for coming to get me."

"These are for you from all of us." Christopher handed Cody the flowers.

"They're beautiful, thank you." Cody gave Christopher a big smile.

"I'm here," Nancy pushed past Christopher to hug Cody.

"Nancy's driving," Riley told Cody.

"That's right, squirt," Nancy grinned.

"With a broken wrist?" Cody looked at Nancy with raised eyebrows.

"Well, my mom is at her quilting club, and we couldn't get ahold of Steven..." Nancy shrugged.

"She drove really, really, really, slowly!" Aiden rolled his eyes. "I swear I saw a tortoise pass us."

"Hey," Nancy glared at Aiden. "I was being extra cautious."

"You were driving like a snail." Aiden shook his head.

"Don't worry," Steven knocked on the door. "If Cody doesn't mind, I'll drive you all back to the Inn."

"Can you give Steven and me a moment, please," Cody asked everyone in the room.

"Uh..." Christopher frowned and looked at Steven, who nodded. "Okay, everyone out. We'll meet you in the waiting room." He pulled the door closed on his way out.

"I won't drive you if you don't want me to," Steven said.

"Thank you, but I would appreciate you driving us home." Cody looked at him. "Carla told me about your house renovations. You're welcome to stay at the Inn. We do have two rooms available."

"That's such a relief. Thank you, Cody." Steven stepped up to hug her, but she stepped back.

"This doesn't mean that things between us are good again." Cody watched Steven's smile fade from his face. "I understand why you did what you did. But you should've trusted me to talk to my son and not go behind my back like you did. You had no right to do that. I don't think I'll ever trust you again."

"I completely understand that." Steven nodded.

"That being said...." Cody looked into his eyes. They were shadowed with regret. "We're all going to be living under the same roof now. The kids adore you, and Christopher needs your support. So, you are welcome to come to family gatherings again."

"Thank you, Cody." Steven gave her a small smile. "I appreciate that."

"Now, I would really like to get out of this hospital and go home." Cody allowed Steven to open the door for her.

They walked through to the waiting area where Cody's family was waiting to take her home.

Chapter Nine
A VISIT FROM THE EX

"If I hadn't become a doctor, I was going to own a seaside restaurant." Carla sat at the beachfront restaurant Cody had told her about, sipping her glass of white wine.

"I couldn't imagine you running a restaurant." Brandon Newton laughed. "You're not the best people person."

"True." Carla grinned. "But before my mother died, I was."

"Your mother is the one part of your life you never really opened up about." Brandon leaned forward on the table and looked her in the eyes. "Yet, I know how much you loved her."

"I guess it's something I've never really gotten over," Carla said honestly. "My father and I were close right up until I was about fourteen. I think that's the year he started cheating on my mother." She watched the wine swirl in her glass.

"Have you gone to see him yet?" Brandon asked Carla.

"No." Carla shook her head. "I want to go over the contents of his folder first." She tapped the large brown envelope Brandon had given her when he'd arrived in Nantucket earlier that day.

"When are we going to open it?" Brandon raised his eyebrows.

"I'm not sure I want to," Carla admitted. "You've seen the DNA report."

"All the more reason to open it." Brandon smiled encouragingly.

"Do you want me to do it? Like when I opened your results for you in university?"

"Would you?" Carla pulled a face.

"Sure." Brandon reached over and picked up the thick envelope. "I wonder what is in here?"

"You know how thorough that P.I. is." Carla had been surprised that Brandon had even agreed to ask the investigator he'd used to help him. There was bad blood between Brandon and the man.

"Like you said, he's thorough, and he has the right contacts." Brandon shrugged. "We needed information only he could get us."

"Brand, one day, you need to give him the benefit of the doubt and listen to what he has to say," Carla said softly.

"I'd rather not," Brandon's face became a mask. "He made his bed and has had to deal with the consequences. I won't let my family be dragged down by him again."

"Yet, whenever you need him, he drops everything to help," Carla pointed out. "Why won't you look a little deeper? Didn't you ever think that everything about that case was just a little too neatly packaged?"

"We've been over this," Brandon looked at her warningly. "That case is closed." He pulled the contents out of the folder.

"No, it's not," Carla persisted. "Until you and he sort it out, it will never be closed and will leave a big hole inside of you."

"Like you and your father?" Brandon hit the ball back into her court.

"My situation is nothing like yours." Carla hissed. "And you know it. You also know I'm right about you, and...!"

"Can we change the subject?" Brandon looked at her. "This subject always gets out of hand with us."

"Whatever, Brand," Carla said, annoyed. "What's in the envelope?"

"When did you say your uncle went missing?" Brandon frowned as he read one of the pages.

"Tenth of March, nineteen-ninety-three." Carla looked at Brandon curiously.

"According to this, your uncle was seen on Nantucket on the

eleventh of March nineteen-ninety-three." Brandon's eyes widened as he looked up at her. "He made a trip to the island just after eight that morning and then took the last ferry off the island that night."

"That's impossible. The sheriff's office said Uncle Luis left in June the previous year and was never seen on the island again. Even his house had been closed up since that day." Carla's frown deepened. "So where did he go after he took the last ferry off the island? He never went back to Boston or Martha's Vineyard. Unless my grandparents lied to me."

"Would you put it past your grandparents to lie?" Brandon raised his eyebrows. "You know how reliable they were."

"That's true," Carla agreed. "But why would my uncle leave without even saying goodbye to me?" She shook her head. "He was the only one that supported me through that awful time."

"I don't know," Brandon shook his head. "This whole thing doesn't make sense." He put two official-looking documents in front of her. "It seems like a lot of trouble to cover up something like this."

"What else is in there?" Carla asked Brandon, looking at the envelope. "Did he manage to find the adoption papers?"

"No, there's a note that they were missing," Brandon shook his head. "That shouldn't be a surprise to us, considering everything about this situation doesn't make sense."

"Can I see the rest of the investigation files?" Carla took them from Brandon and started going through them. "What do you think this means?" She showed him an encrypted letter.

"Isn't that your handwriting?" Brandon looked at Carla.

"You're right. It does look similar to my handwriting, right down to the crossed sevens." Carla cocked her head and looked at the page. "But I didn't write this, nor do I know whatever kind of language or code this is written in."

"I know someone who could decode this for us," Brandon offered. "Are you sure you didn't write it?"

"No," Carla stressed. "I would've remembered writing something like that."

"I'll give it to my contact," Brandon put the note to one side.

"Carla, I don't like this. My gut is screaming at me to tell you to leave sleeping dogs alone."

"You know I can't do that. If there's one person who can shed some more light on this, it's my uncle, and I refuse to believe he's dead." Carla took another sip of wine as the hairs on her arm stood up again. She looked around the restaurant and out onto the beach.

"Got that feeling again?" Brandon asked her.

"You know me too well." Carla grinned at him. "But yes, I feel like someone's watching us."

"I couldn't perchance be a tall, dark-haired man with glaring blue eyes, could it?" Brandon raised an eyebrow.

"What?" Carla turned to see Steven standing to the side, staring at her. "Oh!"

"Let me guess, that's Steven Stanford?" Brandon leaned forward. "He doesn't look so happy to see me sitting with you."

"Steven," Carla called him over.

"Hi," Steven walked over to their table. "I see you found this place after all?"

"Yes." Carla nodded, scooping up the papers on the table. "I'd like you to meet Dr. Brandon Newton. Brand, this is Dr. Steven Stanford."

"Hi." Brandon stood up and shook hands with Steven.

"Nice to meet you," Steven said politely.

"Steven," a waitress called him. "Your orders are ready."

"I better get that order back to Cody Bay." Steven looked from Carla to Brandon, "Enjoy the rest of your afternoon." He nodded and walked off.

"Well, that wasn't at all awkward," Brandon teased Carla. "I think that man has a giant crush on the gorgeous Dr. Carla Newton."

"Stop it, Brandon," Carla said, a little irritated.

"You have to tell him the truth, Carla," Brandon said more seriously. "I have a terrible feeling we've poked some giant sleeping bear here." He pointed to the envelope. "Someone is going to find out we're snooping into all this."

"I know," Carla breathed. "Steven's just dealing with so much right now."

"And you aren't?" Brandon sat back. "Tinker Bell, I'm not here to help you if anything goes wrong, and now that I've seen how Steven looked at you, I think he would be there for you without question."

"I will," Carla promised. "But there's someone I need to confront first." She shoved the papers back into the envelope and dropped it into her purse. "Will you let me know as soon as you get the note decrypted?"

"You know I will." Brandon looked at his watch. "I best get going. I have to get Sophia from my parents' house before eight tonight."

"Give her a hug from me." Carla walked out of the restaurant with Brandon.

"Will do. She's going to love the outfit," Brandon held up the shopping bag. "You spoil her."

"I can; I'm the cool aunt." Carla grinned and gave him a kiss as he slid into his car. "Call me when you're back in Boston."

"Will do," Brandon blew her a kiss. "Love you, Tinker Bell."

"Love you too, Brand." Carla waved him off.

Carla stood watching his car pull out of the parking lot. A chill crept up her spine once again, and a soft wind blew over her making her shiver. Carla turned her head to look around her. She had the feeling she was being watched again. Carla turned on her heel and headed for her car.

Carla stood at her car, fumbling with her keys and feeling really uneasy when a hand touched her shoulder. Carla screamed, dropped her keys, and swung her large purse around, aiming for the head.

"Ow!" Steven hissed. "Good grief! I was just coming to ask if you were okay."

Carla stood holding her chest, which rose and fell in time with her rapid heartbeat.

"You scared me half to death!" Carla rasped.

"I'm sorry," Steven held the side of his head. "I had to come back for the ice cream." He held up the tub in one hand. "I saw you rush to your car like you were being chased."

"Sorry." Carla swallowed as her nerves settled.

"What the hell do you have in that purse?" Steven rubbed the small lump forming on his temple.

"Let me have a look." Carla's lips started to twitch as she started to see the funny side of what just happened. "You'll live." She swallowed and put her hand over her mouth.

"Are you laughing at my pain?" Steven glared at her, but he, too, couldn't stop his lips from twitching.

"Do you want to have a sundowner at Cody Bay with me?" Carla asked him impulsively. "Cody told me you moved in."

"I did," Steven confirmed. "And I'd love to join you for a sundowner. Where's the other Dr. Newton?"

"He's gone back to Boston and his daughter," Carla told him.

"Shall I pick you up at say seven?" Steven asked her as he dropped down and picked up her car keys.

"Perfect." Carla smiled and took her keys. "You might want to put some ice on that bump."

"Good advice." Steven gave her a sexy smile as he held the car door open for her.

Carla waved to him as she pulled out of the parking lot. Her heart was beating in her throat and the crazy butterflies that tormented her every time Steven was near her were back.

"Steven was wrong; Dr. Brandon Newton's not good-looking. The man's gorgeous, sexy, and incredibly wealthy." Nancy spun the monitor around for Christopher to see.

The three of them were sitting in Cody's office while Cody was at the Marine Life Center.

"Huh." Christopher pulled a face. "I could see why women would think he was good-looking." He looked at Steven teasingly. "I can see your problem."

"He's not a problem," Steven shook his head as Nancy and Christopher grinned. "The two Dr. Newtons are divorced."

"Why do you think she's kept his surname?" Nancy frowned and took in a breath. "Holy moly." Her eyes widened. "You'll never guess who his mother is."

"Some famous supermodel?" Steven guessed.

"She's as beautiful as a supermodel, and I think you'd feel better if she was one." Nancy raised her eyebrows and turned the screen around. "His mother is Wendy Barr."

"Dr. Wendy Barr?" Steven's eyes widened.

Nancy nodded and bit her bottom lip.

"Oh, great!" Steven sighed and threw his hands in the air.

"Who is Dr. Wendy Barr?" Christopher asked.

"Only one of the top neurosurgeons in the world!" Nancy told Christopher. "Not just America," Nancy gestured with her hands. "The world!"

"Dr. Wendy Barr came into surgery at a time when it was mostly dominated by men," Steven explained. "She started in general surgery before specializing in neurology. Within ten years, her name was basically synonymous with neurosurgery."

"She's amazing," Nancy said excitedly. "Dr. Barr took on surgeries no other doctor would touch, and they say she's never lost a patient."

"I'm sure that's not true," Christopher was skeptical. "Every doctor has lost at least one patient."

"They call her the Evel Knievel of neurosurgery." Nancy's eyes narrowed as she looked at Steven. "If I had to have someone work on my brain, I'd want it to be Dr. Barr."

"Nice," Christopher drawled.

"Oh, sorry, did that touch a nerve," Nancy said smugly.

"Funny," Christopher threw the pencil he was holding at her.

"Why would someone with Dr. Brandon Newton's credentials and famous mother want to work at Nantucket General?" Steven wondered.

"Because Carla's here?" Nancy grinned.

"They're divorced, and Carla said they got divorced because they found they were better as friends," Steven told them.

"Are you trying to convince yourself or us that's true?" Christopher asked his older brother.

"Look at it this way—you'll be his boss!" Nancy pointed out.

"You know what," Steven sat down in front of the desk. "We're here to discuss what we found and where we will go from here."

"You don't want to know who Brandon's father is?" Nancy asked cheekily.

"NO!" Steven and Christopher said together.

"Fine!" Nancy clicked off the page she was on. "I went to get my adoption records from Social Services."

"And?" Steven asked. He felt his heart lodge in his throat.

"Here," Nancy gave him the document she'd gotten from them. "My birth parents are marked as unknown. I was brought to Social Services by someone with the initials LV."

"This is the birth certificate that was given to my parents." Nancy handed Steven her birth certificate. "I wasn't even born on Nantucket."

"But you were taken to Social Services by someone with the initials LV." Christopher steepled his finger in front of him. "Why would LV try to hide who you were?"

"Maybe LV didn't know who I was?" Nancy shrugged.

"How did the Honeys come to adopt you?" Christopher asked her. "You were a newborn baby; there are waiting lists to adopt newborns."

"I have no idea." Nancy shook her head. "No one at Social Services could tell me; there are no reports, only those adoption papers."

"If you were Charlene's daughter and for some reason someone was trying to cover up who your parents were, why give you to the Honeys here in Nantucket?" Christopher frowned. "Maybe we need to find out who LV is and then go ask?"

"I think we should have our DNA tested and try to get some of Carla's. That would be one way of proving I was the child of your brother, Lance, and Charlene Baxter." Nancy suggested.

"NO!" Steven's voice was gruff. He ran his hand nervously through his hair. "If you're Charlene's daughter, Lance wasn't your father."

"But wasn't Charlene the girl he was about to ask to marry him?" Christopher looked at his brother, confused.

"No... yes!" Steven squeezed his eyes shut and pinched the bridge of his nose. "It was a little more complicated than that."

"I remember the night of the accident. I came to call you because Mom and Dad were fighting." Christopher stared at Steven as he remembered. "I remember Charlene being passed out on the sofa in the outside locker room of the clubhouse." He looked at Steven. "You told me to stay with her while you and Lance went to sort out our parents."

Steven pursed his lips and closed his eyes as the memory of that night came back to haunt him.

"Lance was going to drive Dad home. He was angry and you made him calm down." Christopher stared off through Cody's office window. "I heard you offering to drive Charlene home when she was ready to leave the party." He looked at Steven. "What made Lance so angry?"

"What's going on...." Nancy looked from Steven to Christopher. "What am I missing?"

"If you are Charlene's daughter, Nancy, Lance wouldn't..." Steven said softly, swallowing down his guilt. "Lance wouldn't be your father..." He closed his eyes and shook his head before looking Nancy in the eyes. "I'd be your father."

"WHAT?" Nancy and Christopher choked in shock.

Steven watched Nancy and Christopher gaping at him. He clenched his jaw. "There's a lot none of you know about what's going on this island," he said softly.

"You bastard!" Christopher hissed once he was over his shock. "What the hell, Steven!" He glared at his older brother. "You know how crazy Lance was about Charlene Baxter."

"It haunts me every day." Steven's voice was hoarse with emotion. "But there's also a lot you don't know about Lance either."

"You told Lance on his birthday that you and Charlene had cheated on him?" Christopher sneered.

"Christopher!" Nancy glared at him. "Don't go pointing fingers at your brother because you have three pointing back at you, dude!"

"I never stole my brother's girlfriend!" Christopher glared back at Nancy.

"Didn't you?" Nancy raised her eyebrows. "Should I tell the story of how you and Cody met?" She asked.

"Oh for goodness sakes, that's not the same," Christopher argued. "She was a kid, and Steven was way too old for her."

"I've never loved or even looked at Cody as anything but a little sister," Steven admitted and cleared that misconception up once and for all.

"Still, you have no right to berate your brother after what you did to your family," Nancy reminded Christopher. "This is not the time to get into a family spat."

"Nancy's right," Christopher said grudgingly. "We need to find out why all the secrecy surrounding Nancy's birth and birth parents."

"Do you think your mother knew about Charlene's pregnancy?" Nancy asked.

"No," Steven shook his head. "I didn't even know until the night of the accident."

"You found out on Lance's birthday?" Christopher hissed.

"I don't think either myself or Lance was meant to find out ever," Steven told them. "We both found out purely by accident on that night."

"So, how did he and you find out that Charlene was pregnant?" Christopher looked at Steven with contempt.

"From what Charlene told me when I was driving her home, Lance had found her pregnancy test." Steven sighed. It was time to tell Christopher the truth about that summer in Nantucket. Or at least the beginning of it.

Chapter Ten
A FATEFULLY TRAGIC NIGHT

June 1992

The weeks since April had gone by far too quickly. The month had rolled over into May in a blink of an eye, and now May was ending abruptly. There were only two weeks left until Steven's life was going to change forever one way or the other.

"Hey, sleepyhead," Charlene's soft voice whispered in his ear. "You've been sleeping for two hours."

Charlene's beautiful violet eyes shone with happiness, and her smile dimpled her left cheek. Every time Steven looked into her eyes, she took his breath away, and he fell deeper in love with her. They'd met two days after her grandmother's funeral. She'd gone to Nantucket General to get stitches in her hand after breaking a vase. Steven had been the intern assigned to stitch her up.

The minute their eyes had met, they had felt the strong connection between them. Only, on that day, her eyes were haunted with secrets and shadowed by sorrow. Charlene was his last patient for the day, and he'd impulsively asked her if she wanted to get a pizza with him. To his surprise, she'd said yes, and they'd spent every day together since that day. Steven hadn't meant for it to happen. He'd know who she was, and every day he swallowed his guilt to follow his treacherous heart.

"You shouldn't have let me sleep." Steven pulled her to him and kissed her soft pink lips.

"You needed it," Charlene put her head on his chest and cuddled up to him. "You've been burning the candle on both ends lately."

"When you get to do your internship, you'll quickly learn how to stay sharp and function on very little sleep." Steven kissed the top of her head. "I wish I wasn't on a shift at the hospital tonight."

"I do too, but it's worked out nicely because my uncle is back, and I promised I'd have dinner with him," Charlene told Steven. "I'll miss you, though."

"You know we're going to have to speak about the elephant in the room some time," Steven said softly. "We have two weeks left before my family comes back to Nantucket."

"I know." Charlene rolled off Steven's bed, grabbed his hand, and pulled him up. "You're not on duty for another two hours; let's go get a milkshake, and we can discuss this as we walk along the beach." She smiled up at him. "Let's go to Cody Bay beach."

"You know I can never say no to you." Steven sighed, grabbed his shirt and car keys as they rushed through his parents' Nantucket home.

Steven's eyes connected with a picture of his brother, Lance. His eyes bore into Steven's soul, fueling Steven's guilt. He swallowed as his eyes moved from Lance to their youngest brother Christopher. *What was he doing?* Steven ran a hand through his hair, feeling like the biggest traitor ever. He was the older brother—the example. And what kind of example was he setting?

"Steven?" Charlene's voice made his heartstrings pull. "Are you coming?"

"I'll be right there," Steven called. He reached out and touched the photograph of Lance. "I'm sorry little brother." He swallowed and closed his eyes.

Steven had known what kind of people his parents were since he was nine years old. He'd vowed then that he'd never be anything like them, and he'd do whatever it took to protect his two younger brothers. Steven had taken it upon himself to be their example and teach them how to be decent human beings. It hadn't been hard, as their parents mostly left them with the nanny unless they were needed as props to show off the Stanfords' perfect family.

Both his brothers trusted Steven and looked up to him, and here he was breaking that trust because he'd fallen in love with Charlene Baxter. Steven's heart was torn, and although he'd managed to push it to the back of his mind these past months, he knew he couldn't ignore his conscience forever.

He knew what he had to do. Steven took a deep breath. His hand shook as he closed the front door. Steven was between a rock and a hard place. Either way he turned, he was going to come out bruised, and someone he loved was going to get hurt. There was no middle ground.

Charlene had been walking around in a daze for the past two weeks. She felt like she was turned inside out and used as a punchbag. Every part of Charlene ached, and there was no medicine, cream, or miracle cure for what was ailing her. Only time would heal the emotional wounds that were torn into her soul and bleeding heart.

Charlene couldn't even hate the man who'd broken her heart because she'd always known there was no way their romance could have a happy ending. She knew he loved her as much as she loved him. Charlene knew Steven would have to make a difficult choice when the time came. And she loved him even more for making the right one, which wasn't her.

She wiped tears from her cheeks as she walked into Cody Bay Inn.

"Hello, Charlene," the owner, Mrs. Moore, greeted her. "Are you okay, honey?"

"Sorry," Charlene sniffed and swiped more stray tears from her cheeks. "I'm fine. May I use the bathroom?"

"Of course," Mrs. Moore smiled. "When you're done, why

don't you come and have some chamomile tea in my office with me?"

"Thank you," Charlene sniffed again and forced a smile on her face.

Charlene closed and locked the bathroom door. She stood looking at herself in the large mirror that hung over the basin. *Please, please, please, don't let it be true!* She drew in a shaky breath and took the test from her bag. Charlene couldn't believe this was happening to her.

Her mother's voice ran through her head. *Charlene, honey, you know what happens when you play with fire. Don't tempt fate, honey!* She smiled, remembering her mother. She missed her so much, and right now, she could really have used her support. Charlene looked down at the test in her hand. She'd been carrying it around in her purse for the past four days, and it was time.

Charlene squared her shoulders. She was brave and now an adult. She had to act like one and take responsibility for her actions, no matter the consequences. Charlene marched into the toilet stall and closed the door. The next minute was the longest of her life. Charlene deliberately didn't look at the stick that held her life in the balance but kept her eyes on her watch as it ticked away sixty seconds. At first, she couldn't bring herself to look at the results until she dropped the darn test. She bent to pick it up, and her heart froze in her chest.

*

Charlene sat on the sand staring out over the Atlantic Ocean as it rolled lazily onto the shore of Cody Bay. She couldn't remember how long she'd sat there and knew she had to go back inside and apologize for running out and ignoring Mrs. Moore's call. The shock waves still zinged through her body, and she felt like she was in some surreal alternative dimension in someone else's body living out their life.

"Hello," a young voice greeted her. "I'm Cody."

Charlene wiped her eyes and plastered a smile on her face. "Hi,

I'm Charlene." She looked at the pretty young girl standing with her long hair in pigtails. She was carrying a bucket full of shells.

"I'm collecting shells to take with us on a trip," Cody explained to Charlene. "Charlene is a very pretty name."

"Thank you, so is Cody," Charlene smiled. "Like the Bay."

"That's right," Cody nodded. "My grandparents own it," she said proudly.

"So, where are you going on your trip?" Charlene asked Cody.

"My parents travel all over the world on various expeditions studying marine life and the effect of pollution on the oceans," Cody said. "I go with them."

"You're so lucky. That must be so interesting," Charlene smiled.

"Do you want to collect some shells with me?" Cody asked her.

"Sure," Charlene said and stood up. "You have quite a nice collection there."

"My mom and I usually collect them, but she's at the Marine Life Center with my dad," Cody bent down and picked up a soft blue shell. "It's my birthday tomorrow."

"Oh, and how old are you going to be?" Charlene asked, thinking what a coincidence that Cody shared a birthday with Lance Stanford.

"Eleven." Cody picked up another shell.

"A friend of mine also has a birthday tomorrow, but he's going to be nineteen," Charlene shared with Cody.

"That's awesome." Cody grinned. "Do you want to come for some tea with my grandma and me?"

"I would like that very much," Charlene felt tears sting her eyes when Cody put her hand into Charlene's as they walked along the beach towards the Inn.

A soft breeze picked up and drifted over them. Charlene shuddered.

"Don't worry." Cody looked up at Charlene. "Grams says that if the breeze caresses you, it's the bay trying to tell you something. But you can't listen to it with your ears. You have to open your heart to let it in so it can whisper to your soul and show you the way."

"That's lovely, Cody." Charlene shivered again as the breeze tickled her skin.

"I can't do this now, Steven," Charlene hissed. "Please, just let me walk away. I'm going to break it off with Lance on Monday, so I don't ruin his birthday weekend, and then I'm going back to Harvard early."

They were standing at the back of the Nantucket Country Club. Inside, the club music played, and people danced and laughed as they celebrated Lance Stanford's nineteenth birthday.

"I can't let you walk away," Steven's voice was hoarse with emotion. "These past two weeks have been torture without you. I know my brother is going to hate me, but I love you, Charlene."

Steven stepped towards her, but Charlene knew if he put his arms around her, she wouldn't have the strength to do what was right. Charlene may have ruined her own life, but she wasn't going to pull Steven down with her.

"No," Charlene took a step back. "Let's not ruin your brother's birthday."

"Sure." Steven's face looked like she'd slapped him. But he backed off. "We better go inside." He stepped aside for Charlene to go in first. "I'll be right in."

Charlene swallowed down her tears, once again plastered a smile on her face, and walked to where Lance was waiting for her. Her guilt was eating away at her as the night wore on. Her eyes kept roaming to the bar where Steven was chatting to a beautiful woman who'd been monopolizing his time the entire night.

After another hour, Charlene needed some air, so she slipped outside. She was going to get a taxi to take her home. His uncle was originally going to take her home, but he'd had to leave a few hours ago because he wasn't feeling well. He'd made Lance promise to get her home safely at the end of the night. But Charlene wanted to go home now. She was once again feeling queasy, and she was not having fun.

"Hey, there you are," Lance came up next to her. "Are you okay?"

"I have a bit of a headache," Charlene told a little white lie. "I was thinking about calling a cab to take me home."

"Nonsense," Lance smiled at her. "I'll go get my father's keys and drive you home."

"You can't do that—it's your party." Charlene fiddled in her purse for a tissue. When she pulled it out of her bag, the pregnancy test came with it and fell to the ground.

"What the..." Lance bent down before Charlene could and scooped it up. He stared at it in shock. "Is this yours?"

"Lance..." Charlene stepped forward to grab the stick from his hand when her eyes locked with Steven's.

Steven was frozen in the doorway, staring at the stick in Lance's hand. Charlene's breath caught in her throat, and she felt the world start to spin. The floor tilted, and Charlene felt the blood drain from her brain as she struggled to breathe. She swayed. From a distance, she heard her name being called before the world started to fade from her vision.

"Quick, bring her in here," Lance jimmied open the men's outdoor locker room.

Steven had rushed forward and caught Charlene before she hit the ground. His mind was reeling, and his chest was tight. Was Lance holding what Steven thought he'd been holding?

"Did you know about this?" Lance held the test up to Steven.

"No," Steven said honestly.

"Mom was right," Lance said angrily and punched the door jam.

"You need to calm down. I know this has been a shock to you..." Steven warned Lance.

"You think it's mine?" Lance hissed. "It's not mine, but I'm pretty sure I know whose it is. He did it again, didn't he? Just like he did to you with Judy."

"Judy?" Steven's brow furrowed together in confusion.

93

Steven's mind was trying to sift through the implications of the test that Lance was waving through the air like a wand. He was only partly concentrating on what Lance was saying.

"We need to help Charlene," Steven advised Lance.

"You help her," Lance was seething. "I'm going to punch someone in the face."

"What?" Steven looked at Lance. "Who are you going to ...."

"Lance, Steve, come quick..." Christopher came to find them. "Mom and Dad are having a horrendous fight. I think it's time to take dad home."

"Christopher," Steven managed to claw his way out of the brain fog that shrouded his mind. "Can you look after Charlene until I get back?"

"What happened to her?" Christopher raised his eyebrows.

"She wasn't feeling well," Steven explained as he looked past Christopher to see Lance storm out of the room. "Stay here."

Steven ran after Lance.

"Lance," Steven barked. "Slow down, little brother." He reached out and took the pregnancy test from Lance and shoved it into his back pocket.

"I need that," Lance argued.

"No, you don't." Steven held his brother at bay. "You don't know the truth about anything yet. Don't go throwing around accusations. No matter how you feel, imagine how Charlene is feeling. If it is her test, I'm sure she doesn't want the world to know."

"She's been cheating on me, Steve," Lance swallowed. "I can't believe Charlene would do that to me."

"Listen to yourself and remember what you told me a few days ago," Steven reminded Lance. "You know about wanting to end things with Charlene because of the other woman you met in April and had been seeing."

"That was a mistake; I knew it as soon as I saw Charlene again." Lance's eyes still glittered angrily.

"Really?" Steven was still a little hurt over his brother's confession a few days after Steven had broken it off with Charlene. "I had

94

to talk you out of bringing your new girlfriend to Nantucket because you hadn't broken up with your current one."

"I..." Lance swallowed and closed his eyes. "I'm sorry. Charlene and I have been together forever, you know." He shook his head. "Just the thought of that man with her makes me so mad."

"What man?" Steven didn't get an answer from Lance because their mother stormed over to them.

"Get your father's keys for him," Margaret Stanford said angrily. "He needs to go home and sleep it off." She stormed inside.

"Lance," their father walked over to them. "It doesn't matter what your mother says. I never had an affair with your girlfriend. I have cancer, and I am getting treatment." He slurred and swayed.

"Dad!" Lance and Steven looked at their father in shock. "I'll take him home." Lance offered.

"I'll take Charlene home and come back to get mom," Steven said.

"Thanks, big brother," Lance gave Steven a hug. "Please don't tell Charlene about Peggy. I'll do it and you're right; I need to hear her story about the other thing."

"Charlene's asking for you," Christopher told Steven.

"She probably wants a lift home." Steven shrugged, and Lance nodded.

"Thanks, Steve," Lance looked relieved before he propped up their father. "Come on, Dad, I'll take you home. Then tomorrow you need to tell us what the hell is going on with you and why you'd be drinking on top of treatment."

"Can I come with you?" Christopher asked Lance. "Steve, will you tell Mom I've gone with them?"

"Sure," Steven hugged Christopher. "Oh, here, I found Dad's phone on the bar. Can you take it?"

Christopher took the phone and followed Lance and their father to the car.

Steven watched them pull off before he ducked into the locker room, where Charlene was sitting up waiting for him.

"Were you going to tell me?" Steven pulled the test out of his pocket and handed it back to her.

"No," Charlene shook her head. "Because there's nothing to tell. I went to the clinic, and their test was negative."

"Are you sure?" Steven's eyes narrowed. "Those home tests are pretty accurate."

"I'm sure." Charlene nodded. "Would you take me home, please?"

"Sure." Steven nodded. "Do you have everything?"

"I do. I was about to call a cab when Lance found me," Charlene admitted. "But if you're busy, I can still call a cab."

"No, I promised Lance I'd take you home." Steven didn't know what to say to her.

It was like they were suddenly strangers. His heart ached for her, but now there seemed to be nothing but debris between them, pushing them apart. As Steven stepped out into the night, he didn't realize just how much his life was about to change and be turned upside down. He had no idea he was about to lose two people he loved dearly, and his world would have a tear in it that couldn't be fixed.

Chapter Eleven
FINDING NANCY'S PARENTS

Present Day

"Lance died not knowing you'd cheated with his girlfriend?" It was Nancy glaring at Steven this time. "Unbelievable."

"I'm not proud of what I did," Steven assured Nancy. "I know it's not an excuse, but what I felt for Charlene was more powerful than anything I'd felt before or have again."

"Aw," Nancy mocked him. "I'm sorry, but what you did goes against every moral code in the book."

"Nancy!" Christopher shook his head at her. "I can understand what Steven went through. You've probably never felt the kind of love that automatically links your heart and tethers your souls."

"How do you know?" Nancy challenged Christopher. "I've been in love... once... maybe twice."

"I'm not talking about surface love, Nancy. That's more to do with chemistry and a physical connection. I'm talking about deep soul-disturbing love you only experience once," Christopher explained. "When that love is ripped from you, it takes a piece of your soul with it. A piece that no one else quite fits into but the one."

"So, you're saying there's only one great love for everyone?" Nancy raised an eyebrow.

"No." Christopher shook his head. "You can have many great loves, Nancy, but you'll only ever have one epic one."

"Good to know." Nancy tapped her chin with her fingers. "So Steven's excuse for cheating with his brother's girlfriend is because Charlene was Steven's epic love."

"She was... is still my epic love," Steven confirmed. "She always will be."

"What would Carla be then if we find out she's not Charlene after all, but a relative?" Nancy asked Steven. "Because the way you look at her seems pretty epic to me!"

"Can we change the subject and move back to the mystery about the secrecy surrounding your birth?" Steven looked from Christopher to Nancy, who were both glaring at each other.

They really did look like they were related right down to their steely eyed stares. Steven ran a hand through his hair. *Is Nancy my daughter?* He glanced at the young woman. *Did Charlene lie to me when she said her blood test at the clinic came back negative?* He looked down at his hands. *Why would she have lied to me?* The familiar ache throbbed through his heart like it did every time he thought of Charlene or looked into Carla's eyes.

"I think Carla is Charlene," Steven looked at Nancy and then Christopher. "I have since the minute I laid eyes on her at a conference in Boston."

"No, she's not." Nancy sighed as she tried to scratch her finger through the plaster cast on her one hand. She pulled out a ruler from Cody's drawer to help her scratch her arm beneath the plaster. "I just found her marriage certificate to Dr. Sexy Brandon Newton."

"How did you..." Steven decided it was better not knowing how Nancy managed to get into whatever state records she'd gotten into to find that information. "And don't put a ruler into your cast." He snatched the ruler from Nancy.

"My arm is itchy beneath the plaster," Nancy hissed and gave Steven a dirty look before turning back to the computer. "Carla Vern married Brandon Newton on the twentieth of November in the year two-thousand."

"Did you say Vern?" Steven leaned forward to look at the document Nancy had on the screen.

"I did," Nancy confirmed. "Carla is the daughter of the late Michaela Vern. There is no father listed." She sighed.

"Vern... LV...." Something dawned on Steven. "Luis Vern." He snapped his fingers.

"The chauffeur?" Christopher asked Steven.

"Luis Vern was not just a chauffeur; he was Dad's head of security." Some pieces of the puzzle started to fall into place for Steven. "He disappeared the night of Dad's accident."

"I thought Mother fired him because she blamed him for the accident," Christopher said. "If he hadn't gone home sick, Lance wouldn't have driven Dad home that night."

"No, Mom didn't fire him," Steven informed Christopher. "And it was Mom who sent him home, if you remember." He looked at Christopher. "Luis Vern was reassigned to Boston and our grandparents' estate."

"That would make sense because that's where Dad went after he got out of the hospital," Christopher suddenly realized. "I really should've visited the grandparents more."

"You hated going to their estate," Steven reminded Christopher.

"That's true," Christopher admitted.

"So, Carla is Luis Vern's daughter?" Nancy looked confused.

"No." Steven grinned. "Not if Michaela Vern is her mother, because Luis was Michaela's older brother, so he'd be Carla's uncle." He kissed Nancy on the head. "You've just proved to me exactly who Carla is."

"I'm as lost as Nancy here, bro." Christopher and Nancy were both looking at him with deep frowns on their faces.

"Oh my God," Nancy breathed. "You both have to see this. I've just found Charlene Baxter's old driver's license."

"What did you find..." Steven and Christopher both stood behind Nancy and looked over her shoulder at the screen. "I told you so!" He gave them a smug smile.

"Cody..." Carla knocked on the door and pushed it open. "Oh, sorry, I was looking for Cody." She held up a first-aid kit. "I need to check her wound."

Three pairs of eyes stared at her as if she'd grown three heads.

"What?" Carla looked around her nervously. "Is there a spider?" She jumped back from the door frame.

"No." Steven straightened up from over the computer screen in front of Nancy. "There's no spider." He folded his arms across his chest, and his eyes narrowed.

Okay... Carla thought. *What's going on here?* "Is something wrong?" she asked cautiously.

"You tell us?" Nancy leaned back in Cody's leather office chair.

"I'm not sure what's going on?" Carla gave them a sideways glance.

"I once knew someone who was afraid of spiders," Steven started telling Carla a story. "You remind me a *LOT* of her. In fact, the two of you could be sisters."

"Twins, really," Nancy piped up.

"I don't have any siblings," Carla told them. Her heart started to race. *Uh-oh!* Carla thought, and her mind screamed at her to run.

"Interesting," Nancy said as she typed something on the computer. "Oh!" She pointed to the monitor for Steven and Christopher, who were both now standing behind the desk next to her, to see. "Whose DNA tests did you order the other day, Dr. Newton?"

"That's confidential information." Carla's eyes narrowed. *Run! Go Now!* Her instincts screamed. *No!* Carla refused to run anymore, and she was tired of hiding.

"It looks like whoever this test was for, it confirmed the maternity of the subject," Nancy tapped her chin. "Oh, and look here, the subject's blood type matches mine. This test was started on the day I had my dirt bike accident. Weren't you the one that took away the tray with my bloody swabs on it?"

"Okay, would you believe I was trying to help you find your birth parents?" Carla's brows drew together. *Drat, they're onto me!*

"How would you know who my mother was to get her DNA, or..." Nancy brought up another report, "know who my father was to get his DNA?" She pulled a face. "Strange how you'd know that!"

"I had a hunch," Carla told her truthfully. "You look a lot like the Stanfords."

"Nancy also looks a lot like you!" Christopher raised his eyebrows. "Right down to the hereditary dimple in her left cheek."

Carla's cheeks reddened. *Oh, yes, the cat was definitely out of the bag!* Three sets of eyes bore into her. She chewed on her bottom lip for a minute, staring back at them. *Maybe they could help me?* Carla thought, and suddenly a breeze gusted through the office door and wrapped around her like a soothing balm. A little girl's voice from years ago echoed through her mind: *You have to open your heart to let it in so it can whisper to your soul and show you the way!*

Okay, breeze, let's hear what you have to say! Carla took a deep breath in and let herself relax. She felt a warmth in her stomach and instantly looked up at Steven. He held her gaze, and that's when she felt it. It was like a tug on her heart, and she instinctively knew what she had to do. Carla stepped into Cody's office and closed the door behind her.

"If I tell you everything you want to hear, I'm going to need all of your help with something," Carla bargained with them.

"What do you need help with?" Nancy asked, intrigued. "Does it have something to do with Dr. Sexy Brandon Newton?" She asked, hopefully.

"No." Carla shook her head and frowned at Nancy. "This has nothing to do with Brand."

"Brand!" Nancy tested the name. "I like that."

"Do we have a deal?" Carla asked the three of them.

"Is it dangerous?" Nancy asked.

"Possibly," Carla said honestly.

"Okay, well, I'm in." Nancy raised her hand.

"Really?" Christopher shook his head at Nancy. "What is it with you and danger?"

"We live on a little island!" Nancy gestured with her hands. "When adventure, mystery, and intrigue presents itself, I'm the first in line for the ride."

"As my doctor, are you saying you'll allow me to help?" Christopher asked Carla.

"Within reason," Carla told him.

"I'll take that," Christopher nodded. "I'm in too."

"Steven?" Christopher looked at his brother, who was staring at Carla.

"I have some questions." Steven's eyes narrowed.

"Okay," Carla folded her arms across her chest and looked him in the eye. "Ask away."

"Me, first!" Nancy raised her hand.

"Sure," Carla shrugged.

"Are you my mother?"

"Yes," Carla answered. "I believe I am."

"Is Steven my father?" Nancy asked another question.

Her eyes flew to Steven's again, and his eyelids narrowed to slits; a nerve ticked at the side of his jaw, and his shoulders stiffened.

"Well?" Steven gritted. "Are you going to answer, Nancy?"

"Yes," Carla swallowed and held Steven's gaze. "Steven is your father, Nancy."

"So you're telling us that you're really...." Nancy gave Carla a sideways look.

"I am who you suspected me to be," Carla confirmed. As soon as the words were out of her mouth, she felt a weight lift from her chest. The gentle breeze brushed through her hair and danced around her before disappearing.

"So, I was born at Martha's Vineyard?" Nancy picked up the one birth certificate. "Why was I given to the Honeys?"

"I don't know," Carla answered Nancy honestly. She swallowed down the haunting memories of those months she spent in Martha's Vineyard and the day of Nancy's birth.

"So you just handed me over like I was nothing and walked away?" Nancy's eyes darkened with emotion.

"No." Carla shook her head. "I didn't hand you over..." She swallowed, fighting back the emotion that still overwhelmed her when she thought of that day. "I...."

The office door swung open, and Cody stopped at the threshold when she saw the four of them in her office.

"I didn't realize my office was booked for the afternoon!" Cody looked at all of them questioningly. "Are you using my laptop too?" She looked pointedly at Nancy.

"I... err..." Nancy's eyes narrowed. "I had to look something up."

"Sorry, Cody," Christopher started walking towards her. "Just discussing some family business."

"May I suggest the lounge?" Cody folded her arms, waiting for them to pile out of her office.

"I actually came here to check on your stitches," Carla told Cody.

"Can we do my checkup a little later?" Cody asked Carla as Lana rushed into the room with a thick white binder under her arm. "Lana, myself, and Connie have some things to discuss."

"Sure, let me know when you're ready," Carla stepped around Lana and waited for Nancy to leave before she followed behind her.

"Sorry we took over your office," Nancy gave Cody a sheepish smile before heading to the lounge with Carla and Christopher.

"*L*et's not make it a habit," Cody said before turning towards her desk and stopping when she saw there was still one person left behind. "Steven?"

Steven felt like he'd been frozen to the floor. He'd had a hunch about who Carla was, and when he'd seen Nancy's birth certificate, deep down inside, it was like he instinctively knew. But then it was all just hearsay. Now that Carla had confirmed it, he'd frozen.

Steven had so many questions, but he'd lost his voice. All he could do was stand there with his heart pounding in his ears and looking dumb.

"Steven, what's wrong?" Carla walked up to him. "Why don't you come and sit down?"

"She is who I thought she was all along." Steven managed to say. "She lied to me all those years ago and then disappeared when she could have brought some light to a dark time."

"Lana, would you get that chair?" Cody asked her.

"Oh, dear, is Steven okay?" Connie walked into the room carrying a tray.

"I think he's had a bit of a shock." Cody looked up at Connie.

"Here you go," Lana wheeled one of the chairs over to him.

"Thanks," Steven sat down.

"Do you want to tell us what's going on?" Lana asked him. "You look like you need to talk."

"I wouldn't know where to start." Steven breathed and ran a shaky hand through his hair.

"The beginning is always the best place," Connie poured him some tea and put one of her pastries on a plate for him. "Here, this will make you feel better."

"I don't want to intrude on..." Steven looked at the folder Lana had put on Cody's desk. "Your wedding plans."

"Oh, no," Lana waved it off. "We need a break from this stuff, anyway."

"So, out with it." Cody looked at him. "I take it this little meeting had something to do with Nancy and Carla?"

"Yes," Steven confirmed. "I just found out that I'm a father to a twenty-eight-year-old daughter."

"Congratulations?" Lana's brow furrowed.

"Thank you," Steven gave a small mocking laugh.

"You're Nancy's biological father?" Connie looked stricken. "Are you sure?"

"Are these yours and Nancy's DNA paternal reports?" Cody looked at her computer screen, where the records Nancy had dug up were still open.

"Yes," Steven looked at the computer.

"Can you excuse me for a minute?" Connie stood up. "I'm going to get another cup; we're one short."

Steven smiled at Connie, "I'm sorry, Connie, I didn't even realize how this would upset you."

"Oh, no, Steven," Connie leaned forward and touched his hand. "I'm glad Nancy finally knows who her father is. She's plagued me for years about it." She smiled. "I'll be back in a minute."

"Why don't you fill us in from the beginning?" Cody smiled.

"You don't look surprised." Steven looked from Cody to Lana, "Neither of you do, for that matter."

"Lana noticed the likeness between you and Nancy quite a few times," Cody told Steven. "I always had a feeling the two of you were related. Even though you both weren't aware of it, you had a special bond."

"When I mentioned how alike you and Nancy were, Cody told me how you always looked out for Nancy," Lana smiled at him. "Like a big brother."

"I've taken care of her since she was a baby," Steven's hand shook as he took another sip of his tea. "The Honeys would bring her in to see me for all her vaccinations, checkups, cuts, scrapes...." He swallowed, and his eyes glistened with unshed tears. "Do you know how many times I set her broken bones?" He shook his head and smiled. "She was such a tomboy and so adventurous. I always admired how the Honeys never tried to tame her spirit but let her spread her wings."

"Nancy really was a handful," Cody said. She frowned and looked at Steven, "Do you think the Honeys knew she was your daughter?" Cody asked.

"My name's not listed on her birth certificate," Steven said. "So how could the Honeys have known?"

"So, are you going to tell us how the Honeys ended up adopting your daughter?" Lana poured herself and Cody some tea.

"It's a long story," Steven told them.

"I'm not going anywhere." Lana settled back with her tea and a cupcake.

"Let's hear it." Cody settled back into her office chair.

Connie's legs felt like jelly as she rushed through to her cottage at the back of the Inn. She made sure Nancy was still out of the house before pulling out her mobile phone and calling a contact on it. Connie had to force her hands to stop shaking as she held the phone to her ear.

"Why are you calling me?" The person on the other side of the phone was not happy to hear from her.

"We need to meet," Connie's voice was low. "It turns out you were right; someone was investigating the child's birth parents." She hissed.

"Unacceptable!" the voice on the other end gritted. "*You know who* is not going to be happy about this."

"Well, *you know who* can go to hell for all I care," Connie said vehemently. "I'm tired of all the guilt, secrecy, and having to keep quiet."

"Connie, don't do anything stupid," the person warned her.

"Did you know who the real father of the child was?" Connie asked.

"What are you talking about?" the person asked her. "We all know who the father is."

"No." Connie shook her head. "Turns out we were wrong."

"Impossible," the person said. "We have all the evidence pointing to the father."

"How about actual DNA proof from both the mother and the father?" Connie asked. "All we had was circumstantial and the word of that…."

"I get it," the person cut her off. "And no, we never had DNA proof. With everything that was going on over that time…."

"We ruined the lives of three people," Connie said angrily. "You better round up the committee, or I'm going to tell them everything, including the real story behind the accident."

"Connie…" the person warned her, "I'm warning you again not

to do anything stupid. Remember what happened the last time someone tried to step on *you know who's* toes."

"Well, it's time someone squashed those toes and put that arrogant...." Connie drew in a deep angry breath. "When did things get so out of control?" She shook her head. "This was not what the committee was supposed to be about."

"I know," the person agreed with her. "Please, promise me you'll give me a few days to organize something before you do anything crazy." There was silence for a few seconds. "Remember what we're working for here."

"Fine, but get the committee together because they're onto us, and I would much rather tell them the truth than have them find it out on their own and hate us all for it," Connie said.

"Give me a few days," the person promised. "Who is the real father, Connie?"

"I'll tell you when I have the attention of the rest of the committee." Connie hung up the phone.

Connie stared at her phone for a few seconds before deciding to call the one person she knew she could always count on to be in her corner. Her call was answered after the third ring.

"Hello, Pete," Connie greeted him. "I need your help."

Chapter Twelve
GOODBYE CHARLENE BAXTER

Carla stood on her balcony looking out over the sea, trying to draw in some of its calm as it gently swayed back and forth onto the rocks below. She didn't know if Steven was still going to show for their date tonight, but she'd gotten ready just in case he did. Carla looked at her watch and closed her eyes, breathing in some of the cool salty air. It was already ten minutes past the time Steven was supposed to pick her up.

Carla felt relieved that Nancy now knew the truth about what had happened. Nancy and Christopher had grilled her for what seemed like hours after they'd left Cody's office. Steven had not joined them in the lounge, and he was nowhere to be found when Nancy and Christopher were called away by Riley, Grace, and Aiden. Carla was left alone with her thoughts and the remnants of her painful past.

Carla always knew that one day she'd have to face them and thought she'd be prepared for it. But she wasn't. As soon as she pulled the lid off them, the memories came flooding back, packed with all the pain and torment she'd gone through. Only now, she had the added bonus of seeing all the mistakes she'd made as clear as day. For years, Carla had blamed her uncle, her father, and that evil woman, Margaret Stanford, for her pain.

The truth is, Carla had other options, but she'd let them back her into that corner. Carla had let them lie to her even though deep down she'd always known the truth. She'd taken the easy way out because she couldn't take any more pain, and their way offered her closure. Well, at least she thought it would. But as the years ticked by and the rawness started to fade into a dull ache, her need to know the truth took over.

Carla turned and walked back into her suite. She was about to go down to the dining room and order some food to bring back to her room when there was a knock at her door. Her heart skipped a beat as she stood frozen for a few seconds until there was another knock. Carla pulled herself together and answered the door.

"Hi," Carla greeted Steven. "I wasn't sure you were going to show."

"I wasn't sure either," Steven admitted. "But, we have a lot to talk about."

"We do," Carla agreed. "Where do you want to go?"

"I know this is probably not the best occasion for this," Steven said. "But I thought we could go sit on the beach. Connie packed us a picnic basket, and Cody has set up a cabana for our use. It's private, and we can sit there for as long as we need."

"Can I change into some jeans quickly?" Carla asked because she was wearing a dress and heels.

"Of course." Steven nodded. "Although you look lovely."

"Thank you," Carla felt the heat creep over her cheekbones at the compliment. "But I feel overdressed."

"I'll meet you in the lobby." Steven gave her a tight smile and walked off.

Carla closed her door and leaned against it for a few seconds. Her heart was beating quickly, and her nerves were making her feel like a plate of jelly. Carla couldn't believe this was happening. She'd gone over how she'd finally tell Steven the truth over and over in her head millions of times. None of those scenarios had her feeling like a nervous wreck about to walk to her execution. In her version, she was calm, cool, and collected as she discussed the situation with him.

Carla gave herself a mocking laugh. In her version, she was in a conference room and treating the bomb she was about to explode in his life like a neat PowerPoint presentation. Only, real life wasn't so clean and simple. It was messy, complicated, and full of emotional landmines that exploded in your face when you least expected it to. Carla slipped into some jeans, a cotton shirt, a pair of sneakers, and grabbed a sweater. She looked at herself in the mirror and took a deep breath, squared her shoulders, and breathed out.

"This is it, Carla," Carla gave her reflection a pep-talk. "The day of reckoning. You faced Nancy, and now it is time to face Steven." She lifted her chin up. "Whatever happens, you'll accept the consequences with dignity and respect the other person's decision."

"It's going to be fine." Cody gave Steven a warm smile. "Just give her a chance to explain, and remember to listen. Don't let your emotions get the better of you, Steven."

"If you need us, we'll be here," Lana promised Steven. "Just don't mind us if you see us on the widow's walk with binoculars." She grinned.

"We won't be on the widow's walk," Cody shook her head at Lana.

"But we want to know what happens because we're invested now," Lana told Steven. "But really, Steven, Cody's right. No matter how hard it is and what emotions get stirred up, listen to her and think before you respond."

"Thanks, both of you." Steven smiled at them, his attention turning to Carla coming down the stairs. "I'll see you tomorrow at breakfast."

"We'll be there," Lana assured him. "Waiting to hear what happened."

"When did you become such a busybody?" Carla grinned at Lana.

"I'm not," Lana told her. "This is just such a...." She swallowed and wiped a tear from her eye, "a heartbreaking story. It makes me want to be a writer."

"I think someone has premarital blues," Cody pointed out.

"Hi," Carla greeted the three of them.

"Hi," Cody and Lana said in unison.

"Shall we?" Steven picked up the picnic basket.

"Enjoy your evening," Cody said, ushering Lana into the lounge before she could say anything else.

"Wow, this is lovely." Carla looked at the cabana.

The tall blue structure stood protectively over a groundsheet that had a small table set between two beach chairs loaded with cushions and soft throw rugs. There were even cushions stacked up on a soft shaggy rug on the ground in case they wanted to sit there. There were fairy lights strung up around the inside of the roof, and a few lanterns were dotted strategically around them.

"Cody and Lana did it." Steven put the basket down on the table and pulled the top open. "Would you like something to drink or eat?"

"What do we have?" Carla peered into the basket.

"Wine, soda, fruit juice, and mineral water." Steven pulled the neatly packed beverages out of the basket. The glasses were already neatly stacked on the table for them.

"A glass of wine, please." Carla chose one of the beach chairs to sit in.

Steven poured the wine and handed her a glass before taking a seat in the other chair. They sat in an awkward silence, staring out at the ocean and sipping their drinks.

"Steven, I'm sorry you had to find out about Nancy like you did." Carla decided to break the silence.

"It was a shock." Steven didn't look at her; he kept his gaze fixed on the ocean. "Do you know I've taken care of Nancy since the day the Honeys adopted her?"

"I saw her file," Carla admitted. "When I found out she may be my daughter, I pulled everything I could find on her." She swirled her wine in her glass. "I used her recent dirt bike accident as an excuse to check her medical history."

"Clever." Steven glanced over at her but still couldn't look her in the eye.

"I never told you that I was pregnant because I didn't want to put you in that position with your brother," Carla swallowed and looked into her wine. "It took everything I had to make up my mind to walk away." She closed her eyes. "Then the accident happened."

Images of that night, even after all these years, were as vivid as if they'd happened yesterday.

"You should've let me decide that" Steven's voice was low and hoarse. "Why did you give her up?" He stared into his wine.

"I didn't." Carla swallowed. "She was taken from me."

"How..." Steven looked at her. His blue eyes were dark with emotion, and his brow was furrowed.

"You need to know the whole story," Carla cleared her throat and closed her eyes, leaning her head back.

"We have all night," Steven told her.

"Are you sure you're ready to hear the truth?" Carla pinched the bridge of her nose. "Because you're not going to like what I have to say."

"Let's hear it," Steven picked up the bottle of wine and topped up their glasses.

June 1992

Charlene paced the hospital halls. She had Steven's leather jacket on. She couldn't believe what had happened. Tears stained her cheeks, her hands were stained with blood, and she felt numb inside. Charlene had never seen anything so horrible in all her life. She felt the tears starting to sting her eyes once again as she remembered Lance's lifeless eyes as they pulled him from the car. There was so much carnage on the road. The smell of gasoline and smoke stained her nostrils, making the bile rise in her stomach.

Charlene started to feel woozy. She put her forehead against the cool hospital wall willing herself not to faint or get sick. Charlene drew in a shaky breath and knew she had to get to the bathroom fast. She dashed down the hallway to the bathroom. Charlene didn't check to see who was in there. She rushed into the first available stall, fell to her knees, and got sick. Once she was done, she fell back into a sitting position on the floor, pulled her knees up, and sobbed her heart out.

"Are you okay?" a nurse asked her a little while later.

Charlene let the woman help her up.

"Are you hurt?" The nurse looked pointedly at the blood staining Charlene's hands and clothes.

"No," Charlene's face crumpled as the tears flowed again. "It's from the... the... accident, Steven...."

"Oh, my goodness," the nurse wrapped her arms around Charlene and let her cry some more. "I'm so sorry."

"I'm okay," Charlene took the tissue the nurse gave her and cleaned herself up a bit. "Thank you."

"I'll get Dr. Stanford for you," the nurse told her. "I know his wounds have been tended to. His hands were badly cut open from rescuing that little girl."

"He punched through the glass to get her out of the car," Charlene sucked in a shaky breath.

"Dr. Stanford is a hero." The nurse gave Charlene a smile. "The paramedics told me by the time they'd got there, Dr. Stanford had pulled everyone he could from the two vehicles."

"It was as if he was possessed with a sudden surge of strength and drive," Charlene sucked in another shaky breath.

"Come on. I'll take you to Dr. Stanford." The nurse walked Charlene from the bathroom. "You'll find him in room 334."

"I..." Charlene stopped walking when she saw Margaret Stanford coming from the opposite direction. Their eyes met, and

Margaret's were filled with what Charlene could only define as disgust. "Can I call a taxi to take me home?"

"You don't want to go see Dr. Stanford?" The nurse frowned up at her.

"No, he's with his family," Charlene swallowed. "I'll see him tomorrow. It's been a long night."

"I understand," the nurse said. "I'll take you to the nurse's station. You can use the phone there."

"Thank you." Charlene followed the nurse and called a taxi.

Charlene stood outside the entrance of Nantucket General, waiting for her taxi to arrive, when her uncle Luis seemed to appear from nowhere.

"Uncle Luis?" Charlene's brows drew together. "What are you doing here?"

"You have to come with me," Luis told her.

"I'm going home," Charlene didn't like the look in her uncle's eyes.

"I'm sorry, honey, but I can't let you do that," Luis said softly. "I'm asking you to come with and trust me."

"Uncle Luis, you're scaring me." Charlene took a few steps back away from him.

"Please, Charlene, don't make this difficult," Luis watched her like a cat watching a trapped mouse.

"Let me go call my father first," Charlene tried to step around him to run inside.

"Your father is the one that asked me to do this," Luis gave her a sad smile. "You've got to trust me."

Charlene turned to look inside the hospital, and her eyes met those of Margaret Stanford's once again.

"We have to go, now!" Luis grabbed Charlene's hand and yanked her along with him.

"What is going on," Charlene tried to struggle, but her uncle had her wrist in a vice grip.

"I'll explain everything when we're safe," Luis opened his car door and pushed her in.

Charlene didn't understand, "Why aren't we safe, Uncle Luis?"

She asked as her uncle pulled off and raced out of the hospital parking lot.

Charlene's head was spinning. *What is going on?* When they pulled up at the ferry, Charlene was even more alarmed.

"What are we doing here?" Charlene looked at her uncle, who hadn't said two words to her since they'd raced off.

"Honey, remember I told you I'd always look out for you?" Luis smiled at her. "That's what I'm doing now. One day you'll understand why I've done this. But for now, you need to get some sleep." He glanced at her stomach. "You shouldn't be stressed out in your condition."

"How do you...." Charlene didn't get to finish her sentence. Luis lifted a hand with a handkerchief in it and put it over her nose and mouth, making her pass out.

When Charlene woke up, she was in her mother's childhood room on her grandparent's estate in Martha's Vineyard. Her father had come to see her that day. He'd told her that the little girl from the accident was badly injured, but she'd survived, and Christopher was in a coma. Charlene had asked after Mr. Stanford, and it had made her father angry when she'd mentioned his name. Her father had told her never to mention Mr. Stanford's name ever again.

Charlene had felt quite shocked and confused about his outburst.

"Father, why am I here?" Charlene moved the subject away from the Stanfords. "Why can't I go home?"

"It's best for you to stay here until after the baby is born," her father told her. "There's a reason why I never wanted you to get involved with that family."

"I can't imagine why?" Charlene's eyes narrowed.

"Because Margaret and Christopher Stanford Senior are not nice people." Dr. Baxter's eyes flashed angrily. "I suspect they were somehow responsible for...." He clenched his jaw and closed his eyes for a moment.

"How did you know I was pregnant?" Charlene asked him suspiciously.

"The clinic called me," Dr. Baxter told her. "Did you think they wouldn't?"

"I'm nineteen. Isn't that breaking patient confidentiality?" Charlene felt the anger start to burn inside her. *How dare they?*

"They only called me because they found someone else snooping around your records," Dr. Baxter informed her. "She also found the letter."

"What?" Charlene frowned.

"I know you're mad with me and Uncle Luis right now." Dr. Baxter looked at her. "But you'll see this is for the best and the only way to keep you out of the clutches of that witch."

"Witch?" Charlene looked at her father, confused. "You mean Margaret Stanford?" She glared at him. "The woman you cheated on Mom with?"

"I..." Dr. Baxter looked at her wide-eyed. "It's not what you think."

"Really?" Charlene raised her eyebrows. "I saw you two together the day of Mom's funeral." Her voice was hoarse with anger. "I heard you tell her the reason we couldn't get hold of you was because you were with her."

"Calm down, Charlene," Dr. Baxter held up his hands. "You don't know what you're talking about."

"I do," Charlene hissed. "If you don't let me call the baby's father, I'm going to march downstairs and tell Mom's family everything about your sordid affair."

"You will NEVER speak to the baby's father again, is that clear?" Dr. Baxter stood to his full six-foot-three height. With his solid muscular physique, he could be an imposing figure.

Charlene took a step back at the fury distorting the features of his incredibly handsome face. "You can't stop me," Charlene breathed. "I'm nineteen, and you no longer have a say."

"I promise you this," Grant Baxter stared down his defiant daughter. "If I ever find that man came into contact with you again..." a muscle ticked in his chiseled jaw, "I'll end him myself this time." His eyes narrowed dangerously, and his eyes darkened.

"And I can guarantee you, I won't mess it up." He turned and stormed out of her room.

Charlene stood staring at her bedroom door in shock. Her heart was beating like a jackhammer. She'd never seen her father so angry. It was the first time she'd seen a dark, dangerous side of him. Charlene and her father had their fair share of father-daughter spats, but he'd never lost his cool or even raised his voice to her. This was the first time she'd ever feared him, and what did he mean about ending Steven? Nothing made any sense. Her father hadn't even flinched when she'd confronted him about Margaret Stanford. He'd completely ignored her threats about telling her mother's family about his affair.

Charlene walked to her closet and opened it. She reached into the back of it and pulled out Steven's leather jacket. She held it up to her face and breathed in his scent.

"I'm so sorry," Charlene whispered and hugged the jacket.

Charlene felt like she was in some weird parallel dimension and living someone else's life. She sat on her bed, holding Steven's jacket. She didn't know how long she'd sat there when there was a soft knock at her bedroom door.

"Charlene, honey, it's Nanny. Can I come in?" Nanny called through the door.

"Nanny?" Charlene hid Steven's jacket under her pillows and went to open the door.

"Hi, honey," Nanny hugged Charlene. "Your grandparents asked me to come and keep you company while you stay here."

"It's good to see you," Charlene smiled. "But you know I'm nineteen now and no longer need a nanny."

"I can see what a beautiful woman you've grown into," Nanny admired her. "You look just like your mother." Her voice caught. "I'm sorry about your mother."

"Thank you." Charlene smiled. "I'm glad you're here."

"Why don't you come and have some tea with me in the garden?" Nanny asked her.

"Can you give me five minutes?" Charlene asked her. "I'll be right down."

"Of course, honey," Nanny smiled. "I'll go arrange the tea and meet you on the back veranda. Then you can catch me up on what's been going on."

Charlene closed her bedroom door and went to hide Steven's jacket. She'd been really shocked at how much her father disliked the Stanfords, especially considering his relationship with Margaret.

Charlene slipped a pair of sandals on and headed downstairs. When she passed her grandfather's study, she heard voices having a heated conversation. Charlene stood still and listened.

"Keep her safe until after the baby is born," Dr. Grant Baxter's voice was low. "Don't let her call anyone; is that clear?"

"You are being unreasonable, Grant," Charlene's grandfather told him. "Have you even asked her about it?"

"No need," Grant said. "You've seen all the evidence. Now, can I count on all three of you?"

Charlene frowned. *Am I to be held here like a captive until the baby is born?* Her eyes narrowed as her mind raced with an escape plan. Charlene once again felt so alone. She couldn't even turn to Steven because he already had a lot to deal with. Images of the accident sprung to her mind, and tears stung her eyes again. *Oh God, Lance!* She may have fallen in love with Steven, but she still loved Lance. They'd had a lot of history together.

Charlene turned and quietly made her way to the back veranda to meet Nanny.

Charlene spent the next seven months studying and living with her grandparents at their estates. Charlene hadn't seen her father again after that first night. He hadn't even called her. But her Uncle Luis visited him as often as he could. Charlene was kept company by Nanny and her grandparents, but she spent most of her time studying and keeping to herself.

Charlene felt like her family and Nanny was always trying to interrogate her about the Stanfords. As a result, Charlene was exhausted at having to always keep her guard up and watch what she said. When she was studying, she was left alone, so she threw herself into learning. All Charlene wanted to do was get herself and the baby as far away from Nantucket, Martha's Vineyard, and Boston as she could.

On the ninth of March, Charlene went into labor, and it lasted into the early hours of the morning. She finally gave birth at three o'clock in the morning of the tenth of March. There were complications, and Charlene had to have a cesarean. When she woke up, her grandmother told her that her son was stillborn. They were going to bury the baby in a few days. Her grandparents wouldn't let her see her baby, and they buried him in the family plot.

Charlene spent the days after the funeral locked in her room, and she refused to speak to anyone. She'd felt like the bottom had fallen out of her life, and it tipped her into a big black hole. By the beginning of April, Charlene had decided it was time to move on with her life. She was going to go to study medicine like she'd always planned to and become a top surgeon. Charlene pulled the shoebox of her mother's memories from the back of the closet. She'd found the box the first week she'd been brought to Nantucket. In the box, she'd found a letter from one of her mother's best friends—a friend Charlene knew her mother had kept in contact with over the years.

It took a few days, but Charlene eventually managed to track her mother's best friend down. She wrote the woman a letter and went to the post office herself to post it. She was not trusting anyone ever again, not even her family. Over the past months that Charlene had been stranded in Martha's Vineyard, she'd learned just what kind of people her family was.

The one person Charlene still trusted had disappeared the day after her baby had been born. Uncle Luis had been missing for weeks now, and her grandparents told her they hadn't heard from him either and were worried about him. Since the moment her uncle had abducted her and brought her to Martha's Vineyard, Charlene had felt there was something going on. That feeling had only intensified the longer she stayed.

While she was in town, Charlene headed to the bank to find out how she could gain access to her funds. It was a trust fund her mother had set up for her when she was born. The bank manager was only too happy to help her and set about sorting her money out for her. Her money was the one thing her family was unable to touch or control; her mother had seen to that, and now Charlene knew why. Her mother probably didn't trust her family or husband either.

Each day Charlene walked into the town to check if she had mail in the small postbox she'd rented. The first letter to arrive in the new secret mailbox was one from Harvard canceling her studies with them. A smile split Charlene's face when she saw the letter. This was going to make her father a little bit angry. Two days later, Charlene received a letter back from her mother's best friend, and four days later, she stood in a hotel room in New York.

Charlene had left her grandparent's estate early that morning, taking only her wallet, her baby's death certificate, the letter from her mother's friend, a few clothes, and Steven's jacket with her. That night Charlene spent her last night wandering around New York, buying some new clothes, and saying goodbye to her old life. A week later, Charlene Carla Baxter left America bound for London as Carla Vern. She was met at Heathrow by the renowned Wendy Barr and her handsome son Brandon Newton.

Wendy Barr became a second mother to Carla and welcomed her into her home. Her husband was a famous movie producer and one of the most brilliant men Carla had ever met. Carla became part of the Newton family even before she married Brandon. Charlene Baxter was dead and buried along with her life in Nantucket. Although the shadows of pain still remained from her past, Carla managed to build an entirely new life for herself. After two emotional and physically challenging miscarriages, Carla was told she could never have kids. It had been a bad blow to both her and Brandon.

After only three years of marriage, Carla and Brandon got a divorce in order to save their friendship. He'd been her rock since she landed in England and always would be. Brandon knew her better than anyone else as she did him. After that, her career was all she had, and she threw herself into it with Dr. Wendy Barr and Carla's mother, Michela Vern, as her role models.

Carla's father had over the years kept track of her and wrote to her at least five times a year. She never bothered to open the mail and always made a point of sending it back unopened. Then a month or two before Steven approached Carla about helping his brother, Carla had received a letter from Nantucket from someone claiming to be her child. A child she'd thought was dead.

The moment Carla had set foot back in America and accepted the post in Boston, thoughts of her baby ran through her mind. When she'd bumped into Steven at a medical conference, it had taken everything inside of her not to give herself away. She and Steven had stayed in touch after that conference. Not a day went by when Carla hadn't wanted to break down and tell him everything, but once again, the time wasn't right. Carla had resigned herself into thinking the time would never be right for her and Steven.

Once again, fate had intervened, and Steven offered her a post at Nantucket General. It was the opportunity she needed to investigate the letter she'd gotten and her Uncle Luis's disappearance.

Chapter Thirteen
WHERE DO WE GO FROM HERE?

"Your grandparents told you that the baby was stillborn?" Steven looked shocked. "That must've been so heartbreaking for you."

"I couldn't stop wondering if it was something I did wrong," Carla's voice was thick with emotion. "I even named him Steven."

"Carla..." Steven didn't know what to say. "I'm so sorry you had to go through that."

"I came to find you the night of the accident," Steven told Carla. "A nurse told me she'd found you in the bathroom, and you were heartbroken."

"I was heartbroken over Lance and over you," Carla said. "I couldn't believe Lance was gone. I didn't even say goodbye, and we left things on such a bad note. The pain of his loss and the guilt of him never knowing how sorry I was to have caused him all that pain."

"Lance never blamed you for a second," Steven gave Carla a smile. "I know Lance loved you. But do you really think, even if we hadn't gotten together, that the two of you wouldn't have moved in opposite directions?"

"We'd been together for years, so I guess we'd both just become used to being together," Carla admitted. "I think by the time he and I went off to college, we both already knew we were soon going to break up."

"When I couldn't find you at the hospital, I went to your house later that day, but your housekeeper said you weren't there." Steven took a sip of his wine. "Then I went to your father's surgery and asked him where you were."

"You went looking for me?" Carla looked at him, amazed.

"I did," Steven nodded. "Your father said you'd left the island and wouldn't be coming back anytime soon and warned my family and me to stay away from you." He took another sip of his wine. "He said if one Stanford ever went near you again, we'd end up regretting it."

"Why does my father dislike your family so much, especially when..." Carla stopped mid-sentence.

"When what?" Steven's eyes narrowed.

"When he's spent a lot of time with your mother over the years," Carla said softly.

"It's okay, Carla," Steven assured her. "I've known about your father and my mother since the night of Lance's accident. When I finally went home that day, it was to find my mother crying rather intimately on your father's shoulder."

"Oh!" Carla's eyes widened. "Was that before or after you went to find out about me?"

"After," Steven told her. "It was a shock after what he'd said to me to find him with my mother. But, your father was her doctor, so at first, I thought he'd come to give her a sedative." He took a sip of his wine. "And then I heard them talking."

"I found out about my father and your mother at my mother's funeral." Carla looked at him apologetically. "I know I should've told you. But how do you bring that up in a conversation?"

"It's okay." Steven smiled at her. "We had enough outside forces threatening our happy few months, and that would've just been a little more awkwardness we didn't need back then."

"What was Nancy like as a baby?" Carla asked Steven.

"She was very, very cute." Steven smiled. "When she was four months old, she got a bad ear infection. Nancy was never a loud baby. Even the Honeys were concerned that she hardly made any noise." He swirled his wine. "That was the first time they'd heard her scream her little lungs out."

"You know, even though she's sassy and high-spirited," Carla looked at Steven. "She's not loud. Her voice is soft but with a commanding presence."

"I know exactly what you mean." Steven topped up their wine glasses. "It was a joy to watch her grow up. The Honeys doted on her. Nancy was their everything, and she was so loved."

"Nancy told me about the Honeys," Carla told Steven about the conversation she'd had with Nancy.

"The Andersons were bad news." Steven raised his eyebrows. "Nancy's teachers called me to the school quite often when Nancy was in that couple's care."

"Nancy wouldn't tell me much about the Andersons," Carla shook her head. "But I remember Deke Anderson. He was no good, even when he was at school."

"That's right. You and Lance went to school with Deke." Steven's eyes glittered with anger. "Deke liked to use the top of Nancy's arms as punching bags. Once or twice she even ended up with a black eye and a swollen jaw."

"Oh, my God!" Carla looked horrified. "That makes me so angry. I want to march over there and punch him."

"Someone did." Steven took a sip of his wine. "When Nancy finally ran away, she was thirteen. She first went to Uncle Pete's, and he took her to Cody Bay."

"I remember Uncle Pete." Carla took a grape from the plate Steven had put out.

"Yes, he's a good guy." Steven put his glass down on the table and crossed his long legs. "As soon as the Andersons found out where Nancy was, they came to the Bay to get her."

"Oh, no." Carla looked stricken.

"Don't worry—Deke was greeted by Uncle Pete, Dr. Baxter, and Mr. Moore." Steven looked over at Carla. "They kept Deke busy until Social Services got there and witnessed what the Andersons were really like. Needless to say, they've never fostered another child."

"Thank goodness for that," Carla said with meaning. "How do people like the Andersons pass the vetting stages?"

"Some people are really good at window dressing." Steven shook his head. "Then the poor kids that end up with those kinds of foster parents end up suffering."

"I'm glad she ended up with Connie." Carla took another grape. "I can't believe I missed so much of our daughter's life." She shook her head. "I know I shouldn't, but I feel so angry and cheated."

"You have every right to feel that way," Steven assured her. "Now that I know about Nancy, I feel the same way. But at least I was lucky enough to still be a part of her life all these years, even if I didn't know she was my daughter. The strange thing is, Nancy and I always had a bond. Whenever she was in trouble at school or during one of her many adventures, I was always the one she called first."

"I'm glad Nancy grew up in front of you," Carla said softly.

"I got to see her take her first steps." Steven grinned. "Nancy never crawled. She pulled herself along on her butt. Mr. Honey often took her to work with him. It was so cute. She had a tiny hard hat, boots, and a protective jacket."

"Aww." Carla's face softened, and her brows knitted together.

"Mr. Honey would carry her in a baby carrier." Steven laughed. "His construction crew loved Nancy. Like I said, she was such a special, endearing baby."

"Look at you with your fatherly pride!" Carla grinned at him.

"One day when Nancy was around ten months old, Mr. Honey stepped on a nail," Steven explained. "So, he came in to see me at the hospital. Nancy was playing on the floor in my exam room. All of a sudden, she just stood, took two steps, fell, rolled onto her back, and giggled."

"Oh, my word!" Carla's eyes grew wide.

"Now that I know she's my daughter, I keep recalling special times while she was growing up." Steven looked out over the darkening sea with a big smile on his face.

Carla sniffed, grabbing Steven's attention, and he turned to see her wiping tears from her eyes.

"Oh, God, Carla, I'm sorry." His face fell. "That was insensitive of me."

"No." Carla shook her head. "I'm glad I get to see at least a part of her life growing up through your eyes."

"I think Connie has all the Honey's photos and various scrapbooks they made about Nancy growing up right up until she was eleven." Steven stood up and walked over to the basket. "I'm sure Connie wouldn't mind sharing them with you."

"I'd like that," Carla nodded. "But I don't want to make Connie feel uncomfortable. This is such an awkward situation."

"It's a strange situation." Steven pulled out some cheese and biscuits. "Are you hungry?"

"I am," Carla admitted. "Why didn't you ever get married?"

"I got engaged to a wonderful woman in two-thousand and eight." Steven put the cheese and biscuits on a board with some more fruit. "It was the same year that Christopher started to get worse with his mood swings, blackouts, and headaches."

"Oh. Was she another doctor?" Carla put some cheese and biscuits on a plate.

"She was," Steven confirmed. "I started to pull away from her because I needed to take care of Christopher—especially when his marriage fell apart."

"That's so typical of you." Carla looked over at him. "You always put others before yourself."

"That's not true," Steven contradicted. "I can think of a few times I indulged in my own selfishness."

"Name one time." Carla challenged him.

"Can I think about it and get back to you?" Steven asked playfully.

"Exactly, my point." Carla shook her head. "You are the kindest, most caring, selfless person I've ever known."

"I'm not sure if that's a compliment, but I'm going to take it as one." Steven grinned.

"Good." Carla told him and laughed.

"Hi," Nancy's voice startled them, and they turned to see her standing at the side of the cabana. She was holding a box in her hands. "Is this a bad time?"

"No, not at all." Carla invited her to join them. "What's in the box?"

"I hope it's not too soon..." Nancy said. "But I brought you my life in case you wanted to look through it to get to know me."

"I would love that." Carla's eyes misted over.

"I would love it too." Steven swallowed down the lump burning his throat.

Steven couldn't stop wondering what all their lives would've been like if they'd been allowed to be a family.

"Should we sit here?" Nancy took a seat on the shaggy rug piled with cushions. "That way, you can sit on either side of me, and we can go through my memories."

"Absolutely," Carla sat on Nancy's left while Steven sat on the right.

"Can I get a glass of wine?" Nancy looked at Steven. "Before you go all dad on me, remember I'm well over the drinking age."

"I was thinking more about the antibiotics I put you on earlier because of that infection you have under your cast." Steven raised his eyebrows at her. "But I'll get you grape juice."

"Fine!" Nancy huffed.

"You have an infection?" Carla asked her, a little alarmed. "Steven, are you going to change her cast?"

"He's already made the appointment for tomorrow." Nancy sighed.

"Here you go." Steven handed Nancy some grape juice. "Do you want something to eat?"

"Is that a trick question?" Nancy looked up at him.

"Of course." Steven shook his head. "I forgot to mention. There has never been anything wrong with Nancy's appetite."

"My mother was like that," Carla told Nancy. "She ate like a horse and never put on weight, just like you."

"Good to know I've got some good genes." Nancy smiled at Carla.

The evening flew by as Steven, Carla, and Nancy laughed at Nancy's stories and went through her albums. Steven and Carla told Nancy about their childhoods, and Carla told Nancy everything she knew about the day of her birth. When they looked again, it was nearly two in the morning when they called it a night and packed up the cabana.

"We talked until all hours of the morning," Nancy told Cody between bites of her breakfast.

"I'm so glad you've finally found your birth parents, Nancy." Cody sipped her coffee, watching Nancy eat her breakfast. "You shouldn't have intruded on their date, though."

"They were fine with it." Nancy poured some more coffee and looked at her watch. "I have a shift at Doctor Baxter's office this morning. He said he was going to be coming in for a few hours today."

"How's the new doctor working out?" Cody suppressed a shudder. There was something about Doctor Stein that made the hairs on her arms stand on end.

"He seems very good, and the patients all love him." Nancy downed her coffee. "I better get moving."

"Enjoy your day, Nancy." Cody watched the young woman gather all her things and take the last sip of her coffee before rushing off.

"See you later." Nancy waved as she ran out of the door.

"So, how did it go?" Lana walked into the dining room not long after Nancy had left.

"It seems they are working things out between them," Cody told Lana.

"It's such a sad story," Lana slipped into the seat Nancy had vacated.

"I know. Nancy has always been such a well-adjusted person even after everything she went through in young life." Cody finished her coffee. "What time is the appointment at the bridal shop?"

"At three," Lana told her. "Are you working at the Marine Life Center today?"

"No." Cody shook her head. "I have to catch up with the accountant for the Inn today."

"Augh." Lana shuddered. "That's one thing I hate is doing finances."

"My beautician friend said she can do the make-up for the wedding." Cody ticked that off the list she found herself carrying around with her lately.

"You're a star." Lana pulled a face. "I just wanted a nice, quiet, quick wedding." She poured herself a coffee when the waiter brought her a clean cup. "You know, close friends and family on the beach with a BBQ afterward."

"Lana, if that's what you really want, you must do it." Cody leaned forward with her elbows on the table. "This is your wedding. Not your family's or your friend's. Yours!"

"I never in a million years thought I'd have to plan two weddings for myself." Lana sighed.

"You know, Lana, we can still have your beach wedding if you want it." Cody's mind raced with possibilities for Lana. "The arch you're having built can be adjusted to stand on the sand." Cody stood up. "Come on, let's get you the wedding you want."

"There's still going to be so many people." Lana groaned. "Wait, I want to pour my coffee into a to-go mug."

"How are you holding up?" Christopher asked Steven while they stood watching Carter and his team close up the cave entrance in the cove.

129

"It's been quite a shock," Steven admitted. "But I think, on some level, I always felt that there was something special about Nancy."

"What about Carla?" Christopher watched his older brother closely.

"I'm not sure." Steven looked down at the sand. "I feel there is so much murky water between us."

"I think we need to find out why Carla's family thought it was necessary to lie to Carla about her child," Christopher said. "There is one person that would know that."

"Dr. Baxter!" Steven shook his head. "How do you approach that when the man's recovering from a stroke?"

"That's another thing that doesn't make sense." Steven's brow furrowed. "Carla asked me to check on Dr. Baxter's hospital records because she couldn't get into them."

"Isn't she your second in command as the medical director of the hospital?" Christopher asked him.

"I know, she has full access.... But get this," Steven lowered his voice. "I couldn't get into them either. They were locked, and I'm sure it flagged some security alert."

"That's weird." Christopher frowned. "Why would his medical records be locked?"

"I'm not sure, but I'm going to check," Steven told Christopher. "Dr. Mann is listed as his doctor, which is also strange because he's retired."

"Where is Carla at the moment?" Christopher asked Steven.

"I'm not sure," Steven's brows drew together as he looked at his brother. "Why?"

"We can go around and around about this, or we can go directly to the source and ask him," Christopher suggested. "As there is strength in numbers, why don't all four of us go to him today?"

"Nancy's at work," Steven told Christopher. "But I know she's only on for half a day. So, I guess we could go when her shift was over."

"Great, let's arrange it." Christopher patted his brother on the shoulder. "Today we'll get you, Carla, and Nancy your answers."

Chapter Fourteen
CONFRONTATIONS

"Hi, we're here to see Dr. Baxter," Carla didn't know the new housekeeper who'd answered the door.

"Dr. Baxter is in a meeting right now," the housekeeper said frostily. "Are you related to him?"

"Molly, who was at the...." Dr. Baxter stopped when his eyes met Carla's. "Charlie?" His voice dropped.

"Hello," Carla's eyes narrowed. "You look rather well for someone recovering from a stroke!"

"I..." Dr. Baxter couldn't take his eyes off Carla. "You look so different."

"That's what happens when people grow up," Carla's voice was laced with ice. "Now that your meeting seems to be over, we'd like to have a word with you."

"Come in," Dr. Baxter welcomed them into his home. "Would you like something to eat or drink?"

"I would love a soda," Nancy replied.

"Molly will get that for you," Dr. Baxter looked at his housekeeper, who nodded and walked off. "Please, come in and take a seat in the living room." He ushered them into the front lounge of his big house.

"This room has changed," Carla looked around the lounge that used to be her television room.

"A lot has changed since you left," Dr. Baxter told her. "Would you excuse me for a few minutes?" He left them in the sitting room.

"I wonder where he's going?" Carla said suspiciously.

"So… Charlie, huh?" Nancy looked at Carla with a teasing smile.

"It used to be cute when I was young," Carla warned Nancy. "And I don't use that old name anymore."

"Noted." Nancy nodded. "So you grew up in this house?"

"Yes." Carla looked around the room they were in. "I used to love this lounge. It had all my favorite things in it."

"I take it the room didn't have these plush leather sofas back then?" Christopher admired the furniture.

"No." Carla smiled. "It was a lot more child-friendly back then."

Molly, Dr. Baxter's housekeeper, walked back carrying a tray filled with snacks and refreshments. She put them on the center coffee table.

"Dr. Baxter had to take a phone call; he will be right with you," Molly informed them before leaving the room.

"Well, she's a delight, isn't she?" Christopher watched the stiff housekeeper leave the room.

"I wonder what happened to Lucinda?" Carla frowned.

"She moved away quite a few years ago," Nancy told Carla. "I'm not sure why, though. Maybe she retired from housekeeping."

"Lucinda went to stay with her son and his family in Boston." Dr. Baxter walked into the room. "Sorry about that, but I had to take a phone call."

"How are you feeling, Dr. Baxter?" Nancy sipped on a glass of soda.

"I'm a lot better, thank you, Nancy," Dr. Baxter sat down in one of the armchairs. "It's so nice to see you all."

"Why did you do it?" Carla wasn't about to sit and play nice. She was not a confused and hurt nineteen-year-old anymore.

"Do what?" Dr. Baxter looked at her, confused.

"Don't play dumb." Carla's anger rose up inside her like a tidal wave. "You know why the four of us are here."

Carla had rehearsed what she would say to her father if she ever saw him again over and over in her head a million times. Only, in her head, she was going to be cool, calm, and collected. Carla hadn't counted on having just found out that he'd lied, manipulated, and stolen from her all those years ago. Or, that all the pent-up hurt and anger would surface like a bolt of lightning striking her and ripping through her core.

"Charlie, I'm not sure what you're talking about." Dr. Baxter's brows furrowed. "Honey, I've been trying to contact you for years."

"Stop it!" Carla's eyes flashed angrily. "And for God's sake, stop calling me Charlie. My name is Carla. Charlene died a long, long time ago."

"Maybe, I should handle this?" Nancy, who was seated in-between Carla and Steven on the biggest sofa, patted Carla's hand.

"Go ahead," Carla said exasperatedly. "But trust me, unless you have something wrong with, he won't listen."

"Dr. Baxter," Nancy began and looked at Steven. He'd not said one word, not even hello, when they'd arrived. He sat, glaring at Dr. Baxter with his jaw clenched. "Were you aware that I am the daughter of Dr. Carla Newton and Dr. Steven Stanford?"

"What?" Dr. Baxter's face paled with shock as he looked from Carla to Steven. "You're Nancy's father?"

"Don't act like you didn't know!" Carla sneered. "You made it very clear to me all those years ago when you trapped me at my grandparents' house that I was never to contact the Stanfords again!"

Carla pulled two DNA reports from her purse plus a copy of his letter he'd written to her and slapped them on the coffee table. Dr. Baxter leaned over and picked the documents up. His brow was deeply furrowed as he went through them.

"You're a doctor. I'm sure you'll be able to read those reports." Carla stood up. "This was a mistake." Her features softened when she looked at Nancy. "Let's go."

"Char... Carla." Dr. Baxter stopped Carla from walking out. "I swear, I didn't know about Steven."

"Really?" Carla was not convinced. "You forbade me to call him for seven months. In fact, you forbade me to ever come back to Nantucket, if I remember correctly."

"No." Dr. Baxter shook his head. "I never forbid you from coming back to Nantucket. I told your grandparents it was best that you go back to Harvard in Boston as soon as you felt up to it."

"I don't believe you!" Carla's voice was gruff with anger. "Why would my grandparents lie to me?"

"I have no idea?" Dr. Baxter told her truthfully. "Maybe you didn't know your grandparents as well as you thought you did?"

"I found out the hard way that I knew very little about the kinds of people my family was all those years ago," Carla looked at Dr. Baxter like he was something nasty she'd just trod in. "But, I was lucky because I was taken in by an amazing family."

"Wendy Barr?" Dr. Baxter raised his eyebrows, and his voice got dangerously low.

"Okay," Nancy stood up with her hands held out between Carla and Dr. Baxter, like a referee.

"This is getting us nowhere," Nancy told both of them. "Please sit down." She looked pleadingly at Carla. "Let me take the floor on this one. Let's find out Dr. Baxter's side of the story about what happened twenty-nine years ago."

"Okay." Carla gave Nancy a tight smile. "I owe you that much." She reached out and squeezed Nancy's arm lovingly.

"Thank you," Nancy said gratefully. "It means a lot to me."

Carla sat back down in the seat she'd vacated.

"I can't believe you trained with Wendy Barr." Nancy looked at Carla in amazement. "She's always been an inspiration to me."

"I'll introduce you one day, I promise." Carla smiled warmly at Nancy.

"Dr. Baxter, can you honestly say you didn't know I was Nancy's father?" Steven spoke for the first time since they'd arrived at Dr. Baxter's house.

"Steven, I honestly didn't know," Dr. Baxter said earnestly.

"Did you think Lance was my father?" Nancy asked Dr. Baxter.

"No." Dr. Baxter shook his head, surprising them all with his answer. "Lance had a football accident when he was sixteen, which made him sterile."

"Who the hell did you think was Nancy's father?" Carla questioned Dr. Baxter.

"Do you mind if I keep these?" Dr. Baxter sighed, gathering up the papers Carla had given him. Carla shook her head. He stood up. "Come with me. I have something you need to see."

Carla, Nancy, Steven, and Christopher stood up and followed Dr. Baxter to his study.

Dr. Baxter walked over to a safe on his wall, opened it, and pulled out a large brown envelope.

"The day before I had Carla taken to Martha's Vineyard by her uncle, I was attending a medical conference in Boston." Dr. Baxter opened the envelope. "During one of the breaks, this envelope was delivered to me."

Dr. Baxter walked back to his desk. "I was in shock when I saw the contents of the file." He scattered the contents onto his desk. It was photos of Carla with an older man that was familiar to all of them. "Needless to say, I cut my trip short and took the ferry home the very next day."

"What the..." Nancy's eyes narrowed as she picked up one and looked from it to Carla. "Is that who I think it is with you?"

"That's not me!" Carla snatched the photo from Nancy's hand. It was a picture of a woman, who admittedly looked a lot like her, hugging Mr. Stanford Sr. "You thought this was me?" She glared at her father. "I've hardly said ten words to Mr. Stanford, and I have definitely never met him at a hotel."

"It looks exactly like you!" Steven pointed out. "Right down the red birthmark on the side of the face."

"You think this is me as well?" Carla's eyes narrowed. "Wait a minute..."

Carla's anger may have been red hot before, but as a horrible thought dawned on her, it went way past that to exploding. She spun around to face her father. Sparks of anger deepened her violet eyes.

"You thought Nancy's father was...." Carla drew in a breath and shook her head. Carla couldn't bring herself to say his name. "You thought this man was Nancy's father?"

"The evidence is quite incriminating," Dr. Baxter said softly and placed the rest of the pictures on the desk. "What was I supposed to think? I'd just been given these photos, and then the clinic called with your pregnancy results."

Carla's heart was pounding in her chest as everything that had happened to her twenty-nine years ago started to make sense. All the haunting memories she'd locked safely away came flooding back. She felt tears of anger, frustration, and years of locked away pain threaten to overwhelm her.

"Lance was convinced you were seeing someone else as well." Steven frowned. "When he found out about the baby, he was furious and wanted to go have it out with the man whose baby he'd thought it was...." He closed his eyes and pinched the bridge of his nose. "That's why he mentioned Judy."

"Who's, Judy?" Christopher frowned at Steven.

"Never mind," Steven said. His eyes were filled with pain and anger as he looked at Carla. "Why were you meeting my father?" He looked down at the desk and rifled through all the pictures. "You seemed to meet quite often at this hotel."

Pain ripped through Carla at the look of hurt and betrayal on Steven's face. She shook her head, watching Steven go through the pictures.

"I don't know what hurts more," Carla's voice was hoarse, reflecting the sea of emotions drowning her on the inside. "That neither you or Dr. Baxter believes me when I say that is not me or that the two men who were supposed to know me best think that's me."

"If this isn't you, then who is it?" Steven hissed. "A secret twin?"

"Go to hell," Carla said through gritted teeth, clenching her hands at her sides. "Both of you." She glared at Dr. Baxter before turning and started to storm out of the room before she embarrassed herself and burst into tears.

"Are you going to run away again?" Steven taunted her. "If this isn't you...."

"I'm going to the bathroom," Carla's face was flaming. She clenched her fists at her side to keep from shaking. "I'll be back in a minute." She left the room.

"You're both idiots!" Nancy looked from Steven to Dr. Baxter. "Anyone with eyes can see this isn't Carla." She shook her head in disgust. Nancy reached into her purse and pulled out a photo of Carla that she'd given Nancy earlier that morning. "This was taken at Cody Bay the day of the accident, twenty-nine years ago."

"Is that Cody with Carla?" Christopher took the picture before handing it to his brother.

"That woman with your father had shorter hair than Carla, and her birthmark is thicker and more prominent than Carla's." Nancy picked up another photo she'd seen on the desk. "Her figure is also more mature than Carla's was back then."

"Nancy's right. When you look at her closely, you can see she's older than Carla," Christopher examined one of the photos from the desk.

"Did you bother to really look at these pictures at all?" Nancy's eyes narrowed at Dr. Baxter.

"Do you know what a shock it is to see photographic evidence of my beautiful nineteen-year-old daughter having clandestine meetings with a man closer to my age?" Dr. Baxter defended his actions. "Especially as that man was Christopher Sandford Sr.!"

"So you rushed back to Nantucket and kidnapped her?" Nancy raised her eyebrows. "That's a bit excessive!"

"No, young lady, that's not what happened!" Dr. Baxter's eyes glittered dangerously. "I cut my trip short and came back to Nantucket. Char... Carla wasn't home. I was about to go and look for her when the clinic called to tell me about Carla's pregnancy test results."

"So that's when you decided to kidnap her, drag her off to Martha's Vineyard, lie to her about her baby being stillborn, and then steal her child?" Nancy raised her eyebrows and crossed her arms over her chest.

"It's a little more complicated than that," Dr. Baxter assured Nancy.

"Well then, make it less complicated for us," Nancy wasn't backing down. "And why would the clinic phone you?" Nancy asked him. "Isn't that violating patient confidentiality?"

"I didn't ask them," Dr. Baxter told Nancy. "I'd just found out my daughter was seeing a man twice her age, and then I got the news that she was pregnant. I knew she'd been seeing Lance, but as I explained, he couldn't have kids."

"So you put two and two together and came up with a way to ruin three people's lives," Nancy hissed. "Instead of doing what a good parent would do and sit down and have a conversation with Carla."

"Nancy," Steven gave her a warning look. "Let Dr. Baxter finish telling his side of the story."

"Thank you, Steven," Dr. Baxter said graciously. "Would any of you like a drink?" He walked over to a cabinet and pulled out a fine bottle of Scotch.

"Should you be drinking?" Nancy took the glass of scotch he handed her.

"I'm fine," Dr. Baxter told her, handing a glass of scotch to both Christopher and Steven before pouring one for himself.

"I'll take that," Steven took the glass of scotch away from Nancy before she could take a sip. "Miss Honey is on antibiotics."

"Are you okay, Nancy?" Dr. Baxter looked at her with concern.

"I'm fine." Nancy glared at Steven. "Can we get back to the part where you kidnapped your daughter?"

"It was never my intention to ruin anyone's life, Nancy," Dr. Baxter told her. "My only thought was for my daughter's safety and well-being."

"Safety?" Nancy's eyes narrowed. "Was Carla in some sort of danger?"

"All that I can tell you is that things would've been a lot worse for everyone had I not removed Carla from Nantucket when I did." Dr. Baxter, who was sitting on the edge of his desk, swallowed down his drink.

"What's that supposed to mean?" Steven asked Dr. Baxter.

Steven couldn't help but feel there was a lot more to Dr. Baxter than everyone thought. The man had an air of danger around him. Steven had always felt the man was a force to be reckoned with. Right now, Steven couldn't help but feel he was hiding something about the night of the accident that took his brother Lance's life.

"Let's just say, certain people didn't take the news of Char..." Dr. Baxter shook his head. "Carla's pregnancy too well."

"How did anyone even know about it? Did the clinic post it in some Nantucket news bulletin board?" Steven made a mental note to investigate the clinic. He knew it was twenty-nine years ago, but still, what they'd done by calling Dr. Baxter was unethical.

"No," Dr. Baxter shook his head. "If you must know, the clinic only phoned me because someone had taken Carla's file."

"Why didn't you just say that to begin with?" Steven's eyes narrowed.

"Because, like you, my daughter would go down there and cause even more problems." Dr. Baxter raised an eyebrow.

"Damn straight, we're going to the clinic," Nancy said. "I know one sister, Fern, that has been there for over thirty years. She'd remember Carla's pregnancy."

"Do you mean, Fern Taylor?" Dr. Baxter asked Nancy.

"Yes." Nancy nodded. "Fern is my mother's youngest sister. Well, not Carla's, Connie's sister."

"I think the clinic needs to be our next stop," Steven suggested.

"We can go to Fern's house." Nancy looked at her watch. "The clinic closed a while ago."

"I don't think any of you should go harass Fern," Dr. Baxter advised them. "I can tell you that I already asked Fern about the missing file more than once."

"What aren't you telling us?" Carla's voice at the door made them all turn towards her.

"*How* long have you been standing there?" Steven asked Carla.

"Long enough to know that Dr. Baxter's still keeping things from us." Carla glared at the man.

"I have to agree with Carla," Steven looked at Dr. Baxter. "You've given up half-truths, and I think, after what you've done to us, we deserve to know *everything*."

"Don't waste your time trying to pry any more information out of him." Carla looked at Steven. "I remember who came into the clinic that day. I wouldn't have put it past her to have taken it. Especially as she knew I was dating her son."

"Who?" Nancy asked for all of them.

"I might sound paranoid. But at the time, I actually thought she'd followed me to the clinic." Cody shuddered, remembering the cold feeling she'd gotten when the woman had shown up at the clinic. "I'd bumped into her at the drug store earlier that day when I went to get a pregnancy test."

"Let me guess; it was my mother?" Steven's brow furrowed. A memory flitted through his mind of his mother hiding a folder when he'd stormed into her study the day after the accident. "I think I saw her with Carla's file at our house the next day." His eyes met Dr. Baxter's. *Dr. Baxter also saw that file on Margaret's desk!*

"I strongly advise none of you to tell Margaret Stanford about Nancy. She thinks Carla's child died at birth and that it was a boy," Dr. Baxter looked at each of them in turn. "For now, at least. Let me deal with this." He looked at Steven for help.

"Fine," Steven agreed for the four of them. "We'll not tell my mother until you say it's okay to." He saw the questioning look on Christopher's face. "It's for the best."

"If you say so," Christopher nodded. "I do understand."

"I doubt whether the news will take long to reach Margaret

anyway," Nancy told Dr. Baxter. "Everyone at Cody Bay knows about us."

"I don't think anyone there will talk," Dr. Baxter said with confidence. "The Bay protects its own, and Nancy has been one of its own since the day you found out about her."

"How did you know I went to Cody Bay that morning?" Carla looked at Dr. Baxter accusingly.

"Nancy showed us a picture of you and Cody together that morning," Dr. Baxter looked at Nancy for backup.

"Oh, yes, I pointed out the difference between you and...." Nancy picked up a picture of Carla's look-a-like, *her*.

"Can I see that?" Carla took the picture from Nancy and took a closer look at it. "Dr. R. Decker."

"Where do you see that?" Nancy looked at the picture over Carla's shoulder.

"On the coat the woman's carrying." Carla frowned. "What do you think this man behind them is pushing into the hotel?"

"Not sure," Nancy frowned before turning to the pictures on the desk and going through them. She pulled out three others. "Look, here's the same man pushing the same covered-up equipment into the hotel at the same time these two are walking into it."

"It looks like medical equipment, though," Steven pointed out. "Look at the logo on the cover."

"You're right," Carla agreed.

"Give me a minute," Nancy told Carla and pulled out her phone to search for something. "Found her." She held her phone up. "Dr. Rose Decker. She's an oncologist."

I have cancer and have been having private treatment for it! Steven's father's words from the night of the accident came back to him. "My father was having treatment for cancer." Steven looked up from the pictures in Nancy's hands to Carla.

"I remember him saying something like when Lance and you were helping him to the car that night," Christopher backed up Steven's statement.

"Lance still asked him why he'd been drinking if he was having treatment," Steven gave Christopher a sad smile.

"In the car, on the way home," Christopher frowned as a memory came back to him. "I remember Lance telling dad he shouldn't be drinking if he's getting treatment." He looked at the floor as he gathered his thoughts. "Dad said that he hadn't been drinking, and he didn't know why he was feeling drunk." He looked up at Steven.

"Are you sure he said that?" Dr. Baxter had all heads turn to him at the shocked tone in his voice.

"Yes," Christopher nodded. "Because Lance was grilling him about his drinking just before my father passed out and started to snore." He gave a soft laugh.

"Do you know if they did an alcohol test on your father that night?" Dr. Baxter asked Steven.

"Not sure, but I can check. I'm sure the records are somewhere," Steven's eyes narrowed questioningly. "What is going on, Dr. Baxter?"

"Yes, *Dr. Baxter*," Carla's tones were icy. "What are you not telling us?"

"Look," Dr. Baxter pinched the bridge of his nose. "I know none of you trust me right now, and you have a lot of questions." He looked up at the four of them. "But I need you ALL to promise me you'll not look into this any further."

"Not until you tell us what is going on," Carla hissed.

"I can't do that, it will put you all in a great deal of danger, and that is all I can tell you," Dr. Baxter and Steven exchanged a look that Steven understood.

"I think we should do as Dr. Baxter says," Steven looked at Dr. Baxter. "He'll keep us updated on what's going on as soon as he can. Won't you, Dr. Baxter?"

"I will, and I'm sure if I don't, I can expect a visit from the four or you again," Dr. Baxter smiled at them.

"What do you say, Carla?" Steven looked from Carla to Nancy, "Nancy?"

"You have three days," Carla told Dr. Baxter. "And then I'll personally contact Margaret Stanford myself to ask what the hell is going on."

"Deal," Dr. Baxter held out his hand to shake with Carla, but she looked down her nose at him and ignored it.

"Let's go." Carla turned and walked out of Dr. Baxter's office.

"Before you three go," Dr. Baxter lowered his voice. "Make sure no one else knows who Carla is."

Steven felt icy fingers crawl up his back at the look in Dr. Baxter's eyes. The man was truly worried about Carla's safety for some reason.

"We will," Steven did something he never thought he'd ever do and shook Dr. Baxter's hand.

"For what it's worth," Dr. Baxter said to Steven. "I'm glad you're Nancy's father."

Steven nodded and herded Christopher and Nancy out of the office and through the front door to where Carla was waiting for them.

Chapter Fifteen
A DATE WITH CODY – PART 1

"Cody," Christopher knocked on her office door. "Can I have a quick word?"

Cody looked up from her computer. "Of course, come in."

Christopher felt nervous as he walked up to Cody's desk and sat down.

"Are you okay?" Cody's brows drew together.

"I'm feeling great," Christopher lied. He felt like a sixteen-year-old trying to approach the most popular girl in school to ask her on a date. *Pull it together, man!* He gave himself a stern talking to. "I was wondering if you and I could go on a date?"

"Oh!" Cody's eyes widened as she stared at him. "Where were you thinking of going to?"

"The Beachfront Restaurant for dinner tonight?" Christopher asked, hopefully. "I hear they have a local band playing tonight, so we can dance. I hope you still love to dance?"

"I do," Cody smiled and sat back in her chair. "That sounds good. I haven't been out in a while, so it'll be nice."

"Great!" Christopher stood up and nearly knocked over the chair next to him. His heart was beating so fast, and his legs suddenly felt like jelly. "I'll meet you in the lobby of the Inn at seven."

"It's a date." Cody nodded and watched Christopher leave her office.

Christopher pulled Cody's office door shut and leaned against it. He had the urge to do a victory dance but thought better of it.

"She said yes to the date, huh?" Nancy said from the front desk.

"Were you eavesdropping again?" Christopher glared at Nancy.

"I was," Nancy said without any shame. "Good for you!"

"Does this mean you're rooting for Cody and me to get back together?" Christopher's eyes narrowed as he walked closer to her.

"I wouldn't say that...." Nancy shook her head in denial. "But you've really gone out of your way to help me, Carla, and Steven these past few days, so I reckon you deserve a chance."

"That's sweet of you." Christopher eyed Nancy suspiciously. "Are you about to ask me for another favor?"

"No," Nancy looked at him innocently. "But if you were interested in coming with me to my Aunt Fern's for some tea and find out how she's been...."

"Sure," Christopher shrugged. "It will help me pass the time until this evening."

"Are you nervous about your date?" Nancy teased him. "You are!"

"No," Christopher denied. "Not at all."

"I believe the first time you asked her out was right after you punched Matthew Oats in the face." Nancy raised an eyebrow. "I hope you're not planning on punching anyone tonight."

"Who told you that?" Christopher felt his cheeks heat up as his blood boiled, thinking about that pompous oaf who was after Cody.

"My mother, Connie," Nancy grinned.

"The guy was being a jerk," Christopher told her.

"Let's hear your side of the story then?" Nancy was about to lean forward on her elbows when Sheba appeared and hopped up onto the counter. The cat plopped down in front of Nancy and started to purr. "Hi there, Queen Sheba." She started to stroke the enormous cat.

"Are you sure that's a house cat?" Christopher and Sheba didn't get along. Every time the cat was in the room, it didn't let him get close to his children, Cody, or even the dogs. "She hates me."

"No, she doesn't," Nancy assured him. "She's just wary of strangers."

"I've been here for almost two months," Christopher reminded Nancy. "I think it's safe to say the cat and the parrot hate me. It repeats everything I say."

"He's a McCaw!" Nancy gestured with hands. "That's what they do."

"He doesn't do it to anyone else in the house but me. The other night he tried to bite me when I was eating a snack." Christopher groaned.

"Were you eating watermelon?" Nancy hid her grin.

"I was," Christopher confirmed her suspicions.

"Mr. Squawkiness would bite Cody to get her watermelon," Nancy laughed. "Trust me on this."

"Oh, I take it, that's his favorite fruit?" Christopher felt a little better. "Has he ever bitten Cody or the children?" Worry creased his brow.

"No," Nancy looked at him as if he was mad. "Prof. Squawkings was raised by those children, so he wouldn't harm a hair on their head. That's why he went for your watermelon and not theirs." She chortled at his look of outrage.

"I'm being bullied by a parrot and a cat!" Christopher shook his head.

"You need to establish boundaries with the Prof. and this big ball of fluff." Her voice changed to baby talk as she picked up Sheba and gave her love. "See, she's a big ball of love."

"She's all fluffy and cute until I get closer," Christopher sighed.

"So, you were telling me about the first night you asked Cody out on a date when you were younger...." Nancy put Sheba down and looked him in the eye.

"Was I?" Christopher looked at Nancy innocently.

"Yes, you were!" Nancy gave him a smug smile.

"Fine," Christopher gave in. "It was the night of Cody's

sixteenth birthday. I'd met her that day when Steven had dragged me to go say hello to her. Cody was collecting shells on the beach."

"She still does that every year on her birthday; it was something she and her mother did together," Nancy explained.

"I know," Christopher nodded. "When we were married, I'd bring her and the children to Cody Bay for Cody's birthday."

"That was sweet of you." Nancy looked impressed.

"My brother had spoken about Cody a lot since the accident," Christopher reached over and took a piece of candy from the plate on the front desk. "On the day I met her, I realized why; Cody was special. There was this air about her. It was like I could see an aura of pure gold around her."

"Wow, love at first sight!" Nancy looked at him wide-eyed.

"No," Christopher laughed at her. "I was nineteen."

"You saw her light," Nancy pointed out. "Granny Moore would tell you that it was love at first sight. It was her soul making a connection with yours."

"If you say so," Christopher gave Nancy a sideways glance. "I wasn't very nice to her when I first met her. To be honest, I felt a little self-conscious around her."

"See..." Nancy lifted her eyebrows. "Your heart knew."

"Then that night at the Cody Bay Festival dance, I saw that idiot Matthew Oats chatting her up." Christopher's gut tightened, thinking about it. "Mat always had to try and pull smooth moves on the ladies, as he put it."

"You knew him?" Nancy frowned.

"Yeah," Christopher nodded. "We were friends. Played football together and were in the same year at school."

"You punched your friend in the face over a girl?" Nancy shook her head. "Isn't that going against some sort of bro code?"

"What?" Christopher looked confused. "In the nineties, there were no bro codes!"

"No matter the decade," Nancy pointed out to Christopher, "there were always bro codes."

"Okay!" Christopher pulled a face at her. "That night, there were no bro codes, only good manners codes."

147

"That's not a thing!" Nancy shook her head.

"Well, it should be!" Christopher emphasized. "My older brother taught us to always show respect and have good manners around ladies."

"Wow, that's a little old-fashioned, though, don't you think?" Nancy asked. "I mean, yeah, show a woman respect. I agree, but it's a two-way street, you know."

"Nancy, do you want to hear the story or not?" Christopher looked at her questioningly.

"Sorry," Nancy said sheepishly. "I was just thinking about Steven as a father and... never mind, continue with the story."

"You were wondering what it would've been like to have grown up with Steven being in your life?" Christopher smiled at Nancy. "It's natural to wonder about that now you know he is your biological father and the circumstances that led you to be adopted."

"Sorry," Nancy shook her head. "Please continue with your story."

"I've lost track of where I was now," Christopher grinned.

"You saw hunky Mat making moves on Cody, got jealous, and went and punched him in the face," Nancy told him.

"Again, that's not what happened," Christopher said and sighed. "Mat was chatting with Cody, and then she and her friends went to dance. Mat came over to me and told me he was going to score with Cody that night."

"That's when you punched him?" Nancy's eyes darkened. "Good for you!" she said, with admiration shining in her eyes. "I didn't hear that side of the story. According to witnesses, you told Mat you were going to ask Cody out, and you got jealous when he got to her first."

"It happened the way Christopher said it did," Cody had them both turning around to stare at her guiltily. "I was mad at Christopher for hitting Mat in the face. So I helped Mat go get some ice, and I was administering the ice pack when he grabbed me and tried to kiss me."

"I heard Cody shouting angrily and went to help her," Christopher smiled at Cody as they shared the memory.

"Did you hit Mat again?" Nancy asked. "Because I would've."

"No," Cody smiled up at Christopher as their eyes met. "He shouted at Mat to let me go, and he may have given Mat a gentle shove, but he was more concerned that I was okay."

"Aww..." Nancy's brows furrowed together as she looked at the two of them staring into each other's eyes.

"That's when I asked her belatedly if she'd be my date to the dance," Christopher's voice dropped.

"It was the best birthday I'd had in five years," Cody said softly.

"You two are so cute," Nancy grinned. "Oh, Cody, before I forget, here's Connie's grocery list."

"Agghhh," Cody was the first to break hers and Christopher's eye contact as she stepped up to Nancy and took the long list. "We need to hire a shopper."

"I'll do it for you," Christopher offered. "I know you have a busy day today at the Marine Center."

"I'll help you," Nancy volunteered.

"Don't you have a shift at Dr. Baxter's office?" Cody had no sooner asked her when Steven walked into the Inn. He'd just gotten back from a shift at the hospital.

"Nancy!" Steven bellowed. "Dr. Baxter just called me!"

"Uh-oh!" Nancy rolled her eyes. "I think now's a good time to head to the grocery store."

"What's going on, Nancy?" Christopher looked at Nancy, confused.

"Nancy quit her job at Dr. Baxter's office," Steven informed them.

"Is that true, Nancy?" Cody looked at her.

"I don't have to explain myself to anyone. I'm twenty-eight." Nancy picked up her purse and looked at Christopher pleadingly. "Christopher and I have to go shopping, and it'll be good for him to get some exercise."

"You can't go running away from this," Steven looked at her. "You've worked so hard to get your nursing degree. You need these credits."

"No," Nancy shook her head. "I don't. Working with Dr. Baxter was just extra credit. Besides, my aunt has asked me if I want to take over the clinic because she's retiring soon." She shrugged.

"Why didn't you tell me?" Cody looked at Nancy in surprise. "Nancy, that's a wonderful opportunity."

"I didn't want anyone making a fuss," Nancy shrugged. "With everything that's been happening lately, I never found the right time to tell you."

"That's wonderful news, Nancy," Christopher was so proud of her. "There's so much you can do with the clinic."

"Really?" Nancy walked up to Christopher and took the shopping note from Cody. "You'll have to tell me on our way to the grocery store."

"Good idea," Christopher said goodbye to Cody and Steven as he followed Nancy out the door.

"Did I just get out-maneuvered by my daughter?" Steven stood staring after Christopher and Nancy as they walked out of the Inn.

"I believe you did," Cody chuckled. "Welcome to parenthood. You'd have thought at twenty-eight it would've been easier. But I guess not!"

"I think I came on too strong with the father routine." Steven felt awful for having reacted like he had when Dr. Baxter had called him.

"No, you were being a parent," Cody told him. "That gut reaction you got thinking that Nancy was ruining her career shows how much you love her and only want what's best for her."

"I do," Steven ran his hand through his hair. "I know she's put everything into becoming a nurse practitioner. Getting a position with Dr. Baxter was a huge deal."

"Maybe now that Nancy knows who she really is, she feels she didn't get the position fairly," Cody gently pointed out to him. "You've known Nancy her whole life, Steven, and you know that everything she's achieved she'd done on her own—with no special favors and against all odds."

"That's true," Steven sighed. Cody was right, of course. Nancy was a force of nature and always had been. She'd never let life beat her and lived it to the fullest. "She's truly amazing."

"Look at you all shining with fatherly pride," Cody shook her head.

"I wish she'd look into becoming a doctor," Steven said. "She has the scores for it, and it's not that hard a transition from Nurse Practitioner."

"Steven, listen to yourself," Cody warned him. "Nancy has her reasons for becoming a nurse. Maybe you start by asking her why she wanted to become one first before trying to push her to do something else."

"You're right," Steven gave a small laugh. "I have no right to interfere. I just think she could be so much more."

"Talk to her," Cody advised Steven. "But, also remember that Nancy is already so much more!" She smiled. "I have to get to the Marine Life Center." She glanced at her watch.

"Thank you, Cody," Steven grabbed her arm to stop her from walking off. "For everything you've done for all of my family."

Cody nodded before grabbing her keys from behind the counter and leaving the Inn.

Steven stood, staring at the empty doorway. He couldn't believe how much his life had changed in such a short space of time. He'd thought he'd never have kids, only to find out he had a twenty-eight-year-old daughter. Over the past two days, since confronting Dr. Baxter, Steven had found himself wondering how different things would've been if he'd known about Nancy.

Steven was about to go to the dining room to get something to eat when Connie and Uncle Pete walked into the Inn.

"Steven," Connie said. "You're just the person Pete and I were looking for."

"Hello, Connie," Steven looked at Uncle Pete, "Uncle Pete."

"Hello, Steven." Uncle Pete shook hands with Steven.

Uncle Pete looked so different. He was wearing a suit and tie.

His face was clean-shaven, and his silver hair was neatly cut. Connie was also smartly dressed and not in her usual attire of jeans, a t-shirt, sneakers, and apron.

"Have you two been out on a date or something?" Steven asked them curiously.

"Or something," Uncle Pete told him. "Is there a place where we can talk in private where we won't be disturbed or overheard?"

"My suite?" Steven said, thinking it was the only place they wouldn't be disturbed. "I can get out of these scrubs as well."

"I'll get us a pizza and some coffee," Connie offered. "Pete and I will meet you up there in twenty minutes."

"Sure," Steven nodded. "You'd better make two of your delicious pizzas, Connie. I was on night shift, and I'm starving."

"I was going to make two," Connie winked at Steven. "Oh, and Steven, this meeting is just between the three of us."

Steven frowned at the look on Connie's face. She looked both anxious and fearful.

"Of course," Steven promised before heading up to his room, wondering what Uncle Pete and Connie needed to discuss with him.

Chapter Sixteen
A TANGLED WEB

"Hello, little fellow," Cody stroked the baby seal. "You're looking so much better."

"He's such an attention seeker, Aunt Cody," Harper laughed when the little seal nudged Cody's hand, not wanting her to stop stroking him.

"What are you going to name him?" Cody looked from Grace to Harper.

"I was thinking we should call him Solly," Lana walked over. "Hey, little guy."

"Why do you think his mother just let him go?" Grace asked.

"He could've been a twin," Lana explained. "Sometimes, the mother can only keep one alive, so she'll abandon the other one. The mother might have felt threatened for some reason, so she left the baby seal."

"Oh that's so sad," Grace's eyes portrayed her compassion for the young seal. "What's going to happen to him now?"

"We'll keep him for as long as we can until we can find a center that can house him," Lana told them. "Until we know if we can secure more funding to expand the Marine Life Center, we don't have the place or resources to keep him.

"Oh, no, Mom!" Grace's face crumpled as she looked at her mother. "You've got to do something."

"Honey, right now, my hands are tied," Cody's heart also ached for the little seal.

But Cody had to be realistic. They'd recently taken on another dolphin and a baby killer whale that wasn't such a baby anymore. While they were an attraction that brought in visitors, they were trying to make a much larger pool for the orca, which was costing a lot of money. Since the center was down two of its regular donors due to the incident that happened at the beginning of summer, Cody was trying to find more donors to take their place.

"Can't we throw some sort of festival to raise more money for the center so we can keep Solly," Harper suggested.

"That's not a bad idea," Grace's eyes lit with excitement. "We could have shown them the dolphins."

"I can show kids how working with sea life really changed my life," Harper liked Grace's ideas.

"Whoa," Lana reigned the teenagers' imaginations in. "That's a great idea and a nice thought, but arranging even a small festival takes time and money."

"We've got the time," Grace said. "We just need the money."

"We could do a charity drive," Harper suggested. "We could make one of those big barometer money goal chart things."

"How much do we need to be able to expand the center?" Harper asked Cody and Lana.

"Honey, I know you want to help, and those are great ideas," Lana smiled. "Let's put a pin in them for now and revisit them after the wedding. We still have time; this little guy isn't going anywhere for the time being, and the expansion pool is being built for Maxine, our baby orca."

"Okay," Harper and Grace exchanged looks. "Should we go and see the dolphins?"

"Yes," Grace agreed. "I want to check out how George the dolphin is doing with his new prosthetic tail."

"Have fun, girls," Cody called after Harper and Grace as they left the infirmary. "You do know they have no intention of letting up on their fundraising drive ideas, right?"

"I gathered that," Lana laughed. "They are two very stubborn young ladies."

"They take after their mothers," Carter, Lana's fiancé, walked into the room. "How is the little guy doing?" He walked over to the baby seal.

"He is still bugging the life out of Ginny, our resident mothering penguin," Lana told him. "But he's stable and eating now."

"That's something at least," Carter took a fish and handed it to Ginny, who was making a low trumpeting sound at Carter.

"I think Ginny has a crush on you," Cody chuckled. "She basically ignores us, but as soon as you walk into the room, she starts demanding your attention."

"Well, the bird has good taste," Carter grinned and threw Ginny another fish. "I can't believe that a penguin has taken to comforting a baby seal."

"Well, right now, they are both lonely," Lana shook her head as she looked at Ginny.

"Ginny wouldn't be lonely if she wasn't so aggressive towards the other penguins," Cody looked at Ginny.

"She's had a tough time," Carter defended Ginn. "You'd also be aggressive if you were all covered in oil and nearly died."

"True," Cody agreed with Carter.

"Cody, we need to get to that conference call," Carter told her.

"Is that the time already?" Cody glanced at her watch. "I'll check back with you after the meeting," she said to Lana.

"I'll be here," Lana assured her. "I think I know just the dress for your date tonight."

"Date?" Carter looked at Cody with raised eyebrows. "Who's the lucky man?"

"Cody has a date with Christopher," Lana grinned at the dirty look Cody gave Lana.

"Ah." Carter nodded. "Going somewhere special?"

"Dinner and dancing at the Beachfront Restaurant." Cody shrugged. "It's really just a friendly date." She looked at her watch again. "We need to go; we only have seven minutes, and you know what getting onto those conference calls can be like."

The look exchanged between Carter and Lana didn't go unnoticed by Cody as they left to go to Carter's office.

"So why are we really going to see your Aunt Fern?" Christopher asked Nancy as they pulled up outside a house.

"Because Dr. Baxter lied to us." Nancy shrugged. "The clinic didn't phone him that day when he found out that Carla was pregnant."

"Okay," Christopher looked at her with a raised eyebrow. "Then how did he find out?"

"You're not going to like the answer to that question," Nancy told him. "He's not the only one that's been lying to us."

"Are you telling me that Carla or Steven are lying to us?" Christopher looked at her in surprise. "Why would they lie to us?"

"That is what we're going to find out," Nancy gave him a smug smile. "You see, I overheard my mother having a conversation on the phone the day we arrived back from confronting Dr. Baxter."

"Nancy, you really need to stop snooping and eavesdropping," Christopher sighed, but he could not help be intrigued. He was too deep into this mystery now.

"Fine then, I won't tell you what I heard," Nancy shrugged and started to climb out of the car.

"I didn't say I wasn't interested to know what you'd heard," Christopher touched her arm to stop her from getting out of the car. "But I am worried about what you may overhear one day that could land you in trouble."

"Noted," Nancy exclaimed. "I heard my mother speaking to none other than Dr. Baxter about us. My mother sounded like she was both worried and scared of someone and of us finding out the truth about something and that it could unravel a whole lot of trouble for them."

"I wonder what they meant by that?" Christopher frowned.

Christopher had a suspicion there was more going on behind

the scenes at home, at the business, and even on Nantucket than first met the eye. But he'd always put it down to the ticking time bomb in his head, making him paranoid. It was good to know that at least his instincts were still sharp.

"Let's go find out," Nancy's features changed. "There are some things that you are not going to like hearing." She patted his arm. "I was shocked when I heard them."

"You're not going to tell me?" Christopher looked at her accusingly. "You want to torture me, wondering what you know that I don't?"

"No," Nancy shook her head. "I thought it best you hear from the person that was at the clinic that day."

"Fern," Christopher guessed correctly.

"Yup," Nancy pointed to her aunt standing at the now open front door, waving at them.

"That's just mean of you to keep me hanging like this," Christopher mumbled. "It's like getting to the end of the book, and the last few pages are missing."

"She tells it better than I do," Nancy told him as she locked the car when they were both out. "Come along, Uncle." She lightened the mood by teasing him.

Christopher looked at Nancy and smiled. He liked being called uncle. He'd always thought he'd be the cool uncle to his brother's children one day. Up until recently, Christopher didn't think he'd get to be an uncle, and he hadn't really given much thought to being an uncle to Nancy until this minute. Here he was being the cool uncle and helping his niece uncover a mystery. It felt good!

"Hello, earth to Christopher," Nancy snapped her fingers.

"Sorry, I was deep in thought," Christopher greeted Fern when Nancy introduced them.

"Come on in, I have coffee ready," Fern invited them into her home.

"You have a lovely home, Fern," Christopher complimented the neat colonial-style house.

"Nothing grand like yours," Fern beamed from the compliment. "But it's been home to me since I was a girl."

"My mom gave the house to Fern when their parents passed away," Nancy explained to Christopher.

"It's good it gets kept in the family," Christopher looked at the pictures on the wall. "Look at what the town center looked like in the early nineteen-hundreds."

"Oh yes," Fern stopped and looked at the pictures Christopher was admiring. "We have loads of old pictures, paintings, and pictures in the attic."

"Who drew this one?" Christopher asked, admiring the sketch of the old town.

"My grandfather," Fern said proudly. "He was quite the artist."

"Is that the old clubhouse?" Christopher pointed to a very old black-and-white picture.

The picture was in an elaborately carved wooden picture frame. At the top of the frame was a hand-painted coat of arms of a whale in the middle of a sun. Christopher had seen that coat of arms somewhere else. There was a motto at the bottom of the coat of arms; *Nos defendat, cum honore.* Christopher was also sure he'd seen or heard that motto somewhere else on the island.

"No," Fern shook her head. "That was a club or town committee that a few key residents of the island started. It was like a town council, I guess."

"Is it still standing?" Christopher didn't know why but there was something about it that pulled at his memory.

"No." Fern shook her head. "Sadly, it was knocked down years ago."

"That's a pity," Christopher looked at Fern. "I find it so sad that these old historic buildings get pulled down or modernized."

"I agree," Fern turned towards the sitting room. "Make yourselves comfortable in the living room. I'll go get the coffee."

"Thanks, Aunt Fern," Nancy smiled at her aunt. "There are a lot more paintings and pictures in the living room, believe me."

"Yes," Christopher said beneath his breath. "But I want a picture of this one." He pointed to the clubhouse. "There's something about it."

"Okay," Nancy pulled out her phone, glanced down the hallway, and then quickly snapped a picture. "I'll send it to you."

"Thanks," Christopher followed Nancy into the living room. "You weren't kidding about the paintings and pictures."

"No!" Nancy plopped down on one of the overstuffed sofas. "I don't think this room has changed in about a hundred years."

A shiver traveled up Christopher's spine as a draft blew into the room. He looked to find the source of the draft, but the windows were closed.

"Are you okay?" Nancy looked at him worriedly.

"I thought I felt a draft," Christopher looked at the living room windows again. "There must be a gap in the windowpane."

"Must be," Nancy raised an eyebrow. "Or it could be your subconscious mind trying to get your attention."

"Uh-huh," Christopher shook his head at her. "It was nothing and probably just my imagination from being surrounded by all these portraits." He looked around the room.

"I know, right?" Nancy laughed. "I would never stay in the room on my own when I was younger."

"I don't blame you." Christopher took a seat next to Nancy on the sofa. "It's as creepy as hell."

"I keep wanting to clear this room out," Fern admitted as she walked into the room carrying a tray with coffee and cookies on it. She put it down on the center table. "We should've gone to the sunroom at the back, but I'm having it repainted."

"It's not a problem," Christopher shrugged his discomfort off.

Nancy looked down at her phone and shook her head in exasperation. "Shoot," Nancy hissed. "We have to go." She sighed. "Cody messaged to ask when we were coming back with the groceries. They're out of ketchup."

"What?" Christopher's brows furrowed. "We've only just got here...."

"That's okay," Fern stood up. Christopher couldn't help but notice that she looked relieved.

"I'm so sorry, Aunt Fern," Nancy all but pushed Christopher

out of the door. "We'll reschedule." She waved goodbye to her aunt and hurried to the car. "Hurry up." She hissed at Christopher.

Christopher slid into the car. He'd barely closed his door when Nancy started to drive off.

"What the hell, Nancy?" Christopher rasped.

"My aunt was warning us," Nancy told him.

"Where …." Christopher looked at her, confused. "She barely said a few words to us, and you were up and pushing me out the door."

"My Aunt's sunroom was painted three weeks ago," Nancy explained. "She was actually warning us before we came inside." She shook her head. "My aunt doesn't drink coffee."

"How on earth did you know she was warning you?" Christopher snapped his seatbelt into place.

"When I was a rebellious teen, and I would go stay with my aunt, she worked out a way to warn me when my mother had come to pay me a surprise visit," Nancy explained.

"Oh, I get it," Christopher realized what was going on. "You knew the sun lounge had been painted a while ago and that she didn't drink coffee."

"My aunt never serves her guest's coffee unless they specifically ask for it," Nancy pulled a face. "To her, it's considered bad manners."

"That's very British of her," Christopher laughed. "So, what do you think she was warning us about?"

"My mother could've been there," Nancy told him. "What I want to know is how my mother knew we were going to visit my aunt."

"I think you're taking this mystery thing a little too far, Nancy Drew," Christopher raised his eyebrows.

"Oh, really?" Nancy glanced at him. "Well, then how about this. It wasn't your mother that took Carla's folder from the clinic—it was Steven."

"My brother?" Christopher looked at her with disbelief. "Why would he be at the clinic?"

"Your mother called him from the clinic," Nancy told him.

"Your mother asked my Aunt Fern if she could use the clinic phone to call Steven as she wasn't feeling well enough to drive."

"Steven knew Carla was pregnant?" Christopher frowned. "That doesn't make sense."

"It makes perfect sense," Nancy said to Christopher. "What if Steven had also seen those pictures of who Dr. Baxter thought was Carla and your father?"

"No way!" Christopher didn't believe that for a minute.

"Think about it," Nancy said. "He and Carla had been broken up for weeks before she found out she was pregnant."

"You think that Steven thought Carla moved from him to our father and also believed you were my father's child?" Christopher speculated. "No, I'm sorry, I don't believe it."

"Oh, and Dr. Baxter was told about the pregnancy by your mother, not by the clinic," Nancy pointed out. "That's why he didn't want us to go and ask any questions."

"So, the whole banishing Carla to her grandparents, lying to her, and stealing you from her was because they were worried you might be my sister?" Christoper asked her incredulously. "Why? So it would be a little bit of a scandal...."

"That's what we need to find out!" Nancy told him as she pulled up at the grocery store. "Steven knows more than he's letting on," Nancy warned Christopher.

Christopher's head was spinning. So much for being the cool uncle—instead, he felt like he'd been sucked down a rabbit hole with Alice. "I hope you're wrong about Steven."

"Me too," Nancy assured him as she climbed out of the car.

"What are you getting us into?" he whispered when they neared the entrance to the store.

There was something in Steven's expression the other day at Dr. Baxter's house that made Christopher think that maybe Nancy was right about his brother after all. But he shook it off to give Steven the benefit of the doubt until they had time to talk to Steven. But that cold shiver once again crept up his spine as he took a shopping cart and followed Nancy into the store.

Chapter Seventeen
A DATE WITH CODY – PART 2

"That was a lovely meal," Cody took a sip of coffee. "I know I should not be drinking this so late, but the Beachfront Restaurant makes the best cappuccino."

"Is it better than that little cafe we used to go to in Boston?" Christopher looked at her teasingly. "You used to say the same thing about their cappuccino."

"That's right," Cody remembered. "We used to go there every Sunday for lunch."

"You'd always order the chicken salad in the summer with fruit salad dessert and the pumpkin soup and mini loaf in the winter." Christopher surprised Cody by remembering their Sunday ritual.

"That pumpkin soup was the best," Cody breathed in, savoring the memory. "Even you, the pumpkin hater, loved their soup."

"I'm not a pumpkin hater. I just think it's a creepy vegetable," Christopher shuddered.

"I can't believe a grown man is scared of pumpkins," Cody teased him.

Cody was enjoying their evening. She hadn't known what to expect and was hoping it wasn't going to be awkward, but it wasn't. Christopher was relaxed, charming, and had made her laugh. From the moment they'd met in the lobby of the Inn, he'd made her feel relaxed and at ease. He'd even regaled her with his antics with their children over the past weeks he'd been with them.

She knew she shouldn't be, but Cody had found herself thinking about Christopher more often than she should be. The more time they spent together, the more the old feelings for him were starting to resurface. Feelings she had lately admitted to herself that had never gone away she'd just buried them in hopes that time would erode them.

No matter how she tried to fight it or didn't want it to be, Cody knew the moment Christopher had walked back into her life this summer that he was her epic love. Her soulmate! Cody knew that Christopher wanted to try their relationship again. He'd hinted at it many times this summer while he'd been recovering from surgery at Cody Bay. But, how would they ever be able to get over everything that transpired between them, and how would Cody ever be able to trust him again?

"Do I have something on my face?" Christopher asked her. His brows were drawn together as he stared at her. "You're looking at me as if I do."

"No," Cody shook her head. "Sorry, I was deep in thought."

"Can I offer you a million dollars for your thoughts?" Christopher grinned.

Cody laughed at him. Christopher never offered her a penny for her thoughts, always a million dollars, because he was sure her thoughts were worth that much. He could be cold, foreboding, and she'd hate to be on the wrong side of him, but he was also sweet, kind, funny, protective, caring, thoughtful, and so romantic. Well, at least he used to be before he'd changed.

Cody gave herself a mental shake. She now knew why he'd changed, but at the time, she hadn't known he had a tumor, and Cody was always left wondering what had happened. She'd tortured herself all those years ago, thinking it had been something she'd done because she knew he was hurting, but he'd refused to open up to her. Cody smiled at Christopher.

If only they could somehow erase all the bitterly painful memories, things would be so much easier for them and the children.

"I don't think thoughts of putting a nice sun deck or pool on the Widow's walk at the Inn are worth a million dollars," Cody replied.

"Are you thinking of doing that?" Christopher leaned on his elbows.

"I have been for a while, and this summer when I went up there it was so beautiful and such a wasted space," Cody told him.

"I think it's an incredible idea," Christopher said enthusiastically. "I hope you'll let C. Stanford Construction bid on the project?"

"You started your own business?" Cody looked at him in awe. "When and how come I never heard about it?"

"About nine years ago, I finally did it," Christopher sighed. "I'd secured some big contracts and had been operating for three years when my father got sick again, so I was roped back into the shipping business." He leaned back in his chair.

"What about your construction company?" Cody finished her coffee.

"I was still running my new company and acting as chairman of the board for Stanford Shipping in my father's place." Christopher sighed. "It was a tough time. A year after my father got ill, Riley was born, and a year later, Janine got ill again."

"That must've been awful for you." Cody's heart ached for him. "It was also a lot to take on, considering what you had also gone through with the tumor."

"It was a juggling game," Christopher gave her a sad smile. "When my father died, I left nearly everything, including Stanford Shipping!" He shocked Cody by saying.

"What about Steven and your mother?" Cody asked Christopher.

"My dad left my mother a small trust fund and the estate in Boston, which originally belonged to her parents until they went bankrupt, and my father bailed my mother's family out." Christopher shook his head. "Steven was left a letter that only he could open, a hefty trust fund, and Nantucket General."

"Your father owned Nantucket General?" Cody knew she was gaping.

"He was the majority shareholder of the hospital," Christopher smiled. "Oh, Steven also got the house he was living in that he was renting from my father."

"I wonder what was in the envelope your father left Steven?" Cody bit her lip in contemplation.

"I do not know, and I've never asked," Christopher admitted. "I was in such a state at the time because Janine was getting worse by the day. I had two companies to run, Riley to look after, and my mother—who was furious and wanted to contest the will. It was a nightmare."

"So, the Nantucket Estate is yours?" Cody said thoughtfully.

"It is," Christopher nodded. "Why?" He gave her a sideways look.

"The land that runs between the Stanford Estate and the Marine Life Center, I was told, is actually part of the Stanford Estate," Cody leaned forward on her elbows. "We've been trying to buy that land for ages as the center needs to expand."

"Let me guess?" Christopher leaned forward as well. "My mother has been blocking it?"

"I think it's your mother... we keep getting some administration person at Stanford Shipping," Cody told her.

"Why didn't you just come to me?" Christopher asked her.

"I didn't want to trouble you with it or to have you go up against your mother," Cody shrugged. "I thought she was the owner of the property now that your father had passed."

"Well, she doesn't, and she has no right to not forward all business about the estate to me," Christopher assured Cody. "She's only staying there because I let her do so."

"That's a prime piece of land for the Marine Life Center," Cody said.

"How about we discuss this tomorrow," Christopher reached over and took Cody's hand. "Right now, I'd very much like to have a dance with my gorgeous date."

"Fine," Cody shook her head and smiled. "You're lucky I happen to like this song."

"I know you do," Christopher grinned, pulling Cody onto the dance floor and into his arms. "I asked the band to play it especially for you."

"That's so sweet," Cody looked up into his deep blue eyes and sucked in her breath at the emotion she saw shining in their depth.

Cody stepped a little closer and let her head rest on Christopher's shoulder. He rested his head against hers as he swayed them around the dance floor. It felt so right to be held in his arms. The old butterflies that always fluttered in her stomach whenever Christopher was near her dusted off their wings and took flight once again.

"I think we should get an ice cream and go for a walk on the beach," Christopher whispered in her ear. "I'm not ready for the night to end yet."

"That sounds like a good plan," Cody agreed.

When the song ended, Christopher was reluctant to let Cody go. He wanted to hold her close to his heart forever, where she was always supposed to be.

"Should we go?" Cody pulled back and looked up at him. "I'm sure you promised me ice cream."

"I knew you wouldn't be able to resist that offer," Christopher dropped his arms from around her and let her walk back to their table.

Christopher felt empty and cold and had to stop himself from reaching out to touch her hand. Instead, he called their waiter to get the bill. The waiter brought a takeout bag with ice cream in it.

"I see you've already ordered the ice cream." Cody laughed.

"I like to plan ahead." Christopher smiled. "Shall we go to Cody Bay, sit in our favorite spot on the jetty and eat it?"

"Yes, let's go." Cody walked out of the restaurant ahead of Christopher.

"Thank you for a lovely evening," Cody kissed Christopher on the cheek. "It's been a long time since I went out to eat, dance, and had ice cream on the beach."

"I hope we can do it again very soon." Christopher's voice was hoarse.

"I'd like that." Cody slipped out of her car and waited for Christopher to get out so she could lock it.

They walked into the Inn and were surprised to see everyone still up; it was after midnight. Connie, Uncle Pete, Lana, Carter, Harper, Grace, Riley, and Carla were gathered around the reception desk. Tiny and Rage ran to greet Cody and Christopher. They were the only ones that looked excited. Even Sheba looked unsettled as she sat in her favorite spot on the desk next to Professor Squawkings.

"Mom, look what Aiden and Nancy found." Grace pointed to the two puppies that were playing with Tiny and Rage.

"Where on earth did you find them?" Cody looked at Aiden.

"Can we keep them, Aunt Cody?" Riley ran up to her and grabbed her hand. "Please, I've always wanted my own dog, and I still love Tiny and Rage."

"We'll discuss this in the morning," Cody promised Riley.

"Nancy and I were on the roof because, as you know, tonight is the night the guiding star shines over the bay." Aiden started to tell the story.

"Are you and Nancy still looking for that elusive star that guided the first Moore to Cody Bay?" Christopher shook his head.

"Of course," Nancy told him. "It's real, and tonight I got proof of it."

"You saw it?" Christopher looked surprised.

"No," Nancy shook her head. "Not exactly."

"It's part of the story," Aiden told his father impatiently.

"Oh, sorry, son," Christopher looked apologetic.

Cody loved seeing how easily the children had accepted their father back into their lives. She was so proud of them both.

"A woman came up the backstairs of the widow's walk and asked us if we could help her look for two puppies she'd found in a sack on the side of the road." Nancy picked up the story.

"I recognized her as one of your old friends, Mom," Aiden reached into his jeans pocket and pulled out a card. "Her name's Hilda-May, and her family owns a farm on the island."

"Hilda-May is back in Nantucket?" Cody was so pleased. She had to remember to call her and arrange a meetup.'

"We went to help her, and we found these two," Nancy finished the story. "We told Hilda-May that we wouldn't mind taking them."

"That was nice of you," Cody sighed and looked at the two adorable pups harassing Tiny and Rage. "Well, they can stay here tonight, and we'll discuss them in the morning."

"I think we should also discuss the two of you rushing off to help a stranger at night," Christopher looked from Aiden to Nancy.

"Hilda-May wasn't a stranger," Nancy pointed out. "Her family's ancestors were on this island long before any settlers, and her family has been tasked with helping guide all those that need it."

"Hilda-May told us that tonight was the night that her family stayed up the entire night to guide ones in need," Aiden said excitedly. "We asked her about the star, and she told us that we would only see it if we needed to."

"So, are you two going to give up looking for the guiding light every year now that you know that?" Christopher asked them.

"Not a chance," Aiden and Nancy said in unison.

"I think it's way past everyone's bedtime, and we should get these two little pups settled," Cody picked Riley up. "Come, do you want to help me feed them?"

"Yes, please," Riley said excitedly.

*C*hristopher was about to follow Cody when Nancy stopped him.

"Christopher, will you help me with my telescope, please?" Nancy held up her arm. "I battle to take it apart with my arm, and Aiden is clearly too preoccupied with the puppies."

"Sure," Christopher nodded and followed Nancy to the widow's walk.

Chapter Eighteen
THE REAL STORY BEHIND THE PUPPIES

"Thank you for coming to help me," Nancy walked up to her telescope and started to disassemble it without any problems.

"Why am I here?" Christopher suddenly got the feeling this wasn't about the telescope.

"So I could tell you the real story behind the puppies," Nancy lowered her voice.

"I wondered why you, who doesn't like the dark, would go running around in it after puppies with a stranger," Christopher drawled.

"Hilda-May did approach us on the widow's walk." Nancy packed the parts of the telescope into its case. "We did go down to help her because Aiden and I both recognized her. She used to visit with Cody a lot."

"I know who Hilda-May is," Christopher watched Nancy pack her equipment away. "Not many guys on the island don't."

"She's stunning, isn't she," Nancy stopped and looked at Christopher. "I wonder why she's still single?"

"Hilda-May was more about saving the world than settling down," Christopher told her.

"Ah, that makes sense," Nancy nodded. "Anyway, we went to

help her. While we were looking for the pups that supposedly escaped, she walked us towards the black SUV."

"Why don't I like where this is going?" Christopher folded his arms across his chest.

"It was nothing sinister," Nancy stopped and looked at him. "She said that we shouldn't be scared, and there was someone who wanted to talk to me."

"Okay..." Christopher gave her a sideways look.

"Hilda-May introduced Aiden to the puppies she'd found in a bag on the side of the road that day. That part was also true," Nancy disclosed. "While I climbed into the back of the SUV and was introduced to none other than..." she leaned closer to Christopher. "Luis Vern."

"Carla's missing uncle?" Christopher looked at her in surprise.

"Yup," Nancy confirmed.

Earlier That Night

"Thank you both so much for helping me," Hilda-May sounded relieved. "I know they're this way." She pointed down the road with her flashlight.

"No problem," Aiden assured Hilda-May.

Nancy shook her head at the smitten Aiden. The minute Hilda-May had half-scared them to death on the widow's walk, Aiden hadn't been able to take his eyes off the drop-dead gorgeous Hilda-May.

Hilda-May stopped next to a black SUV.

"Okay, now, don't be scared," Hilda-May held up her hands in front of her.

Nancy suddenly got a tingle up her spine. "When people say don't be scared, it usually makes a person scared, wary, or wonder if they are about to be kidnapped." Nancy's eyes narrowed as she and Aiden looked at each other and instinctively moved closer together.

Puppies barking inside the SUV caught Nancy and Aiden's

attention as the back door of the car swung open, and a man Nancy instantly recognized stuck his head out.

"Hello Nancy and Aiden, I'm Luis Vern," Luis introduced himself. He was wearing a familiar-looking baseball hat.

"You're Carla's long-lost uncle?" Nancy gaped at him. "And you're the man in the hat!"

"Is that what you called me?" Luis grinned.

"He's the guy that helped you escape from the Andersons when you were thirteen?" Aiden looked at Nancy. "You're Batman?"

"Yes," Nancy nodded. "He was always there right when I needed him."

"Please don't make his ego any bigger than it already is," Hilda-May laughed at the Batman reference.

"I didn't mean to scare you both," Luis told them. "But this was the only way I could get you alone, Nancy, because I need your help."

"Okay, but I'm not sure why you couldn't just phone, message, or pop in at the surgery?" Nancy frowned.

"Because, like my niece, you're being watched," Luis informed her. "And I can't be seen right now, or it will upset everything."

"Meaning..." Nancy trailed off for Luis to fill in the blanks.

"Aiden, why don't we let the puppies out and leave Luis to talk with Nancy," Hilda-May suggested. "Don't worry. We'll be right over there." She pointed to a grassy spot near the van.

"Sure," Aiden grinned when Hilda-May picked up one of the puppies that was chewing on Luis Vern's sneaker in the car and handed it to him while she took the other one.

Nancy watched as Aiden and Hilda-May walked a little way away from the van.

"I've been presumed dead for quite a while now, and it's best that way," Luis explained. "But Carla is in danger. You both are if you continue to investigate what you have been looking into."

"Ah, you're working with Dr. Baxter!" It all made sense to Nancy.

"No," Luis shook his head. "Well, not directly.... It's complicated."

"That's what Dr. Baxter said too," Nancy folded her arms across her chest.

"I have something for Carla," Luis reached into his jacket pocket and pulled out a sealed envelope. "Would you give it to her for me, please?" He handed it to Nancy.

"Okay." Nancy took the envelope.

"It has information about a meeting place in it." Luis pointed to the envelope. "I'll be there to answer all your questions. It would be best if you, Christopher, and Carla came together."

"Won't that look a little suspicious if you think we're all being watched?" Nancy asked.

"It's coming up for a major checkup for Christopher," Luis pulled a card out of his pocket. "This is the name of a consulting doctor that will call Carla to set up an appointment for him and will ask that both of you be present for the appointment."

"Clever," Nancy said, impressed. "But if we're being watched, won't we be followed to Boston?"

"Bring Aiden, Grace, Riley, and Harper with you for a day trip to Boston," Luis formulated a plan for them. "Caroline West will meet you at the hospital and take the children to do some sightseeing and shopping. You, Christopher, and Carla will go see the doctor, and I'll meet you at the hospital."

"What if Steven wants to come with us?" Nancy asked.

"He won't be able to," Luis gave her a grin. "We'll make sure of that."

"So not even Cody can come with us?" Nancy checked.

"No," Luis shook his head. "Cody doesn't need to know about this just yet."

"Just yet?" Nancy frowned. "What's that supposed to mean?"

Luis drew in a deep breath before answering, "When you hear what I have to say, you'll understand why it would be best not to involve Cody."

"Are you saying not to trust Cody?" Nancy's brows drew tighter together. "Because no matter what you say, I'd trust her with my life."

"And so you should," Luis told her. "Cody is one of the most honest people you'll ever know. But she's been through enough, and I think Christopher needs to hear a few truths before we involve her."

"Okay," Nancy nodded. "So I can tell Carla and Christopher about you."

"Yes," Luis nodded. "But no one else."

"Were you at my aunt's house when Christopher and I were there?" A thought dawned on Nancy.

"No," Luis shook his head. "But I know who it was."

"And how exactly would you know that?" Nancy looked at him questioningly.

"Fern works with us," Luis informed her. "I would trust her before I trusted anyone else in your family, Carla's family, and Christopher's family."

"Noted," Nancy said. "Why did you pick tonight to contact me?"

"Because on this night, every year, you go on the widow's walk to look for the guiding light," Luis surprised her by saying.

"How would you know that?" Nancy asked him warily.

"I've looked out for you, your entire life, Nancy Honey," Luis explained. "Since the day I brought you to the Honeys."

"So it was you that put me with them?" Nancy nodded.

"I did, and I named you," Luis surprised her by saying. "You were named after my grandmother, who, like you, was adopted as a baby."

"Good to know," Nancy said. "I'll give this to Carla." She held up the envelope. "What about the puppies?"

"I was hoping for you and Aiden would take them in for us and give them a good home," Luis' expression changed. "I can't believe someone would just dump them on the side of the road."

"That really happened?" Nancy felt the anger burn in her stomach. "Unbelievable."

"It was nice to finally get to talk to you, Nancy," Luis smiled warmly at her. "There's a number in there that you can get me on at any time, or you can call Hilda-May."

"I'd better get Aiden and our new additions back to the Inn before we are missed," Nancy looked to where Aiden was playing with the puppies. "I'll let him know not to say anything. He's a good kid."

"I know," Luis nodded. "I wouldn't have brought you here if I thought he couldn't be trusted."

Nancy and Aiden said goodbye to Luis and Hilda-May and made their way back to the Inn. While they walked, they got the story about the puppies straight.

"All I heard from that story was that my niece and my son went to help a perfect stranger look for puppies in the dark." Christopher held up his hand to stop Nancy from speaking. "Then you approached a suspect black SUV and spoke to a strange man."

"It sounds bad when you say it like that," Nancy said impatiently.

"What is wrong with both of you?" Christopher glowered.

"We knew Hilda-May," Nancy snarled back. "I also knew the man in the hat. He's the one that helped me escape the Andersons, and he was there when I broke my arm punching Tim Burke. He was also the one that helped Aiden and me at the track when we had our accident."

"So that's supposed to make me feel better?" Christopher looked at Nancy in amazement. "Your helpful stalker was in the van?"

"You're missing the point altogether," Nancy hissed. "I would never have let anything happen to Aiden. But now we have a way of getting our answers. He wants to see you because he has something to tell you as well."

"Or he's leading us into some sort of trap," Christopher was fuming.

"Why are you so mad?" Nancy's eyes narrowed. "What are you hiding?"

175

"Nothing!" Christopher said quickly. "I have nothing to hide; I'm an open book."

"No, you're not." Nancy raised her eyebrow. "Has this got something to do with Hilda-May?"

"No," Christopher's brows creased, "of course not. It's just that you're putting a lot of trust in the man who was the one to kidnap you in the first place."

"He had his reasons, and I want to find them out," Nancy shrugged. "I will do it with or without your help."

"Fine," Christopher sighed. "We'll find Carla in the morning."

"Or maybe now?" Nancy pointed to Carla walking towards them. "I kinda messaged her while you were doing your whole lecture thing."

"You're worse than my teenage children," Christopher moaned at her.

"Why put off tomorrow what you can do today?" Nancy grinned at him.

"I'm sure that doesn't apply to this situation," Christopher sighed again.

"Come on; she's waiting for us in her room." Nancy hurried towards the stairs.

"Unbelievable," Christopher sighed again as he followed Nancy.

Chapter Nineteen
A TRIP TO BOSTON

"It was nice of Cody to lend us the Inn's shuttle van," Carla said as she pulled off the ferry. "It's going to be nice spending a day in Boston."

"I'm looking forward to the trip Aunt Caroline has planned for us," Grace told them excitedly. "She's taking us to Salem for the morning while dad has his checkup."

"I'm looking forward to the trip across on the catamaran," Christopher looked at the information about the trip on his phone. "We may even see a few whales."

"I'm going to eat cheesecake," Riley grinned. "Lots and lots of cheesecake."

"You were not supposed to say that." Harper, who was sitting right at the back with Riley, tickled him, making him laugh.

"Only one piece, bud," Christopher turned in the front passenger seat and looked at his youngest son. "You don't want to get a stomachache."

"Or be zinging around the place on a sugar high." Aiden's eyes widened as he shook his head.

"Aiden, please make sure Riley only has one piece of cheesecake and try to limit the sugar," Christopher looked at his son.

"Don't worry. I have to keep Grace, Harper, and Riley in

177

check," Aiden smiled at Christopher. "When it comes to cakes and anything sweet, Grace and Harper are worse than Riley."

"Hey," Grace punched her brother. "Don't rat us out."

"Suck up," Harper pushed the back of Aiden's seat with her foot.

"Just looking after your health," Aiden told them.

Carla pulled into the hospital parking lot and found a parking space. Once they'd all piled out of the van, they walked to the entrance of the hospital where Caroline was waiting for them.

"Hello, my lovelies," Caroline greeted them all with a hug. "Are you ready for a morning in Salem?"

"Thanks so much, Caroline," Christopher smiled at her. "Please watch Riley with the sweets."

"He'll be fine, won't he?" Caroline took Riley's hand in hers. "Good luck with your check-up." She gave them a knowing smile before herding the teenagers and Riley to her car.

Carla stood with Christopher and Nancy, watching the children walking off with Caroline.

"Carter is so lucky to have a mother like Caroline." Christopher looked wistfully at Caroline, who was laughing and joking with the kids as they walked. "I can't remember my mother ever holding my hand or interacting with me in any way."

"Some mothers aren't motherly at all," Carla put her hand on Christopher's arm comfortingly. "My mother was a lot like Caroline."

"Both of my mothers were, too," Nancy looked up at Christopher. "At least you had Steven."

"Yes, a brother who I've recently found out may not be everything I thought he was," Christopher's eyes were shadowed with pain.

"Let's not judge anyone until we've heard what Luis has to say," Nancy suggested. "We don't know why or even if Steven really did what he did or is keeping secrets from us."

"Nancy's right, Christopher," Carla agreed with Nancy. "Before we go pointing fingers, let's hear what my uncle has to say."

Carla led the way into the hospital. She was met with smiles by the staff that recognized her as she made her way to the room where they were meeting Dr. Decker.

"*I*f you wait here, Dr. Decker will be with you shortly." Dr. Decker's assistant told them before leaving the room.

"Do you think it's the same Dr. Decker that looks like Carla?" Nancy whispered.

"I guess we're going to find out," Carla whispered back.

"That's going to be weird seeing your doppelganger," Christopher joined in the whispering.

"Do you think Dr. R. Decker is related to you?" Nancy asked Carla.

"I'm not sure," Carla frowned. "My mother did have an older sister that left home when she was sixteen after having a massive fight with my grandparents. I only ever met her once, and that was at my mother's grave a few months after she'd died."

"Did she look like your mother?" Nancy asked.

"Very much so," Carla remembered. "I thought they were twins at first. But she's three years older than my mother was."

"Did she have children?" Nancy looked at Carla questioningly.

"I didn't get to talk to her much," Carla admitted. "I was in a horrible place after having lost my mother, and I was putting flowers on her grave when my aunt approached me."

The office door opened, and Dr. Decker's assistant walked in.

"Dr. Decker asked me to take you through to the consultation room." She stepped aside and waited for Christopher, Carla, and Nancy to leave the room. "This way."

She led them to the elevator. "It's on the fifth floor." She smiled at them.

"Thanks," Carla said as she stepped into the elevator with Christopher and Nancy. "That's weird. The fifth floor is being renovated and has been closed for almost a year now."

"Well, that is not creepy or suspicious at all," Christopher mumbled. "You both remember that the man we're about to see kidnapped Nancy, lied to Carla, and has stalked Nancy for nearly twenty-eight years?"

"Oh, come on. He's Carla's uncle," Nancy tried to reassure Christopher.

"I agree with Christopher, actually," Carla suppressed a shudder. "But we're here now, so let's go find out what my uncle has to say."

The elevator stopped at the fifth floor, and they all piled out of it and stopped short when they were greeted by a woman that looked like a slightly older version of Carla.

"Hi," Dr. Decker greeted them with a warm smile. "I'm Rose Decker." She held out her hand. "You must be Carla?" She smiled and shook Carla's hand.

"Good guess," Nancy told Dr. Decker. "My word. It must be like looking in a mirror for the two of you."

"You look like you could be twins," Christopher gaped at Dr. Decker.

"Not twins, but first cousins," Rose cleared up the mystery surrounding her. "My mother was Carla's mother's older sister."

"You were right," Nancy looked at Carla.

"I only met your mother once," Carla told Rose. "A couple of months after my mother's death, I was putting flowers on her grave when your mother came to see me."

"Yes, she told me she met you at the graveside," Rose gave them a sad smile. "I know she really wanted to be at your mother's funeral, but she didn't want to run into her parents."

"How long have you been at Boston General?" Carla asked Rose as they headed down the hallway.

"Since you left... a month or so ago," Rose answered Carla's question. "Here we are." She pushed open the door to one of the wards.

"This place is creepy," Nancy shuddered.

"It's under major construction, and it is going to be incredible when it's done," Rose assured her. "We could use some excellent nurse practitioners here, Nancy."

"How do you know..." Nancy stopped when Luis Vern greeted them.

"I told her," Luis smiled at Nancy.

"Uncle Luis!" Carla felt the blood drain from her face, and her heart started to pound in her chest.

"Hello, sweetheart," Luis greeted her.

"I thought you were dead," Carla swallowed down the emotions bubbling up inside of her. "I've looked for you for years!"

"I know," Luis said apologetically. "I had to disappear and have to stay disappeared until I've cleared up some matters."

"Let's sit down," Rose suggested. "I've put some chairs at the back of the room."

"You could've given me some sign that you were still alive," Carla followed her uncle.

"I'm sorry, sweetheart," Luis stood aside for her to take a seat. "But I couldn't let anyone know where I was. It was better for me, you, Nancy, and Christopher for me to be missing and presumed dead."

"Why?" Christopher frowned.

"Because I know too much, and that makes some people in Nantucket and here in Boston extremely nervous," Luis answered.

"That's not an answer," Nancy sat between Carla and Christopher. "We're getting a little bit tired of getting vague answers to our questions."

"That's why you're all here," Luis informed them. "I thought it was time you all learned a few truths and about my investigations."

"That would be nice," Nice told him.

"It's been a shock to find out that you all thought that Mr. Stanford and I...." Carla couldn't bring herself to say it. "How could you?"

"You have to understand, there was a lot going on behind the scenes at the time," Luis told them. "I hadn't seen my sister Anne, Rose's mother, since she was sixteen and ran away from home. I didn't even know if she was still alive, let alone that she had a daughter."

"My mother and her parents didn't get along," Rose filled in the gaps about her mother. "She took the money her grandparents had left her and put herself through law school."

"Oh, that's amazing," Carla couldn't believe how much Carla and she looked alike. Although, Carla had had the birthmark on her face removed years ago. "How did you end up treating Mr. Stanford?"

"I was specializing in oncology at the time and had taken a post in Boston. Mr. Stanford was a patient of the doctor I was working for, and I was assigned his case." Rose explained. "Mr. Stanford couldn't travel into Boston, so we came to him and met him at a hotel. It was only for two consultations, though."

"It looked like more than one consultation," Nancy raised her eyebrows as she looked at Rose.

"Well, it wasn't," Rose assured them. "We think that Margaret had the other photos doctored."

"Why would my mother do that?" Christopher looked confused.

"Your father had started divorce proceedings," Luis reached behind him and picked up a folder, and handed it to Christopher. "Your father had hired me because he was convinced someone was trying to kill him."

"Seriously?" Christopher looked shocked. "Why would he think that?"

"Probably because someone was," Luis told them. "Your mother was not very happy when she found out your father had cut her out of his will and was about to hand her divorce papers."

"Are you suggesting my mother was trying to kill my father?" Christopher asked in disbelief. "He could be a bit abrupt and demanding, but he was fair and gave my mother everything she ever wanted." He glanced at the folder in his hand. "I don't believe it."

"I hardly ever spoke to Mr. Stanford when I was dating Lance, but he was always the nicer one out Lance's parents." Carla smiled at Christopher. "Lance really respected your father, although Lance was a lot closer to your mother."

"Lance was my mother's favorite. I'm sure of it," Christopher admitted. "Steven was a bit of a wild card because she couldn't control him, and he did his own thing. My mother didn't know how to deal with children until they reached the age of eighteen."

"She never liked me," Carla voiced her suspicions. "I heard her telling Lance how much better he could do than me."

"Margaret probably didn't like you because you looked so much like your mother and mine," Rose looked at Carla. "Margaret and my mother, Anne, used to be best friends until my grandparents were basically forced to leave Nantucket thanks to the Berkleys."

"The Berkleys?" Carla frowned. "You mean Christopher's mother's family?" She looked at Christopher questioningly.

"Yes, my mother was a Berkley," Christopher confirmed Carla's suspicions. "But I don't know anything about them forcing a family to leave Nantucket."

"Margaret, Dr. Baxter, my mother Anne, and Simon Moore were best friends at school," Rose informed them. "Margaret was madly in love with Simon Moore, and they dated when they got to high school."

"Cody's father, Simon Moore, dated Margaret Stanford?" Nancy's jaw nearly dropped on the floor. "No way!"

"Did my father date your mother?" Carla asked, a little shocked.

"No," Rose shook her head. "They were best friends. Dr. Baxter helped my mother through a lot of tough times. As you know, our grandparents are very old-fashioned and conservative. My mother was not!"

"That's an understatement," Luis rolled his eyes. "My sister Anne was a rebel with a cause, and that was to change the world."

"Believe it or not, Margaret was also a rebel, and she and my mother had big plans on how they were going to fight for different causes." Rose smiled at the look on Christopher's face. "Margaret and my mother had planned to go to Harvard Law school together."

"My mother wanted to become a lawyer?" It was Christopher's turn not to let his jaw drop onto the floor. "Then why did she study business?"

"Mr. Berkley had other ideas for Margaret's future, and they included her taking over the family import-export business," Luis explained. "Only, before Margaret finished high school, my sister Anne stumbled across the Berkley's real import-export business."

"To cut a long story short, the Berkleys framed my grandparents for their crimes," Rose continued Luis' story. "That's when they left the island. But Margaret mistakenly confessed to Simon Moore, thinking he'd be on her side."

"The Moores always do what's right," Nancy's eyes narrowed.

"Yes, Simon Moore went to my grandfather with the information Margaret had given him," Rose breathed. "It was enough to open an investigation into the Berkleys. Mr. Berkely was facing jail time. Christopher's grandfather stepped in and offered the Berkleys a solution. He bought out their legitimate import-export business."

"The Stanfords then owned the Berkleys who were forced to move off the island," Luis continued for Rose. "They lived in the Boston residence, which was also now owned by the Stanfords."

"The only way Mr. Berkley could see through this horrible situation was to force Margaret to marry Christopher's father," Luis picked up the story from Rose. "Margaret had hopes of running away with Simon Moore, but he'd already met Cody's mother."

"Margaret then tried to get Dr. Baxter to help her, but he was angry about Margaret's part in getting my grandparents removed from Nantucket." Rose finished off the story.

"So, my mother reluctantly married my father," Christopher shook his head. "No wonder they were never lovable towards each other. They had an arranged marriage."

"I don't see why Margaret would've been so put out about marrying Christopher Stanford Senior. He was a hunk in his day and wealthy," Nancy put her hand on Christopher's shoulder.

"She would've been a fool not to see what a catch your father was."

"Thanks, Nancy, but I've never had any illusions about their relationship," Christopher said sadly.

"Margaret had felt let down and betrayed by both her best friends and boyfriend," Rose shook her head. "She wrote my mother many threatening letters blaming her, Dr. Baxter, and Simon Moore for ruining her life and forcing her into a hateful marriage, as she put it."

"Margaret had to sign a marriage contract that bound her to produce three children and an iron-clad prenup." Luis pointed to the folder in Christopher's hand. "I don't know if you've ever seen that contract?"

"No, I can't say that I have," Christopher looked like he was struggling to take in all the information Luis was giving them.

"Are you okay, Christopher?" Carla leaned forward to look at him. She was worried about how pale he was.

"It's a lot to take in." Christopher smiled back at Carla.

"There's more, Christopher," Rose said softly.

"Christopher, we suspect your mother of setting up the accident that killed your brother and Cody's parents," Luis got straight to the point. "I've been in hiding all these years because she set me up as the one that took the shot."

"Took the shot?" Carla's brows furrowed. "I don't understand!"

"The explosion just before the car started veering out of control," Christopher said. "I wasn't sure what it was, but I thought it might've been the tire that blew."

"The tire was shot out, and there are only three people I know of on the island that could have taken that shot," Luis raised his eyebrows. "One of them is me."

"Who are the other two?" Carla asked.

"I can't tell you that right now," Luis refused to say more on the subject. "But trust me, each one had a motive to do it, including me." He shook his head. "I'm convinced that Margaret put something in my tea that night. I was fine until I drank the tea Margaret gave me."

"That's right, you went home sick," Carla remembered. "That's the night my father said he had to take you to the hospital."

"That's right. I called him from the road that night as I had to pull over. I was so sick. I felt like there was a fire raging in my stomach. I couldn't stop getting sick, and my head felt like it was going to explode," Luis told her.

I feel like there's a fire raging in my head and my stomach. I can't stop getting sick. Please call your dad! Carla's mother's voice echoed through her head as the memory struck her.

"Did you have a skin rash or muscle cramps, Uncle Luis?" Carla asked him.

"Nausea, vomiting, muscle cramps, and a headache," Luis frowned at her. "Why do you ask that?"

"A few months before my mom died, she kept complaining about stomach pain that felt like a fire burning a hole in it. She'd get the chills for no reason, keep throwing up, and had really bad headaches." Carla's mind wandered through the last few months of memories of her mother. "Margaret Stanford was coming to our house quite a lot back then. She and my father would disappear into his study for hours."

"What are you saying here, Carla?" Christopher's eyes narrowed.

"I don't think my mother died of an aneurysm," Carla said. "I need to look up her records when I get back to Nantucket." She looked up and Luis. "Did the hospital tell you what was wrong with you?"

"They said I had a touch of gastroenteritis," Luis looked at Carla curiously. "I know that look!" He eyed Carla with narrowed eyes. "What are you thinking?"

Carla and Rose looked at each other, but before they could say anything, Nancy beat them to it.

"Carla thinks both you and her mother were poisoned with arsenic," Nancy told Luis.

*C*hristopher couldn't believe what he was hearing.

"And you think my mother poisoned them?" Christopher was outraged. "No way. I told you—she may be cold, overbearing, and somewhat controlling, but she's not a killer." He shook his head. "She would never have harmed her own children. Margaret was not the best mother, but she was very protective of her children. Lance's death nearly killed her."

"She would have paid someone else to do her dirty work," Nancy shrugged. "Maybe she didn't count on you and Lance being with your father in the car that night. Because, trust me, after what she did to Cody and your kids, it shouldn't surprise you that she'd poison someone."

"What are you talking about, Nancy?" Christopher looked confused. "My mother was gutted when Cody took the kids to Nantucket and refused to let any of us see them. Cody got a court order ruling me as a danger to her and the kids." He frowned. "Cody hated my mother and wouldn't let her near Cody Bay to see them."

Nancy and Carla gaped at each other before staring at Christopher as if he had three heads.

"What?" Christopher frowned at the four pairs of eyes staring at him.

"Have you ever spoken to Cody about the night you got your mother to kick her out of her home?" Nancy asked Christopher.

"I never kicked Cody out. She left." Christopher swallowed. His eyes darkened with a flicker of pain.

"Christopher," Luis jumped in before Nancy could say anything. "Your mother lied to you about the night Cody and the kids left you."

"Oh, really," Christopher pulled his wallet out of his pocket with shaky hands and pulled out an old folder letter. He opened it and started to read.

Christopher,

I'm sorry, but I've gone through this battle with my grandfather, and it almost killed me. I can't do this to our kids. I live in fear every day that you're going to lose your temper and lash out at them. The damage would be irreversible.

I wish you all the best with your treatment and hope you find some peace.

Cody

"Let me see that," Nancy grabbed the letter before Christopher could stop her. "You think Cody wrote this?" She shook her head. "Well, I can tell you with all certainty that Cody never wrote this!" Nancy shoved the letter under his nose angrily.

"Nancy," Carla touched her arm. "Don't" She shook her head.

"What do you all know that I don't?" Christopher asked them. "Tell me!" he said angrily.

"Calm down," Carla used the soothing doctor voice she used to calm troubled patients. "You can't get upset."

"No!" Christopher looked at Carla warningly. "I've had this feeling my whole life that my family has been keeping things from me. Even my older brother, who'd been my rock my whole life, kept things from me." He ran his hand through his hair. "I always felt Cody and my kids were the one part of my life that wasn't full of secrets and lies."

"I'm sorry, but he has to know," Nancy ignored the glares from the other three people in the room. "Christopher, Cody never left you. Your mother told her that the reason you'd been so aloof and unhappy was because you'd realized you'd made a mistake marrying her."

"Why would she do that?" Christopher looked at Nancy in disbelief. "She adored her grandchildren."

"No, she didn't." Luis looked at Christopher apologetically. "All her grandkids are to Margaret are obstacles in her way of getting full control of Stanford Shipping."

"Why would care about that? My mother had never had any interest in Stanford Shipping," Christopher. "No, you're wrong."

"Christopher, your mother kicked Cody and the kids out into the street and froze all Cody's cards," Nancy related the events of that night to him. "It was your mother that told her you didn't want anything to do with them."

Christopher wanted to yell at them that he didn't believe them. But, deep down, he knew they were telling the truth. Steven had begged Christopher to go and speak to Cody, to tell her the truth and listen to what she had to say.

"I think deep down you know it's the truth," Nancy handed him his note back. "By the way, Cody prefers handwritten letters. This is typed, and anyone could've typed it."

"Will you excuse me for a few minutes?" Christopher stood up. His legs felt like jelly. "I need some air."

"Here's the key for the roof access," Rose gave Christopher the key.

"Is that wise?" Nancy hissed at Rose.

"I'm not going to jump off the roof, Nancy," Christopher took the key. "I just need a few minutes."

Christopher followed the directions Rose had given him to the roof access. He couldn't get out into the open air quick enough. He felt like something had him a giant vice and was squeezing off his air.

Memories flooded his mind and made his head spin. Images of Cody and his kids scared, cold, and alone wandering the streets of Boston tortured him. *What had he done?* Christopher stood looking out over the city of Boston, not really seeing anything but the pain and suffering he'd caused his family. Christopher now realized Steven had tried to tell him the truth many times, but Christopher had cut him off. *When you're ready to hear the truth, you know where to find me.* Steven's words ran through his brain.

All this time, Christopher had thought he'd done the right

thing by letting Cody and his kids go. He knew he couldn't be trusted around him, and he would've done anything to protect them—even if that meant leaving them alone until he was better and more himself again. But he didn't know what his mother had done. No wonder Cody was so wary of him.

Christopher turned, slid down the wall, and sat with his knees up and his head against the wall. He felt like a monster, and even worse, he'd walked up on Cody's doorstep, dumped his son from another woman on them, and left again. He fought the tears burning at the back of his eyes. Christopher felt like he'd been on an emotional roller-coaster since the beginning of summer. He was exhausted.

Christopher couldn't believe that after everything Cody and his kids had thought he'd put them through, they were there for Riley and him when he needed them. They'd forgiven him, taken him and Riley into their home, and helped to heal both of them. No wonder Cody sidestepped all of his attempts at trying a relationship again.

"Are you okay?" Carla walked up to him and sat down next to him.

"How stupid am I?" Christopher laughed mockingly. "When Cody walked away when I was sick the first time, it nearly killed me. I didn't care if I lived or died. I was just going through the motions."

"I know that feeling," Carla put her arm around him and let him put his head on her shoulder.

"I missed my kids so much," Christopher drew in a deep breath and closed his eyes.

"I'm sorry, Christopher," Nancy quietly walked up to them and sat on the other side of Christopher. "I shouldn't have dumped all that on you."

"It's okay, Nancy. I needed to hear that." Christopher sat up. "How do I fix this?"

"You don't," Carla told him. "Cody told me not so long ago that you can't fix things that were broken in the past, but you can choose to get rid of the broken pieces instead of carrying them around as constant reminders."

"That sounds like something Cody would say," Nancy smiled at Carla. "Cody told me that the night of her sixteenth birthday was the night she met her soulmate. That was a few years after you'd broken her heart into a million pieces."

"Thanks for that, Nancy," Christopher looked at her and shook his head, giving a little laugh. "I'm going to overlook the little dig at what I did to Cody and hang onto the soulmate part."

"I didn't mean it like that," Nancy pulled a face. "Sorry, I was trying to emphasize how, after everything, Cody still maintained you were her soulmate."

"I know." Christopher gave her a hug. "I've always wanted a niece so I could be the cool uncle."

"Well, you have been the cool uncle," Nancy put her head on his shoulder. "I've dragged you on my crazy hunt for the truth, and you've followed me all over."

"My uncle had to go, but Rose has all the information he wanted us to have and a report for your checkup for us," Carla filled Christopher in. "He said he'd be in touch, but we must be wary around Steven, Connie, Uncle Pete, my father, and your mother, Christopher."

"That's everyone we know and have contact with on a daily basis," Christopher shook his head.

"He said they all belonged to something called The Committee," Nancy told him. "Well, except for Margaret, but we have to be wary of her for other good reasons."

"The clubhouse!" Christopher said. "The Latin motto—We protect with pride."

"I know that old clubhouse," Carla's eyes widened.

"We need to find it," Christopher suggested.

"We have quite a bit to do when we get back to Nantucket," Carla started to stand up. "But, for now, I say we go find Caroline and kids and get us some cheesecake and have some fun in Boston."

"I'm with you," Christopher stood up.

"You had me at cheesecake," Nancy let Christopher help pull her up. "And, Christopher, we'll help you figure the Cody thing out."

"Yes, we're family, and we're here for you," Carla patted him on the shoulder.

"Thanks, that means a lot," Christopher felt a bit better, and he knew what he had to do if he and Cody ever had a chance of getting back together.

Chapter Twenty
NO MORE SECRETS BETWEEN US

Steven walked down the hallway towards Carla's office. His eyes felt like they had sand in them, and he had a bit of a headache after being on shift for almost three days in a row. Steven knew he was avoiding going home because he didn't want to run into anyone there right now. He had a lot to think about after his meeting with Connie and Uncle Pete.

Steven had decided he didn't care what sacred oath he was breaking. He'd lived with secrets for far too long now. Steven had battled for a few days now, trying to come to terms with knowing that Carla was Charlene. They were the same person, but he knew them as two separate people.

Steven had been struggling with how to move forward with his relationship with Carla. He'd always thought of Charlene as his epic love, his soulmate, and Carla as the woman he was falling in love with. Steven had met Cody for breakfast the other day and had told her how he was feeling. It has been so good to talk with Cody again. He'd missed her.

Cody had told him that he shouldn't be looking at Charlene and Carla as two different people. But rather as a more mature Charlene that had grown up into Carla. Instead of focusing on trying to reconcile the past, they needed to concentrate on the future. Now that there was no more uncertainty and secrets between them, they could finally get to know each other all over again.

Steven was taking Cody's advice. It was time to get rid of all secrets and tell Carla everything. He took a deep breath and knocked on Carla's office door.

"Come in," Carla's voice reached him through the closed door.

"Hi," Steven popped his head into her office. "Do you have a minute?"

Carla looked at her watch. "Yes, it so happens I do." She indicated towards the seats in front of her desk. "Come in. Take a seat. I just need to sign off this patient form."

"No problem," Steven closed her office door and took a seat in front of her.

Steven looked at the folders on her desk and frowned. Carla had the medical files of Luis Vern and Michaela Baxter, her mother, on her desk. It looked like he'd got there just in time.

"Okay, I'm finished." Carla turned and smiled at him. "I haven't seen you in days."

"We keep missing each other because of our shifts," Steven sat back in his chair. "How have you been?"

"Busy," Carla sighed. "Thank you for securing the budget for the new equipment."

"It's going to benefit the hospital," Steven glanced at the files on her desk again. "I see you've pulled your mother's and uncle's hospital files."

"Oh," Carla gathered up the files and shoved them into her drawer. "I was just trying to figure out some family genetics."

Steven knew she was lying to him, but he let it go. "I was wondering if you were free to have lunch with me today?"

"My last appointment is at eleven-thirty today, so I can meet you at twelve-thirty?" Carla accepted his invitation.

"Make it one, and I'll meet you in the foyer at the Inn," Steven grinned. "That way, I've got time to go home, have a nap, and a shower."

"Sounds perfect," Carla agreed.

"I'll see you later today," Steven stood up. "Oh, and thank you for everything you've done for Christopher. I've seen his latest medical reports, and I'm so pleased with the results."

"I'm glad for Christopher too," Carla nodded.

Steven gave her one last smile before leaving her office.

Carla sat staring at the closed door to her office. Her eleven-thirty appointment was a meeting with Christopher, Nancy, and Rose. Carla hadn't expected to see Steven. He wasn't ever supposed to be at the hospital. She didn't know how much longer she could go without speaking to Steven about what they'd found out. She hated keeping things from him.

Carla sighed. It was bad enough that their lives had become a complicated twist knotted by other people who'd been trying to control their lives. Carla rested her head in her hands. All she'd ever wanted was the fairytale family unit with a caring, loving mom and dad. Parents who guided her, not controlled her, and let her build her own value and belief system.

Carla would've loved for her parents to be like Cody Moore. Christopher was very lucky to have had her as the mother of his kids. Aiden and Grace had grown up to be strong, respectful, independent children that weren't afraid to look to their mother for guidance. Carla was so grateful that the Moores had encouraged Connie to take Nancy in and had given both Connie and Nancy a place at Cody Bay.

A knock sounded at her door. "Come in."

"Sorry, we're a bit early," Nancy popped her head in, followed by Christopher.

"Not at all, come sit down," Carla indicated to the chairs in her office. "Nancy, have you been scratching your fingers again?" She frowned at the raw marks on Nancy's fingers.

"It's been a little itchy again," Nancy admitted. "But it's fine."

"No, it's not fine," Carla raised her eyebrows. "When we're done here, we need to take a look at your hand."

"Sure," Nancy agreed.

"I've gone over these files Luis gave us," Christopher put the folders he'd had under his arm on Carla's desk. "I checked them out, and everything checked out."

"I'm sorry, Christopher," Carla shook her head. "I managed to track down my mother's and Luis' medical records." She pulled them out of her drawer. "They never tested for poison, but interestingly enough, the treatment they gave Luis was not for gastro."

"Nancy leaned over and picked up Luis' file. "They gave him a bowel irrigation and medication they'd give a patient who'd been poisoned."

"So my mother did poison Luis' tea?" Christopher closed his eyes and shook his head.

"We're not saying that..." Nancy put her hand on Christopher's arm, "exactly."

"We just can't rule it out," Carla warned him.

"I asked a friend of mine at the sheriff's department to see if they could find anything unusual about my brother's accident," Christopher told them. "I knew it was a long shot. But we need to know if the tire was suspected of having been shot out."

"Do the police keep files for that long?" Nancy looked at Christopher.

"They should," Carla frowned.

"The content in the files on the accident was missing. All there was about the accident was that two cars collided when a tire blew on the Stanford's vehicle." Christopher raised his eyebrows. "

"Uh..." Nancy's eyes narrowed. "The same doctor who treated your mother when she was brought in treated Luis that night when he was diagnosed with gastro."

"I know," Carla nodded. "Dr. Vaughn was a doctor at my father's practice."

"Dr. Vaughn was our doctor," Christopher told them. "I didn't realize he worked at the hospital as well."

"We'd have to check if he had privileges in the hospital or did rotations," Carla frowned at Christopher. "You say he was your family's doctor?"

"Yes," Christopher nodded. "For many years up until he left the island."

"When did he leave the island?" Carla asked.

"You know, I'm not really sure," Christopher told them.

"Found him," Nancy scrolled through the internet on her phone. "Wow, he has quite an impressive resume. He served in the army, and his family is originally from Boston."

"I wonder how he wound up in Nantucket?" Nancy looked up at Carla, who scowled at her. "Are you okay?"

"Remember how Luis said that there were only three people on the island at the time with the skill to shoot out a tire?" Carla looked from Nancy to Christopher. "What if Dr. Vaughn was one of them?"

"And your father, Dr. Baxter, was the other one," Nancy held her phone up again. "This is how Dr. Vaughn landed up in Nantucket. He and your father served together."

"My dad wasn't in the army!" Carla looked confused.

"Says right here Dr. Grant Baxter and his team is to be honored for their bravery and commitment...." Nancy couldn't finish reading because Carla leaned over and snatched the phone from her. "Hey, that's rude!" She glared at Carla. "And I'm not sure how I feel about my mother going through my phone."

Carla froze and looked up at Nancy in shock. It was the first time Nancy had directly referred to Carla as her mother. A lump formed in Carla's throat that she had to frantically swallow down so she wouldn't dissolve into tears.

"Carla, are you okay?" Christopher looked at her worriedly. "You've gone as white as a ghost."

"Sorry, it's a shock to realize how little I know about my father," Carla showed Christopher the article.

"I know how that feels," Christopher mumbled. "I'm right there with you swimming in a big sea of doubt and confusion."

"Why would Dr. Vaughn want to get rid of Mr. Stanford, though?" Nancy shook her head. "I know Dr. Baxter and Luis would've had a reason because they both thought he'd been having an affair with Carla, and she was pregnant."

"Does it say why your father was filing for a divorce from your mother?" Carla looked pointedly at the files Christopher had brought with him.

"Infidelity," Christopher reluctantly revealed. "That's all it says."

"Do you think he knew about Margaret and my father?" Carla asked rhetorically.

"There is nothing in the files about who my mother was having an affair with," Christopher patted his hand on the folder. "Maybe your father and my mother were just friends like they had been at school, and she was having an affair with someone else."

"Someone, like Dr. Vaughn, maybe?" Nancy suggested. "If they were having an affair, he could've quite easily have been your mother's *problem solver,* shall we say?"

"I think it's time we found Dr. Vaughn," Christopher's eyes narrowed. "I would say we confront my mother. But I'd rather she not know we're investigating her."

"I agree," Nancy seconded Christopher's suggestions. "I, for one, don't want to end up with arsenic poisoning or having my car tire shot out."

"Nancy!" Carla admonished her.

"Too soon?" Nancy pulled an innocent face.

"No, it's just bad taste." But Carla secretly shared Nancy's worries about getting on Margaret Stanford's radar. It was pointing more and more to her being the wicked witch of Nantucket.

"It's okay, Nancy," Christopher's shoulders slumped. "I'm starting to accept that my mother is Cruella de Ville after all."

"She's a little eviler than that," Nancy cocked her head. "I'd go with the evil queen from Sleeping Beauty. Because, you know, the poisoned apple and wanting to be the fairest of them all."

"I get it," Christopher assured her.

"Oh, before I forget to tell you, I have a lunch date with Steven," Carla told a shocked Nancy and Christopher.

"I thought we agreed we were *ALL* going to avoid my brother as best we can," Christopher reminded Carla.

"I know, but he saw my mother's and Luis' files on my desk,

and he also looked like he wanted to say something to me but couldn't." Carla defended her actions. "So, I thought why not. Maybe I can get some information from him?"

"Okay, but be careful and check in with us after lunch," Nancy made Carla promise.

"I'm so sorry I'm late, Steven," Carla rushed down the stairs of the Inn towards Steven.

"It's fine," Steven assured her. "You look lovely."

"I wasn't sure where you were taking me," Carla indicated to her semi-casual attire, which included designer jeans, comfortable sandals, and a flowing, button-down cotton shirt.

"You look perfect," Steven smiled. "Shall we?" He graciously stepped aside for her to precede him out the door.

Steven led her to his pickup and opened the door for her.

"Mm, what smells so delicious?" Carla asked Steven as he climbed into the truck.

"That's a surprise," Steven told her, starting up the car and backing out of his parking lot. "I hope you're hungry?"

"I am. I missed breakfast," Carla admitted.

Steven drove along the coast and pulled into a long driveway that ended at the front of a large home that was being renovated.

"Is this your house?" Carla drew in a breath. "It's beautiful."

"Thank you. I'm so glad you like it," Steven pulled a basket from the backseat before leading Carla to the front door and opening it. "Excuse the mess. But while we're here, maybe you could give me some input into decorating the place."

"Really?" Carla asked him excitedly. "I'd love to."

"Well, let's eat first," Steven smiled and led her through the house onto the back porch.

"Oh, my, Steven," Carla drew in another breath. "Your view is breathtaking."

Steven put the basket on the table and looked out over the bright blue sparkling Atlantic Ocean. "It's a very peaceful view

199

when it's a beautiful day. When there's a storm or heavy winds, I love to sit and absorb the power of the ocean as it fights against the storm."

"I can imagine how empowering that can be," Carla looked at the table on the patio already laid out with plates, glasses, cutlery, and a red rose in a vase in the middle of the table. "When we're finished with lunch, I hope you're going to take me for a tour of this magnificent house."

"Of course, I told you I love your input," Steven set the dishes from the basket onto the table. "But Connie would skin me alive if I let her food get cold."

They settled in at the table, and Steven poured them each a glass of wine. He took a swallow of the smooth liquid as he sorted out how he was going to start this awkward conversation.

"Carla, I asked you out for lunch because I really wanted us to have another date and because I need to talk to you," Steven held her eyes.

"Oh," Carla frowned. "This sounds serious."

"When I found out about you and Nancy, I felt like my life had suddenly spun out of orbit and was hurtling towards a black hole," Steven ran his hand through his hair. "I knew it wasn't your fault. You were even more of a victim to our family's manipulation than I was."

"What I couldn't understand was why you chose not to tell me who you really were right up front," Steven's voice dropped. "I've tried to go over and over in my head why you wouldn't trust me with that information."

"Steven," Carla laid her warm hand over his hand on the table. "When I laid eyes on you for the first time at the conference in Boston, I nearly turned tail and fled right out of there."

"You never showed even a flicker of recognition." Steven frowned.

"It took everything I had not to collapse in a heap of jellied nerves," Carla admitted. "When you sought me out in the bar afterward, I thought for sure you could hear my heart beating through my chest."

"You seemed as cool as a cucumber to me," Steven told her. "You know, I never stopped looking for you. Well, Charlene, that is."

"You have no idea how much I wanted to come clean to you on so many different occasions," Carla admitted to Steven. "But, I wasn't ready to face my life on Nantucket. It had taken me years to shed Charlene and overcome all the hurt, anger, and loss that life had cost me."

"I understand," Steven sighed and took another sip of wine. "Why did you run away to England of all places?"

"After I thought our baby had died, I felt like I had nothing left inside of me," Carla swirled the wine in her glass. "I'd lost you and the only connection to you I had."

"I can't imagine how that must've felt." Steven's heart ached for her. "I wish I could turn back time and do everything differently. But a wise friend of mine told us we shouldn't try and reconcile a broken past. She said a mended bridge will always have the old faults in it and is never that strong again."

"She sounds like a very wise friend," Carla took a sip of her wine. "I think the same friend told me something similar." She smiled. "She said it's better to build a new, stronger bridge built on experience and lessons learned from the mistakes made with the old one."

"Do you think we could start to build a new bridge together?" Steven's voice was soft and full of emotion as he held his glass for a clink.

"I would like that," Carla clinked her glass to his. "Here's to building our new bridge."

"In the spirit of building new bridges, I need to tell you everything," Steven took a swallow of his wine.

"Okay," Carla frowned.

"I ended our relationship because I thought I was doing the right thing," Steven told her. "But I realize now I was taking the coward's way out. I was going to tell you everything after my brother's birthday, but I never got the chance."

"I was going to tell you about the baby when you were taking me home, but then you overheard the accident, and things just escalated out of control." Carla entwined her fingers with his, and they held hands across the table.

"I knew you'd gone to the clinic that day because my nosy mother had followed you from the drugstore to Cody Bay and then on to the clinic." Steven once again ran his hair nervously through his hair. "My mother called me to come to get her. When I got there, she told me she'd seen you go into the drugstore and buy a pregnancy test."

"I had gone to the clinic the day before because I didn't want to go to the drugstore for a test," Carla looked out at the sea. "But then I had to know, so I got the test while I waited for the clinic's results. I got the call from the clinic when I was at Cody Bay. I was there the day your mother saw me there to collect my results."

"When I got to the clinic, my mother told me what she'd seen you do," Steven told her. "She then convinced me to take your folder. I was so shocked at hearing you'd gotten a pregnancy test that I went along with her." He closed his eyes and took a deep breath. "When I got the file home to my mother's house, there were no results in it."

"That's because I'd already stolen the page," Carla admitted and reached into her purse to pull out her wallet. She opened the pocket inside the wallet and pulled out the page to hand it to Steven. "I've kept this with me since that day at the clinic."

Steven took the paper and saw the positive pregnancy results.

"Why did you take this?" Steven looked at Carla.

"I knew my father did rounds at the clinic, and he was also in the habit of having his assistant go through all their files to ensure everything was in order," Carla explained her actions. "That's why I was so angry with my father when we all went to confront him. I knew he was lying about the clinic, and I had a hunch Margaret had told him about it."

"When I finally managed to get home after the accident, I heard my mother and your father talking in the study," Steven drew in a breath. "Your father sounded angry with her. I went a little closer to hear what they were talking about."

"I also caught your mother and my father in a study," Carla looked at Steven sympathetically.

"Oh, no, I don't think they were having an affair because I know my mother was having one with Dr. Vaughn. My father had found out about her affair after having my mother followed," Steven told Carla. "Your father and my mother were just friends, and she relied on your father more for moral and emotional support than anything else."

"That's a relief to know," Carla breathed.

"Your father was also assigned with keeping a close eye on Margaret," Steven told her. "There is a club not many people know about called The Committee." He lowered his voice. "They like to think of themselves as the knights of Nantucket. Keeping peace and order and so on."

"Yes, they started in the old clubhouse," Carla nodded. "I was told about them."

"Oh, okay," Steven took another sip of his wine. "Then you must know that your father, Connie, Uncle Pete, and I are all members of The Committee."

"I didn't know you were a member of the committee, though," Carla looked at him wide-eyed.

"Well, I was a member. I resigned my commission a few days ago," Steven told her honestly. "I could no longer carry all these secrets around inside of me. Not when I was ready to share my life with the woman I loved, and I want to do that with an open, secret-free heart and soul."

"I feel the same way, Steven," Carla said softly. Tears were glittering in her eyes. "I also have a lot to tell you."

"I'm not going anywhere. None of us are on duty for two days," Steven grinned. "I wanted to ask you if you'd be my plus one to Carter and Lana's wedding this weekend?"

"I would love to," Carla accepted his invitation.

For the next four hours, Carla and Steven told each other everything. They pulled out all of their hurt, anger, fears, and pain, laying them out in the open for each other to see. As the sun sunk into the ocean, Carla and Steven snuggled up on the patio swing wrapped in each other's arms.

"I love you, Carla," Steven whispered in her ear.

"I love you too, Steven," Carla tilted her head to look up at him as his lips came down on hers.

EPILOGUE

Cody's eyes filled with tears as the judge said, "I now pronounce you husband and wife; you may kiss the bride." Everyone on the beach stood up and cheered. When Carter and Lana walked down the red carpet that spanned from the wedding arch back to Cody Bay Inn, the guests were still applauding. Nancy and Cody, dressed up in their bridesmaid dresses, followed after the newlyweds as they walked into the beautifully decorated room.

A gentle breeze ticked the back of Cody's neck, and she could feel the Bay was settled and at peace for the time being. As the wedding progressed and it started to get late, the bride and groom took off on their honeymoon. Harper stood with Cody, Grace, Aiden, Riley, and Christopher as they waved the newlyweds off.

"Are you okay, honey?" Cody put an arm around Harper's shoulder and gave her a tissue to wipe her eyes.

"I'm so glad Carter is finally my dad," Harper sniffed. "My mother deserves all the happiness he can bring her."

"That's very gracious of you and shows how much you love your mother," Cody said softly. "Should we go in and have some more cake?" She looked at the teens and Riley.

"Yes!" four young voices said in unison.

"Did someone say cake?" Christopher came up behind them.

"Because I could definitely tuck into more of that."

"Who is Nancy's date?" Aiden asked as they walked back into the Inn and saw Nancy saying goodbye to the good-looking man she'd brought as her plus one.

"Dr. Andrew Stein," Cody answered her son. "He's the new doctor helping out at Dr. Baxter's practice."

"I do believe our Nancy is in love," Christopher grinned.

A shiver suddenly crept up Cody's spine, and she frowned. She turned around in time to see three new guests walk into the Inn.

"Hi," the one man greeted them. "I'm Brandon Newton, and this is my brother Trent and my daughter Sophia. We booked a bungalow and one room."

"I'll book them in," Nancy hurried into the Inn. "You go and enjoy the cake."

"So, you were eavesdropping again?" Christopher teased Nancy.

"No, I just heard the word cake," Nancy grinned.

"Of course you did," Christopher rolled his eyes before ushering the children into the dining room.

"Welcome to Cody Bay, Dr. Newton and family." Cody smiled warmly. "I'm Cody Moore, and this is Nancy. She'll get you booked in and settled."

"Thank you," Brandon smiled at her.

"Would you dance with me?" Steven asked Carla.

"Yes," Carla let Steven lead her onto the dance floor. Her heart beat erratically, and her stomach twisted with the anticipation of being wrapped in his strong arms.

But when they got to the middle of the floor, Steven stopped, turned to look at her, and dropped to one knee in front of her. He pulled a beautiful navy blue box from his pocket.

"I love you, Carla. I always have, and I always will." Steven held her eyes with his. "You're my epic love and the missing piece of my soul. Will you marry me and finally provide the missing piece of my life?"

"I love you too, Steven," Carla's eyes opened wide when Steven pulled open the box to reveal the most beautiful ring she'd ever seen. "Yes, I will marry you."

The leftover guests, Cody, Christopher, Grace, Aiden, and Christopher cheered.

Steven stood up, put the ring on Carla's finger, then pulled her against him and crushed his lips to hers.

The Bay was once again stirred up. It had been ever since Dr. Brandon Newton and his family had booked in. Although Cody knew as soon as she saw the Newton family that they were meant to be at Cody Bay, she couldn't help shaking the feeling that they were only part of what was unsettling the Bay.

Cody sighed and shook off the bad feelings. As she turned off the dining room lights in the Inn, the sky started to rumble, and dark clouds rolled in over the sea. Something drew Cody closer to the window as a bolt of lightning split through the sky and lit up the ocean. One of the windows blew open and banged against the frame.

Cody jumped in fright before she rushed to close it before it shattered. While she was securing the lock, a fork of lightning ripped through the sky and flashed into the water like a long finger pointing into the sea. And that's when Cody saw it—a small life raft being bashed around and pushed towards the shore by the angry sea.

Cody's heart lurched into her throat as she leaned forward to get a closer look. Another finger of lightning split the sky as if helping her to see. Cody's heart caught in her throat when she saw there was someone in the raft. Her heart pounded against her ribs as she sprang into action, taking out her phone. She called Steven because he was the closest.

Steven answered on the third ring.

"Steven, come quickly; I need your help," Cody breathed. "Please hurry."

By the time Cody had rushed through to the foyer, she could hear Steven coming down the stairs from his room.

"Cody, what is it?" Steven's eyes were wide with concern.

Cody grabbed two flashlights from behind the counter. She threw one to him and headed to the door, telling him what she'd seen in the water.

"Over there!" Cody put her hand on her forehead to block the rain from blinding her.

"I see it," Steven ran towards the water. "Call the emergency services. I'm going to swim out to the boat."

"Be careful," Cody shouted and took out her phone.

"Do you need help?" A deep voice had her spinning around. "Dr. Newton!"

"It's Brand," Brandon gave her a smile. "Sorry, I was coming to get some milk when I saw you from the window."

Cody told him what was going on, and without another word, Brandon joined Steven as they fought their way through the waves to the lifeboat while Carla called 9-1-1.

Brandon and Steven managed to paddle the boat to shore. Steven secured the boat while Brandon scooped the lifeless woman up in his arms and started to run towards the Inn.

"We need to get her inside; she's freezing cold," Brandon shouted.

"An ambulance is on its way," Cody called and ran after Steven and Brandon.

Cody woke Carla up to come and help, thinking if the woman woke up, she'd feel more comfortable with a female doctor. Between the three doctors, they managed to get the woman warmed up as they waited for the ambulance to arrive.

"Where am I?" The woman slowly opened her eyes and immediately tried to pull away when she saw four pairs of eyes staring down at her.

"It's okay," Cody soothed her. "We found you drifting in a lifeboat."

"I..." the woman's brows furrowed. "I...." Panic lit up her amber eyes. "I can't remember!"

"It's okay," Carla stepped in. "I'm Dr. Newton, this is another Dr. Newton, and this is Dr. Stanford."

"I'm Cody, and you're at my Inn," Cody smiled warmly at the woman.

"I'm..." she swallowed. "I..." she closed her eyes and shook her head. "Why can't I remember who I am?" Sheer panic emanated from her eyes.

"It's okay," Carla told her gently. "We've got an ambulance on its way. I'll come with you to the hospital, and we can get you checked out there."

The woman's wide eyes were filled with fear as her eyes connected with Cody's.

"Will you come with me, please?" Her hand snaked out and grabbed Cody's like it was a lifeline.

"Of course," Cody promised. "Steven would let Christopher and the kids know where I am?" She looked at Steven.

"Thank you," the woman held onto Cody's hand.

"Can you remember anything at all?" Cody asked the woman, who didn't appear to be much older than Cody.

"I'm sorry, but all I can remember was a bright light in the sky. I felt warm like someone had covered me with a blanket, and then I must've passed out."

"It's okay," Cody gave the woman's hand a gentle squeeze.

Sometime later, when the paramedics were taking the woman out on the gurney, Cody noticed the storm had passed as quickly as it had come. As the clouds parted to show off the sparkling stars in the sky, Cody sucked in her breath as her eyes saw the brightest star she'd ever seen. It blinked a few times before vanishing and getting lost in the Milky Way.

Cody knew in that instant that the woman had been brought to Cody Bay by the guiding light and that somehow her fate was entwined with the Bay.

Amy Rafferty
AUTHOR

STAY UPDATED WITH ME

Thank you so much for purchasing or downloading my book! I am grateful to all my amazing readers.

To stay updated on all my latest books, newsletters, freebies and beautiful photos from the fabulous locations I write about, why not join my VIP group?

I will send you regular pictures of La Jolla Cove, San Diego and the Florida Gulf Beaches where I try to spend as much time as I can. I live in San Diego, my own 'Garden Of Eden' and I am in love with the sea and the beaches in the area. They inspire me to write lots of beachy mystery romance fiction to share with my awesome readers like you.

To join me, go to
https://landing.mailerlite.com/webforms/landing/y6w2d2

You will be asked for your email. You also get a FREE BOOK whenever you sign-up!

FREE BOOK

To get your free copy of the prequel to the Amazon #1 Best-Seller 'The Sea Breeze Cottage' go to https://landing.mailerlite.com/web-forms/landing/y6w2d2

THE SEA BREEZE COTTAGE
La Jolla Cove Series

La Jolla, a hilly sea-side coastal town, perched along the rugged shores of the Pacific Ocean forms part of the city of San Diego. Having spent the summers there with her aunt, it was the place Jennifer had called home as a young girl.

It had always been a place filled with the happiest of memories and times for Jennifer. Even as an adult, La Jolla was Jennifer's haven and place to recuperate from the fast-paced world of New York where she had moved to so she could pursue her career after law school.

Now a single mother of three children and a messy divorce behind her, her safe haven is scarred by a tragic accident that rips a hole in her world. Not only does she lose someone she loves dearly, but she unwittingly gets tangled up in a web of betrayal, mystery, and lies.

To read the series, go to https://www.amazon.co.uk/dp/B08SK5TMGV

THE MCCAID SISTERS
A Clearwater Family Series

Fallon and Piper McCaid have not spoken to each other in fifteen years, much to the despair of their younger sister, Ashley. With their brother missing, their grandfather in recovery, and their family home under threat, the sisters are reunited.

The McCaid sisters are forced to put aside their differences to face their fears, unravel a mystery, and confront an unknown enemy.

Stand with them as they battle their demons, fight to protect their family, their home, and salvage their late father's reputation. Journey with them as they get swept away on the high seas of adventure and intrigue while stumbling upon true love and finding the courage to open their hearts to it once again.

Laugh, cry, and fall in love with the McCaid family, broken by loss and tragedy and torn apart by secrets and betrayal. Get lost in a story about the powerful bonds of family and the magic healing ability of love which can drive a person to defeat their worst fears in the face of danger and adversity.

Let the McCaid family show you that love does conquer all and knows no age limit. This timeless love story spans generations as everyone deserves a happily-ever-after.

Escape into this mystery beach series. You'll fall in love with the McCaid family while you visit the warm white sands of Clearwater beach in Florida's Gulf Coast.

To read the series, go to https://www.amazon.co.uk/dp/B08YWP6RQB

A MYSTERY AT SUMMER LODGE
A Coastal Vineyard Series

As Danielle and Nicole Cartwright take on each other's identities they soon come to realize life is not as cushy as they thought it was on the other side.

Join the sisters as they learn how to walk in each other's shoes to come to a realization that they may not be as different as they thought they were.

Embark on an **adrenaline packed journey** through the Amazon jungle with Nicole who is about to find out that her sister is no pampered celebrity chef. Here, Nicole must learn to cook some of the traditional dishes of some of the tribes of the Amazon. But her problems don't only stop at the fact she can't cook. Her sister's TV show is up against a competition show. Nicole must go head to head with the arrogant but gorgeous Zach Goodwin.

Can Nicole manage to pull off impersonating her sister to save

her sister's beloved TV show while trying not to fall in love with a man totally wrong for her?

While Nicole is trying not to burn down the Amazon jungle with her terrible cooking skills, Danielle is roped into pretending to be Nicole. She must quickly learn how to run Summer Enterprises while flawlessly impersonating Nicole because a successful merger depends on it.

Guilted and bribed by her mother to impersonate her sister until after her great-grandmother's ninety-fifth birthday party when the merger will be signed off, Danielle is caught up in a corporate whirlwind of business meetings and galas, and everything she has ever hated about the rich and famous.

If Danielle can pull this off, she would finally be able to elevate Summer Lodge Wines to the prestige it once had.

First, she must solve the mystery of the **curse of the Summer Lodge Winery** which means delving into a vat of hurt and pain.

Escape into this Californian coastal vineyard series. You will fall in love with the Cartwright twins, whilst mysteries are unravelled and love blossoms for all.

To read the series, go to https://www.amazon.co.uk/dp/B094D7ZMJN

SECRETS AT WHITE SANDS COVE
A San Diego Sunset Series

White Sands Cove, packed with sun, white sand, surrounded by the sparkling blue Pacific Ocean in La Jolla, San Diego, is a cove that stood for almost a century shrouded in mystery and danger and is now the proud new business venture of cousins Michael Cooper and Lily Crowley.

Determined to make their love of outdoor adventure and fun into a full-time business the cousins turn a once run down and condemned White Sands Cove into the 'place to be' if you are looking for a day filled with sun, sea, sand, and fun.

Erin Carnegie is uprooting her New York life and heading for the warm shores of La Jolla, to start over.

Some might say she is running away but Erin, her daughter, Kelsey, and

God son Caleb Barnes need a fresh start, somewhere they can heal and regroup.

Thanks to Erin's best friend and former work colleague, their fresh start comes with good weather, white sandy beaches, and people who don't know who they are.

In La Jolla, Michael Cooper and his cousin Lily Crowley are scrambling to get ready to launch the second part of their White Sands Cove resort project — The White Sands Cove hotel.

Nature and forces they can't control around them conspire against the cousins as their first guests arrive to complicate their lives a little more.

Zane McCaid has sailed with his family to La Jolla for a much needed vacation and to celebrate his nieces and nephew's triple wedding. Staying at the White Sands Cove hotel gives Zane and his family the perfect opportunity to go on a treasure hunt and solve a centuries old family mystery.

Join Erin and her family, Zane and his family, cousins Michael and Lilly as they scramble to sort out their lives, while all getting pulled into an adventure of a lifetime. A treasure hunt and mysterious secret beach caves that gets them all trapped in a potentially deadly situation. As they band together to face the dangers ahead, each one learns they may also be in danger of losing their hearts.

Have some fun in the sun on the white sandy beach of White Sands Cove and get lost in an adventure as the characters try to figure out the secrets of White Sands Cove.

To read the series, go to https://www.amazon.co.uk/dp/B097K4XDDS

ABOUT THE AUTHOR

Amazon #1 Best-Seller, Amy Rafferty is a contemporary romance author of feel-good beach romance reads with heartwarming stories embracing humor and love.

Born in New York, previously a Lawyer, she now lives in San Diego with her beautiful children and cats!

Amy Rafferty
AUTHOR

Aside from writing, publishing and running her home, she spends as much time as she can visiting the beautiful San Diego and Florida beaches where she has family and friends. She calls San Diego her 'Garden of Eden', inspiring her to write clean and wholesome romance novels incorporating mystery, suspense and adventures for her characters as they find a way to open their hearts and let true love in.

facebook.com/amyraffertyauthor
instagram.com/amyraffertyauthor

Made in the USA
Monee, IL
21 January 2022